P9-BJW-467

Quiller Balalaika

Quiller
Balalaika

ADAM HALL

An Otto Penzler Book

CARROLL & GRAF PUBLISHERS
NEW YORK

QUILLER BALALAIKA

An Otto Penzler Book
Carroll & Graf Publishers
An Imprint of Avalon Publishing Group Inc.
245 West 17th Street, 11th floor
New York, NY 10011

Copyright © 1996 by Adam Hall

First Carroll & Graf edition 2003

Library of Congress Cataloging-in-Publication Data is available.

ISBN: 0-7867-1265-1

Printed in the United States of America
Interior design by Simon M. Sullivan
Distributed by Publishers Group West

CONTENTS

1 *Snow* *1*

2 *Dazzle* *19*

3 *Cobra* *27*

4 *Smoke* *39*

5 *Diamond* *53*

6 *Motorcade* *57*

7 *Caviar* *65*

8 *Moonlight* *75*

9 *Finito* *83*

10 *Play* *93*

11 *Spin* *107*

12 *Kick* *115*

13 *Marius* *129*

14 *Shadow* *143*

15 *Orion* *155*

16 *Lifeline* *161*

17 *Gulanka* *167*

18 *Bones* *173*

19 *Flashlight* *183*

20 *Midnight* *193*

21 *Key* *197*

22 *Zero* *205*

23 *Overhang* *211*

24 *Sakkas* *217*

Coda by Jean-Pierre Trevor *225*
Afterword by Chaille Trevor *231*

Quiller Balalaika

I
Snow

A S THE TU-154 BOUNCED AND FLOATED and bounced again, I wiped the mist off the window with the back of my hand and the flashing lights out there became brighter, and I could see a white carpet of fire foam with yellow-caped figures wading through it.

The smell of garlic came suddenly on the air as Pyotor leaned across me to take a look. Pyotor had been my fellow passenger all the way from Paris, and I knew the names and ages of his six grandchildren but still wasn't sure what had happened to Sandro, the third-from-youngest: Pyotor been reticent on the details, and all I knew about little Sandro was that he had "been an angel" and that hundreds had sobbed when they'd lowered the casket into the ground, hundreds.

"The last one," Pyotor said now with disgust as he stared through the window at the wrecked jetliner, "was in Tashkent, only a week ago. A Yak-42, with thirty more people on board than there should have been." He shrugged into his black astrakhan collar. "Par for the course—there aren't enough planes." The scene swung in a half circle as the jet made its turn and started rolling toward the terminal, and the question flashed through my mind: Why wasn't I feeling relieved that we were safely down? Because it can never happen to us, that's right. "But it wasn't the extra load," Pyotor told me. "They said there was water in the fuel tanks. It had been refueled in St. Petersburg in the pouring rain." He slumped back into his seat. "Get the water out of the fuel tanks and the vodka out of the pilots, and we'd all sleep easier under our seat belts."

Light snow was falling as we nosed into the runway gate; it had been announced from the flight deck earlier: light snow, the wind at 5 knots, the night temperature 10° below freezing, welcome to Moscow.

Pyotor pumped my hand and presented me with a cellophane-wrapped packet of toothpicks, courtesy of McDonald's. He said he hadn't checked any baggage. Nor had I, but I went off in the direction of the baggage claim because that was where I'd been told that Legge would make contact.

On my way there, I passed an Aeroflot official standing on some kind of box to give him height above the people flocking around him; their faces were blank with disbelief or angry or wet with tears as he tried to reassure them: The rescue teams had now pried the door of the cabin of the crashed plane open and gained access to the passengers; the flight deck had continued to report to the tower since the landing, but "reception was difficult." It was said that some—perhaps many—passengers were alive, together with three of the crew. Hope must be steadfastly maintained, the official told them, until definite news became available; meanwhile, free vodka and other refreshments were to be had at the cafeteria for those who wished to go there. Some of this was half-lost in the wailing of an ashen-faced *babushka* who stood rocking her shawled head back and forth between her hands, a little girl clutching at her skirt, her huge eyes staring at something she had never seen before: the sudden spinning away of the world she had always been told she could trust.

Legge was waiting for me at the baggage claim, watching me from the middle of the crowd until he thought I matched the description he'd been given. I'd never seen him before either; I'm just quick to note when I'm being watched, and no one else knew I was here. All I'd been given was his name, and the code-intro.

"All my eye," he said.

"And Betty Martin."

"You've got no baggage coming through?"

"No."

"This way, then." He was short, energetic, rolled a little in his walk, didn't look round to make sure I was keeping up as we nudged our way between people with wet coats and snow boots, their eyes half-hidden under their fur hats, snow on some of their shoulders: They were in from the street, like this man Legge, to meet passengers. From snatches of conversation I picked up, they were talking about the crash, just heard the news.

"We've got customs clearance for you," Legge said, "but they'll want to see your visa at Intourist." A young woman was coming out of the office with a clipboard, and Legge steered her back and gave her the visa and she checked it and ripped off her section and didn't seem certain whether to give the visa back to Legge or to me, so I took it and put it away.

"If we can be of any help to you at Intourist," she said, "here is our card and you have only to call us." A stunning smile: she knew about the customs waiver and that I had to be some kind of VIP to qualify.

We got into a battered black Audi outside the terminal and the chains began beating a tattoo as we moved off through the rutted ice of the street.

"Ex-Navy?" I asked Legge.

He didn't look at me. "Crystal ball?"

Sometimes a man's walk can tell you more than his eyes, that was all, especially if he doesn't know you're watching him. After a couple of miles, I took another look at the far right top corner of the outside mirror on the passenger's side. The dark gray Volga was still there, keeping station two cars behind.

"That a tail?"

Legge didn't glance up at his mirror. "No. Escort." He lost the rear end for a moment and let the curb kick him back straight, the chains jingling across the ice.

"And the man in front?" The Land Rover had pulled out ahead of us from the terminal and was still there, in front of a Mercedes.

"Escort."

The rear-end maneuver had shifted my weight, and I snapped

the seat belt tighter. Two escorts, call it a bloody motorcade; it worried me. All Hagen had told me over the phone at three o'clock in Paris this morning was that I had to make Aeroflot Flight 307 at 9:51 and that he'd have transport standing by for me and a man called Legge would meet me in the baggage claim at Sheremetyevo on arrival. I was on standby after two weeks' leave, so I couldn't ask any immediate questions; they'd come later if I had any. But it didn't look like a mission per se: I would have been ordered to London first for briefing and clearance.

"Are we in a burned-out field?" I asked Legge. This was what worried me.

"Not as far as I know." He pulled back to let a police car in and we watched it until it went past the Mercedes and got lost in the snow-haze. Dark was already coming down, sheeting the rooftops with steel.

It was the only reason I could think of for an escort fore and aft: there'd been instructions to protect me from the moment I landed, and that could mean that someone had blown his mission out here and left the terrain smoking.

"Where are we going?" I asked Legge. Tried to make it sound casual, wasn't really interested, didn't bring it off; he knew how interested I was—you never ask questions like that when you're dropped into the field in a hurry, on the principle that you'd have been given the answers already if London wanted you to know: yours not to reason why, yours but to do or die, so forth.

"Got a rendezvous." He flashed his lights at someone coming the other way, trying to blind us.

An escort taking us to a rendezvous: someone important, then. Important or desperate or blown or about to be blown. Despite Legge's cool, I could smell panic in the air, the subtle hint of brimstone.

"Looks different," I said, "Moscow." I hadn't been here since it had become the capital of Russia again. The buildings were the same: it was the traffic, quite a bit more of it. "Lots of shiny Mercs and Jags and BMWs." Not *lots*, I suppose, but they stood out from the crowd of local products.

"Mafiya." Legge nodded.

The leading escort began taking us into side streets—we were now inside the Boulevard Ring—and finally slid into the curbside just beyond a small Russian Orthodox church and stood there with its parking lights on. Legge stopped outside the church itself and told me to wait in the car. I watched him go along to the Land Rover through the flurries of snow and talk to the driver. He'd been checking the environment while he was picking his way through the frozen snow with his back to me. He'd stumbled a couple of times, hadn't been watching the ground, even though his head was down. Then he came back and passed the Audi and in the outside mirror I watched him talking to the driver of the rear escort vehicle. There was good streetcraft in his movements and I put him down as someone more important than a local contact or sleeper or agent-in-place, possibly the chief of a major Bureau support group: Moscow was still a major field.

When he came back to the Audi he put his head in the open window and nodded. "We'll be out here. We shan't move." Looking at his watch—"Rendezvous time was for 18:00. Couple of minutes to go, but your contact's already arrived."

I got out of the car. "Code name? Code-intro?" I shouldn't have had to ask.

Legge looked at me with no change in his expression. "You won't need anything like that."

I crossed the crusted pavement, a snowflake settling on my face and burning the skin as it melted. The arched main doors of the church were shut, chained, and padlocked, but the narrow entrance door was unlocked. I went inside, having to get used to the dim lighting in here after the baroque lamps of the street. Security didn't cross my mind: I'd been brought here under escort and Legge had checked the environment—as I had—and my contact for the rdv was already here, would have done his own reconnaissance or been escorted here as I was.

Three candles were burning in a small chapel on my right, their light reflecting from the gilded robes of three plaster saints—

Nikolai, Marius, Igor. At the far end of the nave, I saw movement and more light, flashing on bright silver, silhouetting a dark figure with a bald pink head.

"He's the lay janitor," a voice came from the shadows of the chapel. "We shan't be disturbed."

Croder, by his voice. By his voice and the way he was standing, still and thin as a heron, the steel claw at his left wrist outlined against the dark of his astrakhan coat.

Croder, Chief of Signals.

Hence the motorcade and the formality and Legge's touch of pride when he'd looked at his watch and said, "Rendezvous time was for 18:00. Couple of minutes to go . . ." The Chief of Signals is a punctual man. He is also brilliant, ruthless, and without mercy when the choice is to abandon a mission or the life of its shadow executive in the field, showing compassion only when the cost is nothing. He saved my life, once, and that had been the price.

But I was glad to see him. It always stimulates me to find myself in the presence of excellence—let's forget the other things.

"Shall we sit down?" Croder suggested.

There was a hewn bench below Marius, the saint. Croder's claw hit the carved edge with the sound of a stone dropping onto a coffin, scattering echoes; he's never careful with it, doesn't find it embarrassing: I've seen him open a tin of sardines with it, push in the broken cork of a '92 Pommard, and, once, smash through the window of a Jaguar and hook the driver's throat before he could take off.

"It's so bloody cold in here," I said, and sat down near him. Not too many executives, I suppose, would come so close to telling the Chief of Signals he'd chosen an inconvenient rendezvous.

"Yes, I apologize—you don't like the cold, do you? But we needed total security, as you can imagine, and I rather left things to Legge. But I was glad to see you turn up—I thought you'd crashed."

"Crashed?" I was thinking of the journey here from the airport through the icy streets.

"I heard there was a plane down."

"Oh, that, yes. It didn't have my number on it." *What the hell are you doing in Moscow?* I wanted to ask him. The COS hardly ever leaves the signals room in London: otherwise known as Action Centre, it is the innermost of inner sanctums—once a wine cellar underneath the building—where at any given time half a dozen directors in the field could be calling in their reports to the mission boards and asking for immediate instructions, and where sometimes the voice of a shadow executive with direct access to the shortwave bands is heard for the last time if he's left things too late to pull out of whatever death-trap he's caught in and even his local support group can't get him clear. Only a man with Croder's impregnable nerves could run a place like that—but here he was in Moscow.

"You're on standby," he said, "I believe."

"Yes." He didn't believe; he knew: he would have checked before he sent for me.

"I'm not sure I have anything for you." He watched the man with the bald head at the far end of the nave; I could now see he was polishing some silver candlesticks. "By which I mean," Croder added, "anything you would accept."

I left that. It wasn't like him to hedge, and it alerted me.

"I was with the prime minister late last night."

He waited.

"And how was the prime minister?"

"In a towering rage. He told me in effect that while the US is pouring billions of dollars into the Yeltsin economy and the UK is doing its rather more limited best in the same direction, the Russian mafiya is threatening to destroy that same economy and bring the country to its knees." His narrow head was turned to watch me suddenly from the shadows. "We may remember that quite recently the head of Russia's Analytical Center for Social and Economic Policies warned Yeltsin that the growth in organized crime here could well overturn his government and force Russia, with her back to the wall and at gunpoint, to choose between anarchy and fascism under the leadership of some dangerous fanatic like Zhirinovsky—with twenty-eight thousand nuclear missiles at his command."

"I understand it's on the cards, yes," I said. But that wouldn't account for the "towering rage." I waited again.

"General Mikhail Yegorov, Russia's first deputy interior minister, believes there are upwards of five thousand individual mafiya gangs operating in this country, totalling one hundred thousand active members. Other estimates are double that. Four million business organizations are known to be forced to pay protection money to their local mafiya 'services,' some of them foreign entrepreneurs—American, British, Japanese—with the result that the price of consumer goods is being forced up by more than twenty percent, triggering a runaway inflation and damaging the economy to the point where the Russian man-in-the-street is near destitution at a time when Yeltsin is desperate to keep down the threat of revolution on a scale of the Winter Palace. I'm quoting these few statistics from memory simply to give you a brief picture of events."

"Understood."

Behind Croder's narrow, silhouetted head, snow eddied past the stained-glass windows, black against the acid neon of the street-lamps beyond.

He went on, "But this doesn't explain the prime minister's feeling of an almost personal affront, does it?"

The rage thing. "Not really."

I'd never known the COS take so long to reach the point. Normally he'd get there so fast that if you didn't duck you'd get it right between the eyes. Again, this worried me.

"Most of the *vori v sakone*—the mafiya chiefs—are themselves Russian, though one or two of the Hong Kong triads have moved in, together with a few bold Sicilians, even though the Russian-style syndicates make the Italian and Sicilian operators look like harmless amateurs." The steel claw glinted as Croder turned to face me again. "In Moscow, one of the eight most powerful mafiya overlords is, in fact, a British national."

Got to the point at last, had taken his bloody time. So there it was: While the PM was proposing and authorizing and implementing the transfer of relatively vast sums from the taxpayer's pocket to the Russian economy to keep Yeltsin in power, one British Moscow-based national was busy undermining the process for his own personal gain, a red rag—yes, I could see that—to a man like the prime minister, whose notorious sense of fair play had so far crippled most of his political ambitions.

"Do we know him?" I asked Croder. The Bureau knows a lot of people, some of them on the run, some of them wanted by the police, a few of them useful to us, since in our trade we see blackmail and threats of exposure as valuable tools.

"We know *of* him," Croder said. "His name is Basil Secker, and he uses the Russian alias of Vasyl Sakkas."

"He passes for a Muscovite?"

"Yes."

"Fluent, then?"

"Perfectly."

This time he waited for more questions. The thing is he was being so bloody *slow*, and now that I knew the potential target for the mission I was getting impatient, smelling the blood, glimpsing the shadows, hearing the distant footsteps. Not that I was committed yet: Croder had spelled it out clearly enough— he didn't think he had a mission I would accept. And that could well be true.

"Go on," I told him.

"While he was working in the Foreign Office, Sakkas, who had access to the ultraclassified files, blew his cover because of a woman and was sent down for life on a charge of high treason—this was four years ago. During the final months of the Soviet empire, he escaped from special confinement by killing two guards—quietly with a piano-wire garrote—and commandeering a fishing vessel on the south coast. The owner's body was washed up at Dover three days later with a harpoon still in its throat."

I thought I heard shots in the distance, couldn't be sure: the walls of the church were massive stone.

Croder's head was tilted; perhaps he'd heard the same thing. "Reaching Moscow," he said, "with assistance from a special Soviet escort en route, Sakkas was immediately awarded the Order of Lenin for his services in London and given the rank of colonel in the KGB. A month later he was offered the Order of the Red Banner, the Order of the Patriotic War First Class, and the Order 'For Personal Valor'—presumably for so expertly dispatching the two prison guards at Wormwood Scrubs and the owner of the fishing boat. These bonus honors he refused: in some ways your Vasyl Sakkas is a modest man; or, to put it another way, he doesn't like too much limelight. With the regime on its way out at the time, he may have decided that the Order of Lenin and the other gongs wouldn't mean a great deal to him in the future."

Croder turned and sat down on the bench below the effigy of St. Marius, resting his claw on his knees and looking up at me with his eyes shadowed by the glow of the votive candles. "Sakkas then submerged for a year or two, then resurfaced as a Russian entrepreneur. We got wind of this from a Moscow sleeper who was doing some work for the Ministry of the Interior on the mafiya situation, with permission from London, of course. We informed Scotland Yard as to Sakkas's whereabouts and opened a file on him ourselves. From the same sleeper we were told that he has so far put away fourteen major rivals and three informers, six of them bound together and burned alive in a stolen BMW in a forest outside the city. There was also a criminal-court judge shot down on the steps of his own courthouse only a week ago; he was to try the case of a Sakkas aide brought up on a charge of rape. Sakkas doesn't make personal kills himself anymore; he uses hit men. His bodyguard is said to number thirty-two young former athletes, most of them out of the karate *dojos* and two of them former Olympic bronze medalists in gymnastics."

"Has he got a mistress?" It wasn't a non sequitur: Croder had said that Sakkas—Secker—had got his cover blown in London by a woman.

"Yes. Natalya Antanova, a leading soloist in the Bolshoi and one of the most beautiful women in Russia."

"Does he keep her to himself, or show her off?"

"I'm briefed that he's rather private about her, as he is with the rest of his lifestyle."

"Does he maintain contact with London?"

"Only as far as his entrepreneurship is concerned; he ships price-less icons and Fabergé jewelry there through his Aeroflot network, using the pilots."

"The dossier's quite extensive."

"Legge has your copy, if you decide to take this on."

He'd said it lightly; it had sounded like an aside. It wasn't.

"Have you given it a name yet?" A code name for the mission.

"Balalaika."

At this stage it wasn't important; I didn't know why I'd asked. I knew later, a few minutes later.

"So why aren't the Russian police and security services targeting Sakkas, along with the other top mafiya kicks?" I swung away, took a turn, feeling restless, came back and looked down at the Chief of Signals. He sat perched in the half-light like a hooded crow. "Or are they?"

I caught the slightest hesitation in him, a pause before he spoke. He'd noted the restlessness, and would know what it meant. *Blast* his eyes.

"The Interior Ministry's Organized Crime Section has been sending in some of its special investigators, of course. The RAOCs have also—"

"RAOCs?" I hadn't been in Moscow since it was the capital of the Soviet Union.

"Our own acronym for the regional administrations for fighting organized crime."

"Bureauspeak?"

"No, it's a straight translation from the Russian."

Perhaps he wondered why I wanted to know. It was because I was beginning to want to know *everything*. "Go on," I said.

"The RAOCs have also been sending their people in, but the odds against success are suicidally high, because of the corruption at all levels of government. A large number of civil servants are in the pay of the *organizatsiya*—the mainstream mafiya—and some of them are actually in close touch, so that any incorrupt agents who try to infiltrate the opposition are immediately recognized by their own colleagues and marked down for the hit squads. Part of the problem is that, to a varying extent, every legitimate agent is terrified of the job."

"Terrified of people like Sakkas."

"Of Sakkas particularly."

Something flashed through the mind: I suddenly wanted to meet him, Sakkas. Then it was gone but it left a trace, like a trail of smoke on a screen. It was in the same instant that I knew why I'd asked if the Bureau had got a name for the mission yet: I'd wanted everything brought together—their suddenly pitching me into Moscow, the impact of finding the Chief of Signals here, his hesitant and almost diffident briefing. And there it was: *Balalaika*.

It was also the name for something that hits the nerves of every shadow executive when he hears it.

"That's the only effective method of operation," I said. "Correct?"

Croder nodded. "Yes. Infiltration."

Hits the nerves because to infiltrate the opposition—*any* kind of opposition—exposes you more and more the deeper you go in, so that by the time you reach the center of the web, you daren't even move in case it sends out vibrations. Have you ever seen a spider working on a trapped fly? Most people have. It makes its rush, binds the wings until they stop buzzing, and then stabs with its jaws, taking its time now, sucking out the vital fluids first, relishing them.

You've infiltrated before.

Oh, sure. But what the fuck are you trying to push me into?

Sweat gathering: I could feel it. Worse, Croder would see it. Not on my skin. In my eyes. The first admissibility of commitment to *Balalaika*.

I took another turn, needing urgently to shake the idea out of my mind. It was too early yet to put my life on the line, if that was what

I was going to do. The man with the bald head at the other end of the nave made clanking sounds with his silver candlesticks, trying to be careful not to knock them against each other, perhaps, but not quite managing his veined and sallow hands, his arthritic fingers, vexed with himself because these sacred ornaments were thus far flawless, burnished and gleaming, a glory to God, how satisfactory, how safe to live a life wherein the worst of your concerns is centered on the flawlessness of candlesticks, or isn't that a kind of living death, a perpetuation of all those years of trivia, what do you think, my good friend, what is your honest opinion, now face him again, Croder, pop the question, the next one, the obvious one, the one the bastard is waiting for, perched there on the bench, on my shoulder blades, like a hooded crow.

"If I say no, who will you try next?"

Croder got up, pushed his right hand into the pocket of his coat, let the steel claw dangle. "No one."

I thought about this. He'd asked everyone else? And been turned down? Every time? "Who else have you tried?"

"Fern."

"And?"

"He said his Russian wasn't perfect."

"*Fern's* Russian?" I regretted it immediately, wished I hadn't said it. Croder knew it was a lie, too, but cold feet were cold feet and I've had them myself—pay attention to them and you stand the chance of a longer life. "Who else?" I asked Croder again.

"Teaseman."

"And?" Making me drag it out of him.

"He said it sounded like certain death."

Honest enough. "Who else?"

"No one."

"Why won't you try someone else if I say no?"

The black snow whirled past the colored windows behind his head.

"There isn't anyone else," he said.

"Pelt? Sortese? Vine?"

"There isn't anyone else *capable*."

"So I'm your last shot." Not a question, but he answered it.

"Yes. You've got to understand—"

"So you've come down to the only psychopath you can think of who might say yes to your bloody suicide run."

"You've got to understand that I find myself in an invidious position. I have virtual instructions from the prime minister—" he turned this way, that, the energy coming off him, palpable, his aura burning with it—"to go for Sakkas and bring him down, and in my living memory the Bureau has *never* refused a mission coming directly from its commander in chief."

His guard down now and I admired that: other men would have sheltered behind their authority. "So you accepted it," I said. "This one."

Look, anybody can make a mistake, even the Chief of Signals. Faced with virtual orders from the head of state, he'd refused to believe he couldn't find a shadow to take this one on, and when the door of No. 10 had closed behind him, he'd been committed.

"Yes. I accepted it." He swung toward me. "Should I have?"

"Oh for Christ's sake, I can't tell you the answer to that yet; it's too soon."

"Take your time. Take all the time you need."

And enough rope.

"This is why you're here personally in Moscow?"

"Of course."

"I don't quite see why it's so bloody obvious. You could have signaled me personally in Paris. Or sent an emissary."

Standing close, face to face suddenly. "You're making it very hard for me."

"I've no intention. I'm just looking for the bottom line, that's all."

He swung away again. "The bottom line is perfectly clear if you choose to read it."

So I read it, took a minute, but I think I got it right. Even Croder wasn't prepared to send a man to his almost-certain death over a signals line. It had got to be done face to face, if at all. And he was forcing himself to the issue on the thinnest possible chance: that before my almost-certain death, I could get close enough to the target for the mission—Vasyl Sakkas—to bring him down. And you can interpret that how you please: put him out of business, run him out of Russia, destroy his network or conceivably arrange to have him found spread-eagled among the stinking bric-a-brac of a rubbish dump or floating in the Moscow River or sitting like a cinder at the melted wheel of a Mercedes 206 in Sokolniki Park: The Bureau, too, has its hit men, though I am not one of them. But even if I could pull this thing off, the risk would increase a thousandfold in the final act because of the kill-overkill syndrome.

"Look," I told Croder, "if I take on *Balalaika*, what toys am I going to get?"

Again it was a second before he answered. I don't think he'd been quite ready to believe I'd even consider this one. "I would be your control," he said.

I felt the reaction. When you're offered the Chief of Signals as your control, it's like being handed the Holy Grail on a gilded platter even before you can wipe your feet on the red carpet.

"On a twenty-four–hour watch," I heard him saying, "throughout every phase of the mission." He wasn't turning away from me now, stood birdlike in the shadows, the candles touching his eyes with brightness.

This, too, impressed me. They've got cubicles next to the signals room where the controls can catch some sleep if a mission starts running hot and they have to keep close to the board. But I could remember Croder's mounting a round-the-clock stint only once in the whole of my time with the Bureau, and that was when Flack was stuck in a trap within a mile of the Kremlin with the proceeds of a document snatch that *had* to reach the Ministry of Defence in London before the PM could raise the president of the United States on the red telephone to say whether or not he was prepared to send troops in with the UN forces if an air strike against Iran was ordered first. Croder had lit a fuse under Flack's support group and got the documents out and faxed within three hours and brought Flack home with not much more than a touch of shell shock. Croder is *that* good.

More toys, I'm never satisfied. "Who can I have as my director in the field?"

"Whom would you like?"

"Ferris."

In a moment: "Ferris is directing *Rickshaw* in Beijing. But if—"

"Who's the executive?"

"Tully."

One of the higher-echelon shadows, or he wouldn't have been given Ferris. "Where are they with *Rickshaw?*" I asked Croder.

"Approaching the end phase."

"Does it look sticky?"

"Not at present, though in the end phase anything can happen, of course."

Conscience pricked. "I'd give a lot for Ferris, but—"

"You need give nothing." He was looking down, Croder, saw the problem, was trying to assess my thinking. To take a major DIF away from a top shadow moving into the end phase of a mission was probably unheard-of in the annals of the Bureau. But the trade-off was obvious: If the Chief of Signals was prepared to order it, it meant that he wanted me to have every single advantage he could give me for *Balalaika* because it was that dangerous. How much, then, was I ready to listen to my conscience? How willing was I to go into this one with someone directing me in the field who lacked Ferris's experience, brilliance, intuition, and ability to get me home with a few bones left, to pull me out of God knew what bloodied stew of an end phase where *Balalaika* could leave me foundering?

I have little stomach, my good friend, for the last-ditch eleventh-hour death-or-glory Götterdämmerung favored by some of the shadows—Kruger, Blake, Cosgrove. Bold fellows, but they carry within them the deathwatch beetle, burrowing quietly.

"If you took Ferris off *Rickshaw,* who would replace him?" I asked Croder.

"That is hardly your business."

Perfectly true. I was being offered a director in the field of my own choosing and I could take him or leave him. I wasn't invited to play any part in decision making at the highest control level.

"Then if I agreed to work this one, I'd need Ferris."

Croder's head came up. "You would have him."

"I'm not saying—"

Croder nodded quickly. "You would have him, if you in fact decided to accept the mission. It doesn't commit you."

Croder has—has always had—his scruples. Tonight he was ready to give me anything I asked for as an incentive to get me into *Balalaika,* but he was going to stop short of coercion.

"What about—" I stopped short as the distant thudding of an assault rifle started hammering at the walls of the church—distant but closer, a lot closer than the last shots we'd heard. We waited for it to finish: I would have put it at a three-second burst, quite long enough to bring about what was intended.

"At this point," Croder said, "let me tell you that if you reach final briefing with Legge, he'll impress it upon you that these people in Moscow are not your cozy Sicilian brotherhood. These people kill those of their protectees who refuse to pay, simply as an example. But they also kill policemen, government agents, bankers, judges, whoever gets in their way. I mention this advisedly."

The smell of cordite out there somewhere lacing the snow, blood creeping from the red-running eggshell skull, a hand flung out to clutch at the last vestiges of life the fingers already uncurling, empty.

I suppose I'd been silent for a moment, because I heard Croder saying, "I'm ready for questions, if you have any."

"All right. What about expenses? If I had to infiltrate a *milieu* as affluent as the mafiya I'd need credibility."

"The figure suggested—I have this directly from the prime minister—is one million US dollars in hard currency, immediately available from Barclay's Bank in Moscow."

"And if that isn't adequate?"

"You'd be able to call upon whatever further funds you needed."

"Fair enough. Now tell me about this man Legge."

"Legge has been in Moscow for nearly ten years. He headed the leading support group for *Cossack, Saber Dance,* and *Roulette.* In his last operation—this was post-Yeltsin—he got the executive out of a remote detention camp run by a clandestine cell of former KGB officers by commandeering three armored cars and a mortar unit from a Russian Army garrison in Tashkent. Prisoners were not taken."

"Real pro. How big is his group?"

"He runs fourteen men under constant training, and can recruit more from sleepers and agents-in-place if needed."

"He ever indulge in freelancer bullshit?" A support chief who commandeered armored cars from the host services could be tricky to handle.

"I don't quite follow."

"I mean, he takes orders?"

"From those he respects. I rather think you qualify."

One of the candles guttered, and smoke spiraled upward across the statue of St. Marius.

I hadn't got any more questions.

Took a turn, watched the man down there polishing his sacred artifacts, felt an instant of brotherhood, listened again to the thudding of the rifle and saw again the fingers slowly uncurling, thought of Moira—how long would the rose take to shed the first petal?—thought of Daisy in the Caff, *good luck,* she always said, knowing when we were going out, knowing sometimes more than the superannuated cardinals in Administration, knowing sometimes when a shadow wouldn't come home. Thought of life's continuance against great odds, turned back to Croder.

"Look," I said, "I'll take it as far as I can." I heard the echo of my voice from a niche in the chapel. "That's all I can offer."

Croder's eyes were bright. "That's all I can ask."

The hot wax of the candle drowned the wick at last, and the tendril of smoke vanished into the shadows. I nodded and turned away, going out of the church through the small side door and into the drifting snow.

2
Dazzle

"SUITE 29," LEGGE TOLD ME AS we pulled up outside the Hotel Moskva International. "You're checked in as Dmitri Berinov. Here's the key. I'm going to park the car, then I'll see you there—three knocks, one long, two short, before I ring the bell."

I got out and went up the soaked strip of red carpet they'd laid across the snow under the marquee. The two escort vehicles had peeled off when we'd pulled away from the church: they'd been there to protect the rendezvous, nothing else. From now on I'd be working solo.

It didn't mean, I thought as I went through the revolving door, that Croder had checked me in personally under Dmitri Berinov; it was simply the mission code-name for the executive, applicable to anyone he could get. He'd set things up for *Balalaika* as a certainty as soon as he'd left 10 Downing Street, trusting in whatever pagan gods he granted the privilege of his prayers.

People in the lobby as I went through to the staircase: a group of Japanese entrepreneurs in dark silk suits with leather briefcases; three women in sable coats and hats, one of them wearing too much Chanel No. 5; a Russian in from St. Petersburg, according to the label on the pigskin suitcase that was just being swung onto the porter's trolley; two hotel security men standing near the elevators. The only character here I didn't care for was the Russian sitting in one of the red plush chairs on the far side from the registration desk with a copy of *Pravda* open in front of him. I put him down as a government security peep. I watched his blurred reflection on the pink marble wall as I reached the stairs, but he didn't turn his head—not that he had any reason to: I was a total stranger here and Legge's security had been perfectly sound since I'd met him at the airport. But later there could be peeps on the watch for me, and I would take more notice.

The door of Suite 29 on the second floor was heavy to swing and two inches thick, with a deadbolt at shoulder level; the suite itself was spacious and ornate, with glass-fronted cabinets of Sèvres *objets de vertu* and gilt Louis XIV chairs, a four-poster bed with a red silk fagoted canopy and solid marble furnishings in the bathroom with gold-plated taps. I felt uneasy here, was more used to a back-street safe house with peeling walls and a rusted fire escape at the rear and a scrambler on the phone and total security.

I'd been dead wrong about Croder: he had indeed booked me into this hotel personally as Dmitri Berinov because the five suits laid out on the bed were my size and London-tailored by the firm that works for the Bureau when we need sartorial camouflage more appropriate than something off the rack, our presence requested at an embassy party or a host-country bash. The shoes lined up in a row on the burgundy pile carpet were handmade by Simpson and Webb, and the snow boots were tooled Russian calf. Again I felt uneasy, preferring jeans and a windbreaker and shoes with quiet, flexible rubber soles, the uppers softened with beeswax.

Yes, Croder may have asked Fern and Teaseman if they had the stomach for *Balalaika* before he'd called me in from Paris, but only as reserves in case I came unstuck. He'd put me in the sights as his main target the minute the prime minister had told him what he needed done.

I heard the echo of Croder's voice in the freezing chapel: *There isn't anyone else capable.* A compliment, if you like, or a sentence of death, you choose.

Thai silk shirts and a quilted dressing gown and a box of linen handkerchiefs initialed DVB; a dozen French silk ties—three conservative, the others on the flashy side, the kind a mafiya capo would sport; gold cuff-links and a pleated scarlet cummerbund; a matching set of Givenchy shampoo, aftershave and cologne, but only for show in the bathroom because that stuff can kill you if you leave traces when the hunt is up, and they'd known that when they'd packed it.

Three knocks and the bell rang. I checked the one-way viewer and opened the door.

"Comfortable?" Legge asked me and dropped two attaché cases onto the bed. "The door's metal, as I'm sure you noticed. The windows are bulletproof and there's a direct line to the hotel security switchboard—the white phone over there." He clicked the locks of an attaché case and opened it. "These rooms are updated versions of the royal suite, fitted out for mafiya guests who like privacy; most of the big hotels have come into line and of course there's no charge: they get automatic protection by the syndicates." He began taking things out of the case.

"I want round-the-clock surveillance on those two windows from the street, and people in the corridor, one at each end," I said. As a substitute for the rusting fire escape.

"No problem—I assumed you'd want that done." Legge turned suddenly to swing a look at me, his eyes not quite level because of the plastic surgery to the left frontal area of his skull. He dropped two folders and a bank card onto the bed. "Dossier on Vasyl Sakkas, general information on the Moscow *organizatsiya* with names and modes of operation, Barclay gold card. Did Mr. Croder tell you what funds you've got at your disposal?"

"Yes."

"Okay." He took out ten bundles of bills and dropped them onto the bed. "This is for ready cash, US $100,000. I'll leave you to find a place for it wherever you want." He slid the locks of the other case and opened it and took out three guns. "Heckler and Koch P7, 9mm, squeezecocking, gas-retarded slide locking system for better control. This one's a compact SIG P228 9mm with a magazine capacity of 13 rounds, weight 29 ounces, but it's got a lot of punch. And this one's a Smith and Wesson high-capacity DA auto 12-shot—"

"I don't use guns," I said. I hadn't interrupted him before because I'd been watching the two windows, looking for movement behind the windows opposite across the street. This place was so very exposed.

Legge swung round to look at me again.

"I heard that, yes. But there's something you've got to understand. If you're going to be infiltrating the mafiya, they'll expect you to dress correctly, I mean you get into a bad situation and they frisk you and there's no gun, it's going to look—"

"I'll take care of that when it happens. Who uses that building across there?"

Legge let out a short breath and dropped the guns back into the case. "With respect," he said, an edge to his tone, "my knowledge of this town is more informed than yours at this stage of the game, simply because I've been here close on ten years. I've also studied the mafiya here since they moved in. You want to take on these people without a gun, you'll be walking through a snake pit without even a stick." He turned his eyes on me and they were hard. "As the chief of your support group, I'd like you to reconsider."

I looked away from the windows across the street. "If anything goes wrong, it won't be your fault. You've warned me. Now tell me about that building."

Legge didn't look at the windows, looked down, fitting the guns back into their baize-lined case. "It's an RAOC headquarters." Regional Administration—Croder had spelled it out for me in the church—for fighting Organized Crime. "I wouldn't," Legge said over his shoulder, "have picked a room for you overlooking a building where anyone could put you in the crosshairs, bulletproof glass or no."

Got his back up, the executive in from London turning down his toys, the Heckler and Koch and the SIG and the Smith & Wesson, but I always have trouble going through Clearance when I refuse to draw weapons. What people don't realize is that your hands are always available—you don't have to reach for them in a hurry, and they don't jam.

"You've seen a lot of service," I told Legge. "You're a survivor, like me."

"Sure. That's because my own preference is the Austrian Glock 19, fires fifteen rounds, and since I arrived in this town I've put six notches on it." He snapped the locks of the attaché case and swung it off the bed and put it carefully by the door, coming back and pulling a colored brochure out of the other case and handing it to me, no eye contact. "For transport I've picked you a Mercedes S420, the flagship of the line, luxury sedan V-8, 275 horsepower, a bit on the heavy side so it takes eight seconds to hit sixty from a standing start, but there are things you'll need here in wintertime—you can adjust the traction-control system to give you some wheel spin so the chains can bite through the snow, for one thing. The headlights have got their own heated washer jets and wipers, which'll give you good visibility even in a blizzard, and the outside rearview mirrors fold back at the touch of a button so they won't snap off if you run things close. The headrests also drop on demand to give you a clear view behind. I tried out six cars and this one came up the best: it's got a hundred-thousand–dollar black-market price on it, which in terms of your mafiyosa image is the least a successful capo would want to pay, plus it's got storm windows and all the other stuff." With a shrug—"You want something different, there's more brochures here, but in the meantime this one's in the hotel garage under support surveillance with the engine kept warm every hour on the hour, and it's got chains on. And by the way—you won't like this—I put an AK47 assault rifle in the trunk with two boxes of ammunition." He got out a small black velvet bag with a drawstring and handed it to me. "These are direct from Antwerp."

Three diamonds the size of grapes, all faceted, dazzling under the lamp on the bureau where I took them to have a better look.

"Worth?"

"For all three, the current dealer price is half a million pounds sterling—they're twenty-four-carat. London would like them back if you don't use them to trade anything."

Such as my life. "Your idea?"

"Mr. Croder's."

I put the diamonds back into the velvet bag, the bag into my pocket.

"Micro recorder," Legge said, and put a matte-black Sanyo compact on the bed, "if you need one. Set of tapes." He shut the case and snapped the locks shut. "The cleaning staff will come only when you request it by calling housekeeping. I would advise being here all the time they are, even though they've been carefully screened by the hotel security. People can make mistakes. Don't tip them. Have you got any questions?"

"Safe house?"

"We've got three lined up for you to look at. Addresses and keys are with the Sakkas dossier and the other stuff on the bed. As soon as you've chosen the one you want, let me know. Our contact numbers are there too and I'll be at the base most of the time and you can get me on the beeper if I'm away. My second in command is Zykov, Russian-born, naturalized Englishman, thrown out of the SAS because he wouldn't always obey orders, but I like his creativeness." He looked at me steadily now and the resentment over the weapons thing had at last gone from his eyes. It had taken its time, and I noted that: The chief of any support group in the field is strictly subordinate to the executive at all times; not as a matter of military-style protocol, but as a matter of life and death.

He was waiting for more questions but for the moment I kept them to myself; I was only a few hours in the field and I hadn't yet been briefed by my DIF and I needed time to orient, mentally and physically.

"I think that's it," I said.

"Okay." Legge swung away with that trapped energy of his and turned at the door. "I've got fourteen men, active. Four of them are going to cover the passage outside in two shifts, four more will be on surveillance in the street. That leaves you with only six bodyguards, and if you need more than that, I can call some sleepers in from—"

"No bodyguards."

His head jerked up an inch and he hesitated, working out how he was going to put what he had on his mind: this was my impression. "All the mafiya chiefs have bodyguards," he said carefully, "some of them twenty or thirty. It's as much for show as anything else, prove how big they are, you know? But they also live a lot longer like that. Six isn't too many, and I'd like to bring in—"

I said, "I'll let you know if I need bodyguards. Until I do, keep them well clear. Those are my express instructions." I was getting fed up, that was all, with having to repeat myself so often. Legge stood there for another five seconds, six, then swung to the door. Over his shoulder—"Infiltrating the Moscow mafiya with no weapons and no bodyguards, I give you three days."

"That's not a bad start."

When Legge had gone I used the phone and called the chief of hotel security to come and see me and gave him a hundred-dollar bill and told him he'd get one every week if he looked after me, and if he didn't look after me he'd be found shot dead in the Katerinburg Forest. And by his reaction, it seemed like language he understood.

3
Cobra

I DIDN'T WANT TO WORK TOO close to the Hotel Moskva International, so I walked across the street and went into the RAOC building and told the desk clerk that Inspector Loshak wanted to see me. They said there wasn't any Inspector Loshak there; maybe I was mistaking this branch for the one down on Suharevskij Prospekt. I said they could be right—how would I get there?

Then I got the Mercedes S420 from the garage and drove sixteen blocks and found the other place and left the car halfway on the pavement—*A car like that,* Legge's briefing noted in the Field Information file, *can be left almost anywhere you can find a space. The police won't touch it: the image is distinctly mafiya.*

The snow had stopped in the early hours of this morning; I'd slept for a time and then got up and gone through the whole of the briefing again, committing the essentials to memory and testing it, looking down from one of the windows at intervals to check on the movements of the two surveillance people, bundled in their black leather coats to look like plainclothes policemen, hands pushed into their pockets and snow on their fur hats and their breath clouding as they shifted their feet, giving an oblique glance upward at my windows every time they reached the end of their beat and turned, could have been looking at the sky, wondering when it would clear.

The fax had come just before five this morning.

Yelena and the children arriving Sheremetyevo Airport 18:12 hours today on China Airlines Flight 2129, no need to meet them, will be staying at Hotel Romanov. Have a successful trip. No one called, no messages.

Ferris.

Already I was beginning to feel uneasy about Tully, the shadow executive for *Rickshaw,* out there in Beijing and just going into the end phase with a replacement director in the field less capable than Ferris—*any* DIF would be less capable than Ferris.

Does it look sticky?

St. Pyotr staring down with his plaster eyes, Croder's steel claw flashing in the candlelight.

Not at present, though in the end phase anything can happen, of course.

Yea, verily: the end phase is when the executive goes in close and starts feeling the heat, confronting the risk, taking final chances he'd never have taken earlier, committed at last to bringing the mission home or leaving it wrecked in the field—*You can't win them all, love*—Daisy in the Caff, small comfort, it takes a lot of tea to wash away the penitence, the self-reproach as those sniveling bastards spell it out in blood on the files: *Mission unaccomplished.*

Conscience pricked as I stood under the noon sky watching the RAOC building, this one smaller, shabbier than the one opposite my hotel, red brick and grimy windows, the brass handles of the entrance doors tarnished with age, birds there, pecking at crumbs someone had thrown down.

But you wanted Ferris, didn't you?

Right.

And you've got him. So forget this conscience shit.

Whatever you say.

People starting to leave the building now.

Whatever you say, my good friend, forget it, yes, we've got work to do.

The entrance doors banging back and the birds darting upward to perch on the windowsills, complaining. Most of the office workers came down the steps in groups, with only a couple of men walking alone so far, one of them slipping on the crusted snow and laughing as he found his balance, the sound clear in the cold air, the others turning to look and a girl in a white fur hat giggling, some of them crossing the street now, lurching their way across the deep frozen ruts in the snow, their boots crunching.

In a small building like this, there wouldn't be too many on the staff. I watched them, concentrating, needing only one, just one of them, the right one if I could find her. It had to be a woman, a woman walking alone, independent of groups, easily bored in company, needing to do her own thing in her own way, to hell with the rules and regulations, a tall order, this I admit, small chance of finding someone like that in a government office, a freethinking bureaucrat. But hope springs eternal and I waited patiently, watching the entrance doors, the steps, because this was important; this was the first day of the opening phase for *Balalaika* and I wanted information, a *lot* of information, to give me the one quintessential requirement the mission demanded before anything else could happen, before I could get inside the mafiya infrastructure in Moscow, before I could move in to the target: Vasyl Sakkas.

Access.

It's a heady thing, when you find it. It's the first signal the shadow's going to send, right at the outset of the mission, the one they're waiting for under the floodlit board in Signals, the one they'll scrawl in chalk across the slate.

Executive has access.

The air cold against the face, a blood red leaf circling downward from the black skeletons of the elms, smoke drawing out in a skein as someone lit a cigarette, the flame of the match bright on his cheeks and flashing on his glasses, three more people coming down the steps in a group, one of them swinging a blue woolen scarf round her neck as they went along the pavement under the trees. Suddenly there she was, a young woman walking alone, pulling on her sable-cuffed gloves as she looked around her, not seeing anyone she felt like joining, shaking her head to someone who called her name—Mitzi—and asked her if she was going to the library this evening, shaking her head to tell them no as I began moving, crossing the street behind her, taking care on the ice as a beaten-up

Trabant went past with its front wheels shimmying through the ruts, exhaust gas clouding on the cold noon air.

She went into the fast-food place almost opposite the RAOC building, and I hung back until the door had swung shut and then pushed it open again, going inside. Steam and tobacco smoke and the comfortable smell of cabbage, three servers working hard behind the counter, four people waiting, Mitzi the last in line.

When her battered tin tray was loaded, I shuffled forward a bit too fast and my foot got in the way and she tripped and the soup and the dish of shashlik slid off and crashed onto the floor, much laughter from a couple of workmen who'd just come in, Mitzi's face open with shock and her eyes flashing as she looked at me.

"*Shit!*" she said, to more laughter.

"I'm sorry—I'll order some more, it won't take a minute."

One of the servers came round from behind the counter with a bucket and a mop, looking daggers at me while I apologized again and gave the order, getting the same for myself, the potato soup and kabobs, while Mitzi told the two workmen to shut up, it wasn't funny, I liked her anger, it had a cat's energy. Where did she want to sit, I asked her when I had the two trays in my hands.

I followed her to one of the bare scrubbed tables—"Mind if I join you?"

"Please yourself." She was silent for a while, wanting me to know she didn't forgive easily, then looked up from her soup. "Clumsy oaf," she said, but with a quick bright smile.

"Dead right."

She opened her money pouch and flattened a 4.000-ruble note on the table. "You didn't have to do that."

"One should pay for one's mistakes. Dmitri," I added, "Dmitri Berinov."

"Mitzi Piatilova." She picked up the note and put it away.

I took my time, talked about the snow, the plane crash, the fist-fight they'd had in the Duma last night—it had been in the papers—talked about Zhirinovsky.

"He's a genius," Mitzi said.

"He is?"

"Look"—she leaned across the table, her long eyes serious, intense—"that man has it in him to bring Russia back as an imperial power in the world. I *like* that."

"He'll need to shoot an awful lot of people."

"So? You remember what he said? 'I may have to shoot a hundred thousand people, but the other three hundred million will live in peace.'"

"You're ready for dictatorship?"

"With a man like Zhirinovsky as our leader, yes. He could make real changes, sweeping and dramatic changes, clear out the trash we've been living with for all this time."

"Yeltsin can't do that?"

"Yeltsin is in the pay of America. Russia can get back her place in the world without any help from the almighty dollar. Look at what Zhirinovsky did when he went over there—he spat in their eye. *That's* the message we need to get across—we're an independent, sovereign people, and give us ten years—maybe even five—with a man like that in charge, and we'll be powerful again in our own right, a force to be reckoned with." Her hand slapping the table—"Russia had a *soul* once, and that man can give it life again."

"You're in politics?"

"Politics? No, I'm with the RAOC. But an ordinary citizen can—"

"You work over there, across the street?"

"Yes."

"You don't look like a bureaucrat."

"I'm *not* a bloody bureaucrat." Her eyes flashed again. "We're fighting crime."

"Making much headway?"

"Are you serious?" With a short laugh.

When her glass was empty I went to the counter for some more *vasti* and came back with some pastries as well.

"So why can't you make any headway?"

Mitzi threw her head back. "Against the mafiya? It's a farce! We catch them and put them into the courts and they buy themselves out or get a slap on the wrist for first-degree murder because either the judge is in league with their boss or he's terrified of making a conviction. It's not difficult in this town to get shot; it doesn't make any difference who you are."

"Rather frustrating for you."

"A job is a job." With a shrug—"Corruption's everywhere, you know that. We can fight crime but we can't fight corruption."

"It must be dangerous."

"Dangerous?"

"Fighting crime."

She looked across at a man sitting three tables away, then back to me. "For some of us, yes."

"He's one of them?"

"Who?"

"The man you were looking at."

"You don't miss much." She checked me over with a quick glance. I was wearing the things I'd arrived in last night; black jeans and a padded bomber jacket, not the tra-la tailoring I'd be using later. "He's one of our special investigators," Mitzi said. "They're crazy, you know that? Young bloods after promotion. They think they can take on professional hit men in the street and get away with it. They should leave the mafiya alone."

"You tell your boss that?"

"Of course not. I got this job because there wasn't anything else. None of us working over there has any illusions. I was talking to a Japanese businessman only a couple of days ago, and he put the whole thing in perspective. He says the *organizatsiya* provides a service. You know what he did? He found a contact in one of the most powerful syndicates and made a deal with him. The night he opened his fancy sushi bar, people from three or four other gangs paid their usual visit and told him what percentage they were going to take. He'd known this would happen, and all he had to do was give them the name of his protector—the one he'd made the deal with—and they cleared out and never came back. There's an unwritten rule—you take over a protectee from a rival syndicate and you're dead, I mean within twenty-four hours." She spread her hands. "The Japanese told me that every entrepreneur needs protection, and since the police can't help him he pays his dues to a syndicate—and gets service."

"The way the KGB used to run things. Freedom from trouble for sale."

"Pretty well. The normal abuse of power—nothing's really changed." With a bright laugh—"Except that the mafiya's better organized and makes a lot more money."

The man sitting three tables away was getting up, pushing his chair back and going across to the door. I watched him go out, a young fellow, walking like a cat as he hitched up his belt, a gun there somewhere, adding weight.

I turned back to Mitzi. "So how long has he got?"

She looked round, and her eyes were deep suddenly. "Until morning."

"How do you know?"

In a moment she said, "I think you're being too inquisitive."

I'd been expecting her to say it earlier, had the pitch ready. "You want me to be frank?"

"Just as you please." But suddenly she looked attentive.

"I've got to go over there today."

"Over where?"

"To the RAOC office. I need some help."

"What kind of help?"

I leaned across the table, moving the pastries. "The thing is, I'm not sure which side you're on, Mitzi. I mean, you work for the RAOC, but you say the mafiya provides a useful service."

She watched me steadily. "What do *you* think?"

"I agree."

"You agree?" In a moment. "I don't know who you are. I think it's time I did."

I gave it a beat. "I'll come to that. Do you know any of these people? In the mob? I mean, have you met them in the course of your work?"

She looked down, up again, turning the ring on her middle

finger, the sapphire I'd noticed when we'd sat down at the table. It was small but flawless, not the kind of bauble a government worker could buy on the standard pay. But then she was attractive, would have a boyfriend, at least one. I thought it was interesting, the way her subconscious attention had gone to the ring when I'd asked her if she knew anyone in the mob. "One or two," she said.

"How well?"

"I'm waiting to know who you are."

I finished my *vasti*, taking my time about it. "I'll put it this way. The help I need is for a friend of mine. He's with the Cobra." They had fancy names, the chiefs of the syndicates, according to Legge's briefing, some of them taken from the world of the predators—the Jackal, the Tiger—some from the American motor industry: Stingray, Cutlass, Baretta.

In a moment Mitzi said, "A friend? Or is it yourself?"

"No. I'm an independent entrepreneur."

"A brave man."

"I know what I'm risking."

"I hope so. Anyway, if your friend is with the Cobra, he shouldn't need any help from outside. They look after their own, like the Sicilians."

"Normally, yes. But this is a rape case, and the Cobra doesn't like that. He says it gives the syndicate a bad name."

"We've got rape cases in our files, of course. Has your friend—you want to tell me his name?"

"Let's call him Boris."

"Has he been charged?"

"Yes."

"When?"

"A week ago."

With a shrug—"It's still nothing anyone in the mafiya would need help with. Even if the Cobra refuses, Boris must have more than enough cash on hand to fix the judge."

"For one thing, he gambles—and loses. For another thing, the girl is still in the intensive care unit, and they don't think much of her chances."

QUILLER BALALAIKA · 35

"So it could turn into a rape-murder."

"Yes."

Someone dropped an iron saucepan behind the counter, and Mitzi flinched, took a couple of seconds to recover. "How do you think anyone in the RAOC could help Boris?"

"By taking the heat off him. Admitting to false arrest."

She looked down again, turning the ring. "It would be rather dangerous for you to approach our people over there. I started work with them only a month ago, so I don't know which ones would be open to persuasion. Most of them are loyal to the administration; I do know that. You go to the wrong one and you'd be in trouble yourself. Deep trouble."

"So what do I do?"

"Look," she said in a moment, "you could be anyone. You could be in the RAOC yourself—we've got internal investigators."

I got out my wallet and put my identification card on the table. London had embossed it to read Dmitri Vladimirovich Berinov, Import-Export, Overseas Affiliates.

"What do you deal in?" Mitzi asked me.

"Anything I can find a source for. Antiques—mainly icons—furs, gems, strategic metals, drugs."

"Have you got anything on you?"

I looked around, then pushed a small plastic bag across to her. "Keep it out of sight."

Mitzi opened the zip-locked bag and sniffed the contents, her eyes on me. "Is this coke?"

"You don't recognize it?"

"I'll take your word for it." She zipped the bag shut and passed it back, her hand covering it. What kind of gems?"

"Diamonds, when I can find them. Rubies, opals, tourma-lines, sapphires. That's a nice ring you're wearing. I've been admiring it."

"Thank you." She tugged her black sweater down, perhaps to show off her breasts: she'd done it several times, just as she tossed her head to show off her chestnut brown hair. "So maybe I'll trust you," she said. "Maybe I won't. It depends. This Boris—you mean he hasn't got *any* funds? Because of his gambling?"

"What would you call 'funds'?"

"I don't know—maybe a hundred thousand U.S. dollars."

"He might be able to find fifty thousand."

"That could be enough."

"But you said you don't know the people over there. The ones you might be able to buy."

"I wouldn't do it through them."

"How would you do it?"

Ignoring this—"Ask him if he'll go to fifty thousand. And a thousand for me."

"If he can't find that much, I will."

She took another pastry and bit into it, dropping crumbs, watching me all the time. In a moment, "What guarantee can you give me?"

"My word."

"That doesn't mean a lot in Moscow these days."

"It means a lot to me."

"I like that."

"And you like money."

Laughing, tossing her head back—"It's all I think about. Why shouldn't I?"

"Absolutely no reason. I'm not in import-export for fun, either. Excuse me a minute."

There was only one man in the lavatory and I got out my wallet and did some counting. Back at the table, I stood close to Mitzi and pushed the wad of notes against her arm. "Put it away without looking at it."

When she'd taken it, I sat down. "That's your thousand dollars. I'll hand over the fifty when Boris is off the hook."

She looked at me with her eyes bright. "How long will you give me?"

"He's due in court tomorrow."

"That's rather short notice."

"So you'll have to be quick." The sooner the executive can find access at the outset of the mission, the better it is for his nerves: He's no longer on the prowl in the field, trying to find his direction.

"I can't guarantee anything," Mitzi said.

"That's understood."

"You're a generous man."

"It oils the wheels."

Someone came in and let the door slam and she flinched again, and again tried to cover it with a wry laugh. "Christ, some people are so noisy!"

"Gets on your nerves."

She looked at her watch, a thin Jacques Picquot. "I've only got ten minutes more of my lunch hour." Getting a ballpoint and a piece of paper from her pouch, she began writing. "Tonight I'll be at the Baccarat Club. It's on Nevskiy Prospekt. I'll be sitting at a table near the door. Be there by nine o'clock and give this to the doorman—he'll let you in." She pushed the slip of paper toward me.

"And then?"

"There's a man you should talk to. I want to be there when he shows up. If he doesn't, I'll try and find someone else. But he should be there—he plays poker in a private room, most nights of the week."

"He's mafiya?"

"Yes."

"How big is he?"

"How big?"

"What's his status in the mob?"

She thought about it. "Maybe halfway up the scale. But powerful. And dangerous—treat him with care."

"What's his *reket*?"

"Protection, mainly, but he also deals in sable."

"Nothing else?"

"Not as far as I know. But he keeps a few judges in his pocket. That's why you should talk to him."

"You want to tell me his name?"

"Vishinsky. He calls himself the Cobra."

"How long have you known him?"

"Maybe a month, six weeks. I've talked to him only a couple of times, but I know his reputation. And I see him around."

"At the club?"

"Yes. I'm a spare-time hostess there when I've got nothing else to do."

She looked at her watch again and I said, "I'll be there before nine tonight."

"All right. It's formal dress."

"Black tie?"

"No, just a good suit." She pushed her chair back, tossing her head—"So I'll see you at the club."

I got up and went with her to the door, and as I watched her crossing the street I considered the impression she'd been giving me all the time we'd been sitting together. Mitzi Piatilova was running scared.

4
Smoke

S HE WAS EXTRAORDINARILY SUPPLE, USING THE whole of her body in a wave of sinuous movement that flowed from her arms downward across her hips and into her long, slender legs as she placed her feet with an instinctive precision, following me so closely that I had the feeling we were a single creature prowling through the jungle beat of the music.

Her name was Claudette, and the heavy gold necklace she wore had the flamboyance of solid gold.

Sometimes as we turned I saw Mitzi sitting at the end of the bar, the rainbow colors of its lights playing across her face. She hadn't looked in this direction since my partner and I had moved onto the small raised floor.

"Can you get me in?" I asked Claudette.

"To see him?"

"Yes."

"Why should I?" Her eyes were huge, glinting with the sheen of black sable under snow-light as she watched me, amused, I think, because I couldn't dance with this serpentine grace that she possessed, give me a chance for God's sake, she was the soul of Africa and I was a runt from London.

"Because I want to do business with him," I said. "Mitzi said you might do me a favor."

We were talking about Vishinsky. He was in the private room across there behind the podium where the band was playing. Vishinsky the Cobra. He had come in twenty minutes ago, two of his bodyguards pushing open the twin gilded doors and leading him along the wall past the rose-shaded lamps where people sat with their drinks. Reproduction? They could be original—this was a rich man's haunt, appointed with an understated splendor. The owner was French, Mitzi had told me.

"I'm needed at the bar," she had also told me when Vishinsky and his entourage had swept into the place. "Go and dance with the black girl—her name's Claudette. Tell her I want her to help you."

We turned, turned again, borne along by the music while these huge eyes watched me, never looked away. More than one man must have drowned in them, I thought.

I didn't think Mitzi was needed at the bar. I thought she'd got cold feet at the last minute. We'd been sitting at a table near the doors waiting for Vishinsky to come in, and she'd said she would intercept him and introduce me, but the very pace of his entrance had made any interruption seem unthinkable, and she hadn't even got up.

"Mitzi thought I might do you a favor?" Claudette asked me.

"Yes."

"I don't owe her."

"So will you do me a favor anyway?"

I didn't put a price on it yet. She'd do that if she decided to.

"You say you want to do business with him."

"Yes."

"What kind of business?"

I made the gesture of looking around before I spoke. "I've discovered a source of sable." The Cobra's *reket* was mainly protection, Mitzi had told me in the fast-food café, but he also dealt in sable.

A smile glowed in the huge black eyes. "Vishinsky *is* the source of sable."

"Not all of it."

"All of the highest-quality pelts. The rest aren't worth his attention."

We turned again, her arms undulating like willow boughs stirred by a summer breeze. "I'm told he's taken by you," I said.

"Sometimes he pays me attention, yes. But that doesn't mean I can talk any kind of business with him."

"I don't need you to. Just get me in there and introduce me."

"You make it sound so easy. That's because you don't know the Cobra." The music stopped and we moved to the edge of the floor.

"Would you like a drink?"

She glanced across at the patron, who was standing near the bar, hands tucked behind his dinner jacket, small spade beard, eyes everywhere. "I think so," Claudette said.

She asked for a Fernet Branca; I ordered Narzan, no ice. She watched me with her chin on her folded hands.

"No," I said, "I don't know the Cobra. So tell me about him."

"There isn't very much one can tell about any of those people, without getting beaten up, maybe killed, according to what one has said, and to whom."

"Then just tell me why you can't introduce me to this one."

She shrugged, her bare ebony shoulders lifting and falling like a ballet dancer's. "It might go all right, but then it might not. It would depend on his mood. If I took you in there and he didn't think the business you discussed with him was worth his time, he would have me beaten up for wasting it. What he would do with you, I don't know."

I thought it was time to change my mind, not wait any longer. "I'm not asking you to help me without recompense, Claudette, if that's how you'd prefer things."

The heavy gold earrings swung as she shook her head. "Men don't understand what happens to a woman when she gets beaten up. The bruises are nothing."

And suddenly it was over. Unknowingly, she had presented the one argument that stopped me in my tracks. Before going out on a mission I always tell the clearance officer the same thing: My only bequest is to Home Safe, and when he asks me if it's a bank, I tell him no, it's the abused-women's shelter in Shoreditch.

"Then we'll talk," I said, "about something else."

It took me ten minutes, a little more, to assemble a full picture of the huge ornate room in my mind as we sat talking—had she been born in Africa and, if so, how could her grasp of formal Russian be so perfect? And where had she learned to dance like that?

The patron hadn't moved, was still near the bar, still watching the girls, some of them drinking with members, some of them dancing. There were two heavy-bodied men in dinner jackets, standing and watching the room, like the patron. Bodyguards wouldn't be dressed formally. There were fourteen of them standing around, five of them in black jumpsuits, six in striped track tops, two in clean crisp karate *gis* and black belts, and one in a white workout suit with a gold cobra emblazoned over the left pectoral, like all Vishinsky's team—he'd brought six of them in with him, so there would be five inside the private room behind the podium. This one was guarding the door.

Two of the mob were dancing, one with a Japanese girl in a jade kimono; the men wore London-tailored silk dinner jackets and both sported carnations. Another mafiya boss was at a table against the red velvet–covered wall, sitting with a Russian woman of great beauty. I could tell which bodyguards were in whose employ by their focused attention.

"How long have you been in Moscow?"

"Five or six years." The black sable eyes watching me as Claudette sipped her Fernet. "And you?"

"Since the Reds bit the dust."

In a moment she said, "I would advise you to think again."

I'd looked twice at the door of the private room, often enough to clue her in. This wasn't important in terms of security: She knew why I'd come here. The man guarding the door wasn't big, but thick-necked and a degree muscle-bound: there was too much bulge under the skintight suit.

"Think again about what?" I asked Claudette.

"Trying to see the Cobra. That bodyguard would stop you anyway, and if you tried to insist, he'd have you thrown out of the club. There are five more inside. They are not gentle."

"I appreciate your concern."

"And hopefully my advice."

"The thing is," I said, "it's very important I talk to this man. Strictly *entre nous,* millions are involved." She'd know I wasn't talking in rubles. "Another Fernet?"

"No."

Of course it was perfectly true: In point of fact, it was important that I saw Vishinsky. There were other capos here, but I didn't have even the slender connection to any of them that I had with the Cobra—an acquaintanceship with Mitzi Piatilova. If I left here without seeing him, I would leave here without access for *Balalaika,* and I would not, my good friend, sleep well. Oh, fair enough, the executive doesn't often gain access on the first day of the mission, though a few of us have done it—Vine, Teaseman, myself. I suppose I wanted to do it now out of pride, since the Chief of Signals himself was my control. But if Croder had known my thinking, he would have flayed me with that tongue of his: Pride can be deadly if you give it rein.

"Would you be able to find some club stationery for me?" I asked Claudette.

"I think so."

"Just one sheet and an envelope."

When she came back from the office near the doors I wrote the note and sealed it and put it into my breast pocket. "You've been very kind," I said. "Possibly more than you know."

A shimmering smile, the first I'd seen, a stunner. "Whatever you're going to do," she said, "be very careful."

"But of course."

On my way to the private room I passed Mitzi, and she caught my arm. "Is Claudette going to help you?"

"She already has."

"You're going to talk to Vishinsky right now?"

"I'm going to try."

Mitzi got off her bar stool, her eyes concerned. "Without anyone taking you in there?"

"There would have been a risk for Claudette."

"So you're going in alone."

"Don't worry. I shall use great charm."

"Shit," Mitzi said.

The bodyguard was still at the door, flexing his ankles, eyeing me with a vacant stare as I went up to him.

He said no, of course, when I gave him the envelope. "It's a matter of urgency," I told him. "I need to make sure the Cobra knows what's happened."

He turned the envelope over to scan the other side. "So what's happened?"

"It's for his eyes only. But when he hears the news from someone else and I tell him you stopped me at the door, you'll finish up in the forest. Now move your fucking arse and go in there and give it to him. *Move.*"

His eyes went hard. "So who the fuck are you?"

I wasn't making any headway, so I used a half-fist under the rib cage and he doubled over and I opened the door and went into the private room. It was full of cigar smoke.

Four men were sitting at a table with cards fanned in their hands. They were perfectly still, looking at me. Ash dropped from one of their cigars onto the polished redwood table. The five bodyguards were standing against the walls, one of them moving into a half-crouch because the man outside was moaning and it must have looked quite clear what had happened. I kicked the door shut behind me.

Vishinsky would be the one on the far side of the table. He was watching me in silence, his eyes smoldering with rage, his long, narrow face paler, perhaps, than normal: This was my impression. His hair was cut *à la brosse,* and shone with oil; his mouth was a bloodless cut across the lower part of his face, and I found myself thinking that his smile, if ever it came, would bear semblance to the look on the face of a predator on sighting prey. He was wearing a perfectly cut dinner jacket—they all were, the men at the table— and the bow was black velvet, the corner of the handkerchief in his breast pocket monogrammed. Then at last he moved, with just a jerk of his head, and two of the bodyguards closed in on me, one of them frisking me, and thoroughly.

"Where is your gun?" This from Vishinsky.

"I don't carry one."

"Why not?" His eyes were fixed on me now with a reptilian stare: He'd got the rage out of his system.

"It's not the way I do business. Call me a peaceful trader."

"You're lying. There's no such thing in Moscow."

"There's a first time for everything."

The man outside was still moaning, and Vishinsky looked at one of the guards. "Go outside and take over. Tell him I want to see him at nine o'clock in the morning, unarmed." Looking back to me— "What did you do to him?"

"Nothing very much."

"He sounds in a lot of pain."

"He's just winded."

"Why did you do that to him?" Vishinsky's voice was suddenly very quiet. "What could have made you even contemplate such a thing, with one of my bodyguards?"

"I asked him to bring a note in for you. He refused."

"You haven't answered my question."

At the edge of my vision I was taking in what I could of the other people in the room. Their heads turned to look at Vishinsky when he spoke, to look at me when I answered. They reminded me of the umpire at Wimbledon.

"I thought I had," I told him.

By now I was having to keep the impatience out of my tone. He'd decided to treat me like a schoolboy, possibly for the benefit of the other three men. But there was no point in getting impatient; the thing was to leave here with what I'd come here for: access for *Balalaika*.

"No," Vishinsky said. "You weren't listening. I asked you what made you even contemplate such a thing, with one of *my* bodyguards."

"I came here tonight to do business with you. I don't like being obstructed by minions."

"And do you think I like being insulted?"

"That's just the way you're taking it. I heard you were a businessman, and I came here to talk business. When do we start?"

He left his stare on me, looking for something in my eyes: apprehension. I don't suppose he ever looked into any man's eyes without seeing it. Apprehension or fear. I didn't think the bodyguard would go to see Vishinsky tomorrow; by nine o'clock in the morning I thought he would probably be in St. Petersburg, or out of the country; even with a neck that thick he must have a modicum of sense.

"I do business in my office," Vishinsky said. "Not in gaming rooms."

"It's rather urgent. The shipment just came in, and I want to make a deal as soon as I can."

"You don't listen, you see. I told you I don't do business in gaming rooms."

"As a businessman, you'll see that this can't wait, when I tell you about the pelts, and the price."

In a moment; "Who told you I was a businessman?"

"No one in particular. It's your reputation."

"Reputations are built on what people say. I want to know who said that. I want to know who said anything at all about me."

I decided not to use Mitzi Piatilova's name. She was perfectly right: This man was dangerous, and might take it out on her if he objected to anything I said—he'd already objected to what I'd done. In any case, I hadn't intended to use the Boris thing as my reason for coming here: the proposal of a deal worth only fifty thousand dollars would only enrage him again, and I needed to use him.

"I can't remember who told me about you," I said. "You're quite famous, as I'm sure you know. Everyone respects the Cobra."

"Except you."

"I have the greatest respect for you, or I wouldn't have come here." The cigar smoke was getting to my lungs, and I had to make an effort not to cough; it would be a sign of weakness.

In a moment, Vishinsky laid his fan of cards on the table, and the other three men did the same instantly. "You said you brought a note for me."

I got it out and went closer, and both guards beside me took a sudden grip on my arms, so it was with a certain awkwardness that I dropped the envelope onto the table. When I stood back, my arms were released.

Vishinsky ripped open the envelope and read the note. "So you want to sell some sable."

"More specifically, I want to sell it to *you*."

"And why is that?"

"You deal in only the best."

"You seem to have been listening to a lot of people—whose names you can't remember."

"I think we've been through all that."

"You're rather cocky."

"I'm sorry you think so."

"I do, and I don't like it. Since you've heard so much from so many people, you must know that when I don't like something I take the appropriate action."

I backed off and leaned against the wall, folding my arms. "Vishinsky, you've got a very good brain, but at the moment you're thinking with your gut, and that won't get us anywhere. I want this deal made tonight, and if you're not interested I'll let you get on with your game of poker. So far you seem to be doing rather well."

The stack of banknotes at his end of the table was larger than the other players', but that could just be because they had to let the Cobra win. Or he wouldn't like it.

"I always do well." His voice grew quiet again. "And I don't always play at a table."

"That's encouraging. I respect an intelligent opponent."

"How long have you been dealing in merchandise?"

"Years."

"Legitimately?"

"Of course."

"Then you're not in the brotherhood."

"Actually, I am. But the deals I've made with members of the brotherhood have usually been honest on both sides."

"Usually."

"Yes."

"And when they're not?"

"I take appropriate action. There are things I don't like, either."

Ash dropped again onto the table from one of the cigars, but the man smoking it didn't take any notice, or didn't think it was important. I thought it was important because it emphasized the mood in this room: These three men were totally attentive to Vishinsky's every word, and if he'd told them to go outside and shoot themselves, I think they would have. He was the Cobra, and I was becoming aware of his power, which could have been achieved only by total ruthlessness. This was the most immediate danger: If it amused him to order a hit on me, simply out of caprice, he would do it almost without thinking.

"What do you mean by appropriate action?" he asked me.

"The last man who tried to screw me on a deal jumped out of a window."

"Jumped."

"There was no evidence that anyone had pushed him."

"You made sure there wasn't any."

Nothing but bloody questions, and I decided we ought to start doing some work. "Look," I said, "you're wasting my time, Vishinsky, and in any case I don't like being put through the third degree, bamboo sticks or not."

The stare took on a glitter. "They could be provided. They will, in fact, be provided if you don't satisfy me as to your identity. You should have thought twice, Berinov, before you decided to insult me and come barging into my private room, a complete stranger."

Knew my name because I'd signed the note. I unfolded my arms and stretched, taking my time, doing it thoroughly. If there was going to be any kind of action, the muscles would need to be in tone.

"We'll get better acquainted as we go along," I said. "Now listen carefully. There are exactly four thousand black pelts of Barguzin. This highest quality is a lustrous brown with a bluish undercoat and a darker center stripe. None of them have white underparts. They were tanned by top professionals who've been working all their lives in the region where the sable were trapped. The pelts are in hermetically sealed containers here in Moscow. If I had time to take them to London or Paris my asking price would be one million dollars. But I haven't got time, so I'm ready to unload them here, since I don't normally deal in sable. My price to you would be five hundred thousand. I hope you're beginning to see that I came here to offer you a deal you can hardly refuse. All you have to do is get those pelts shipped to London or Paris yourself."

He'd looked down, just once, to mask his eyes, and I knew he was interested, knew I'd got him. This wasn't surprising: With a deal like this he could pocket half a million dollars for the thirty minutes of his time I'd so far taken up.

When he looked at me again there was no stare: the eyes had intelligence in them, attentiveness. "You say you don't normally deal in sable."

"No."

"What do you normally deal in?"

"Diamonds."

Vishinsky shifted on his chair. "Did you come here tonight with your bodyguards?"

"I haven't got any."

Head on one side. "You say you're in the brotherhood, but you don't use bodyguards and you don't carry a gun, but you deal in diamonds. You see how difficult I'm finding it to fit you into the picture."

I remembered Legge: "There's something you've got to understand. If you're going to be infiltrating the mafiya, they'll expect you to dress correctly, I mean you get into a bad situation and they frisk you and there's no gun, it's going to look—" and I'd interrupted him, told him I'd take care when it happened. But he'd been perfectly right to warn me—Vishinsky was taking me up on it, though it didn't change anything. If I'd worn a gun here tonight, what earthly good would it have been?

"You don't really need to fit me into any picture. You want those pelts? I'll sell them to you."

"How did you get possession of them?"

"Somebody owed me. He gave me the source."

"What did he owe you?"

"I saved one of his sons from getting shot."

Fingers drumming on the table: "You say you normally deal in diamonds. What sort?"

The two closest bodyguards moved as I put a hand into my pocket and went to the table, but Vishinsky stopped any action with a jerk of his head.

"Like these," I said, and rolled the three blue diamonds out of their bag. Under the green-shaded overhead lamps they burned with a brilliant fire. In a moment, Vishinsky picked one up to look at it, and the three other men leaned forward, dazzled.

"Where did you get these?" Vishinsky asked. I could see the reflection of the stones in his eyes.

"They're from the Jagersfontein mines in South Africa and I got them raw in Antwerp and brought them here for cutting."

"What are they worth?"

"Two million pounds sterling."

"You *bought* them in Antwerp?"

"Yes."

"At a dealer's price?"

"At that *particular* dealer's price to me—a discount of fifty percent. I sell him stones from Siberia, and he does very well. These'll be going to Rome." I leaned forward, picking up two of the diamonds, and in a moment Vishinsky gave me the third, looking up at me with a new expression—not quite of respect, but attention.

"Why are you carrying them on you tonight?"

"Because there's nowhere safer."

"You're extraordinarily confident."

"It's just that I know my way around."

"Even on the streets of Moscow."

"Especially on the streets of Moscow."

He dismissed this with a shrug, then for a full minute there was total silence in the room as he looked away from me and down at the cards on the table as he immersed himself in thought. The cigar smoke drifted upward to the lamps, swirling as it met the heat. At last he looked up and said, "I'll have someone inspect the merchandise. Where should he go?"

"By tomorrow night it'll be at the base of the crane on the Simonovskaya dock at Wharf 39. I'll be there at ten o'clock."

Vishinsky looked at one of the men at the table. "Viktor?"

"Sure, *patron*. No problem."

I looked at him, scanning his face and noting the broken nose, the heavy black eyebrows, the stubble. The hair wasn't important: tomorrow night he'd be wearing his fur hat.

"This is Viktor Stroykin," Vishinsky said, "He is my chief lieutenant." The man looked up at me, his eyes indifferent, and we nodded.

"I'll be alone," I told him. "And so will you." In a moment he glanced across at Vishinsky, who looked at me.

"Unlike yourself," Vishinsky said, "we use bodyguards."

"All the same, I want him to go there alone."

"Why?" The dead stare was back.

"I prefer it like that."

"You prefer it."

"That's right."

Silence again.

"I, too, have my preferences, Berinov. There will be four bodyguards accompanying my lieutenant tomorrow night."

"In that case," I said, "the deal is off." I turned to the door, and one of the guards closed in on me, presumably in case Vishinsky didn't want me to leave.

"Berinov."

I turned back.

"You're being very difficult."

"I'm sorry you think so."

"And rather suspect. Why do you want my lieutenant to go to the rendezvous alone?"

"Because we'll need to be discreet, and I don't want an army of minions hanging around. Take it or leave it, deal or no deal—your choice."

We locked eyes, and the silence became absolute, gathering tension until one of the men at the table felt the need to cough, but stifled it. Vishinsky went on waiting for me to break, and it took a long time for him to understand that I wasn't going to.

Finally he turned to Stroykin. "No bodyguards. Is that understood?"

5
Diamond

THE NIGHT AIR WAS SHARP AFTER the warmth of the Baccarat Club, and the caked snow was brittle underfoot as I walked to the Mercedes. The nearest place I'd found to park it was half a block away, but if there'd been anywhere closer I wouldn't have used it. Half a block was the right distance. I took the alley again; its walls were lit faintly by a shred of moonlit cloud drifting across the rooftops.

A group of teenagers straggled past the far end, singing drunk by the sound of things, a girl giving little squeals of laughter. Then there was some hooting from a pair of expensive horns, and a flood of light swept across the snow and there was the crunch of tires sliding. I suppose the teenagers had decided to cross the street without looking. After a while, there was silence again.

I didn't know yet whether I had any kind of access to the opposition, but I thought I would know in a few minutes from now. Ferris would be at the Hotel Romanov by this time, according to his fax and providing the plane hadn't been delayed, or crashed. It would feel satisfactory, when I met him for the initial briefing, if I could tell him we had access. Ferris is one of the really brilliant directors in the field and I would choose him—had chosen him last night—above all others, despite my aversion to some of his little ways: there is the rumor, now established in the unwritten archives of the Bureau, that he strangles mice to entertain himself when he's got nothing more interesting to do. He likes to see them dance, it is said.

The snow, packed into ice along the alley, broke under my feet, and once I staggered, putting a hand out for support, and a cat went flowing along the top of the wall, black in the moonlight. As I kept on going I listened to the echo of my footsteps, and stopped a couple of times to listen instead to the silence, looking back along the alley. I didn't expect anyone to close up on me here: I would have heard them and they would know that.

They'd made a detour, the only choice they'd had, moving faster than I could have done on the packed snow. They were waiting for me in the street, two of them in their smart white workout suits with the cobra in gold on the left side of the chest.

They would have guns on them but hadn't drawn them, hadn't seen any need, with these odds and their training. They stood bouncing on their feet, hands hanging loose, crowding me against the wall as I reached the pavement.

"The diamonds," one of them said.

I used a shin-rake to double him forward and dropped him with a heel-palm under the jaw, feeling it break. The other man was very fast and already had his gun out but I had time to use a sword-hand to the wrist. It gave him a lot of pain but that wouldn't be enough so I used another one across his carotid nerve to stun him as the gun dropped from his hand and I caught it and emptied the chamber and sent it skittering along the pavement and into the gutter. Then I took the other man's gun from its holster and did the same thing with it before I dragged him into the alley and left him there, coming back for his partner and propping them side by side against the wall.

The one with the broken jaw was whimpering a lot and I left him to it; he'd be pretty inarticulate if he tried to talk. I worked on his friend instead, slapping his face to bring him out of the stupor. He was taking his time, so I kicked some of the snow loose and packed it against his forehead, holding it there until he started moaning, I suppose because of the wrist.

"Where is the Cobra's base?" I asked him.

His eyes came open, glinting in the faint light. "Fuck you," he said weakly.

Center-knuckle to the median nerve and he jerked to the pain. "Where is Vishinsky's base?"

He tried to straighten up and get his eyes focused and I let him: I wanted him to be able to reason. But he didn't answer me so I pushed one finger into the trigeminal nerve and he choked off a scream.

"Vishinsky's base," I said. "Where is it?"

He began lolling his head but there was no reason for him to do that—he was just faking syncope—so I went for the trigeminal again and he screamed and I repeated the question and this time got an answer, and I didn't think he was lying because he was in too much pain to think about tricks.

"Hotel," he said, or it sounded like that.

"What?"

"Stay at hotel—"

"Which one?"

"Stay at—"

"Which hotel? I'll give you five seconds—*come on!*"

One, two, three—

"Hotel Ambassador."

"All right. Do you know Vasyl Sakkas?"

His eyes came open wider. "Sakkas?"

"Yes. Have you ever met him?"

"No."

"But you've heard of him?"

"Everyone has heard of Sakkas."

"Where is *his* base?"

"I don't know. Nobody knows. He moves all over the place."

I hadn't expected anything from the last question, but I thought I'd have a try. Croder had told me the same thing, but Sakkas must have a center of operations somewhere and it must be here in Moscow. I would be asking a thousand people in this city where it was, and one day someone would tell me.

"What's your name?" I asked the bodyguard.

"Rogov."

"Listen, Rogov. If you ever see me again, keep your distance or I'll kill you with my bare hands. And that goes for your friend."

I left them propped there against the wall, going into the street again and finding the Mercedes and getting in, 936 Tokmakov Prospekt, accesss of a sort and useful enough to consider the night not wasted.

I phoned the Hotel Romanov from the car and got Ferris on the line and asked him for a rendezvous.

6
Motorcade

ERRIS HAD SAID 10:30 AND IT was only a twenty-minute run, so I took my time, trying out the S420 as I drove it away, getting used to the controls and instrument panel and pushing some of the buttons and folding the outside mirrors back and dropping the headrests and activating the headlight washer jets. I suppose most of this stuff had been put into the design to give the dealers something to sing about in the showrooms; but if I ever had to drive this car through an ambush or a blizzard or do any fancy footwork with it, the extras would give me a distinct edge on the opposition.

Found the button for the traction control and gunned up and got normal wheelspin until the chains dug through the snow and we moved off, not a lot of acceleration with a car this heavy but you can't have everything—the thick storm windows and door panels would absorb or deflect oblique fire and that could raise the chances of survival if things began running hot.

I shut down all the whistles and bells and slowed to a steady pace and turned north toward the ring road, checking the time at 10:15. Dried blood inside one of the fingers of my right glove was sticking to the knuckle, the one I'd used on Rogov's nerve points, and I eased it clear, watching the BMW in the mirror and making a square circuit when it didn't go away, but this was just for practice because the Mercedes was completely clean: It hadn't been within sight of the two bodyguards when I'd driven away, and there hadn't been enough action to draw attention to me personally.

By 10:29 I was making my first pass through the rendezvous zone near the Borovickaja metro station under a clear night sky with less than full-contrast shadow from the first-quarter moon. The taxi moved in soon after 10:30, and I took up the tail along Vozdvizenka and when it made a right turn and stopped, I left the Mercedes with the offside wheels on the pavement and locked it and watched the alarm flasher shut down and then walked through the dry snow to the taxi and got in.

"How was Beijing?" I asked Ferris.

"Terrible smog, horrible food."

"It's not what I meant."

"I know." He told the driver, "This is Berinov, the executive." The man looked round, just enough to show some of his face underneath the big fur hat. "Charlie Tolz, one of our sleepers." Tolz faced his front again. "Let's just keep moving, Charlie, anywhere you like. And you can leave the radio on."

Rachmaninoff, the Prelude in G. "How's *Rickshaw?*" I asked Ferris, spelling it out this time. In the presence of a Bureau sleeper, there's total security.

Ferris looked down at the folders on his lap, his thin, sensitive face catching light from a passing car. "It could go either way."

"Shit," I said.

"Don't worry, they've sent a perfectly capable replacement in."

"Who?"

"That's not important. The important thing is to get you debriefed before the heating in this thing chokes us to death." He switched on his tape recorder. "We're running."

I wanted to ask him about Tully—how did Tully feel about getting his DIF suddenly replaced in the end phase of a mission that "could go either way"? But Ferris wouldn't say any more than he had already even if I asked him, so I shifted round a bit on the seat and started debriefing. "I've made contact with a woman called Mitzi Piatilova who offically works for the RAOC branch office in my area. She also tries to make tentative connections with the mob because she likes money. She could be useful." I filled in the details, her night work at the club, her thoughts on Zhirinovsky as a potential dictator, and so forth. "I've also—"

"Spell her name."

I spelled it for him. Debriefing always sounds stilted when we do it on a recorder: The tape's going to be reviewed and examined and picked apart by half a dozen Bureau analysts in London and then put into a computer that's going to leave our every word carved in stone, and we're aware of this. "I've also made contact," I went on, "with a medium-weight mafiyosa named Vishinsky. I muscled my way in to talk to him—he was playing poker at the Baccarat Club—and pitched him the story that I had some sable for sale and told him the deal could make him half a million US dollars. He liked it, but when I showed him the diamonds to prove—"

"The diamonds?"

"Legge gave me some for bartering chips. When I showed them to Vishinsky to prove I was a pro in good standing, he took the bait and decided that two million pounds sterling was better than half a million dollars and sent a couple of his bodyguards after me when I left the club. They—"

"For the stones?"

"Yes. It was the only way I could isolate them for working on. One of them gave me the location of Vishinsky's headquarters."

"Really," Ferris said, his pale eyes watching me in the shifting light from the street. He wasn't showing any excitement, but he should have been.

"Of course, he could have been lying."

"You know when someone is lying under duress," Ferris said.

"All right, then he wasn't."

Watching me. "This looks like access."

"No need to get excited."

Ferris hit the stop and ran back and cleared the last bit and replayed and took it as far as "access."

"Anything more?"

"I don't think so. Obviously I've blown my image the first day out. Vishinsky's going to keep watch for me."

"It was worth it, for the access."

Charlie had been watching the mirrors a lot in the last few minutes. And now he made a couple of left turns and a couple of rights, and there were no more lights behind us. Ferris dropped the folders onto my knees. "Moscow information, mainly, that Legge wouldn't have access to. And your complete legend. I picked it up from the embassy when I flew in."

I looked at him. "How much does the embassy know?"

"Nothing. This one is very hot indeed." Ferris shifted on the seat now to look at me, stretching his long thin legs. "Let me tell you exactly how hot." When he spoke again his voice was muted. "Mr. Croder is out on a limb."

It was like saying that God had blundered.

"I got some vibrations," I said, "when he briefed me last night."

"That doesn't surprise me. The thing is, he's not only committed himself to *Balalaika,* but if you can't bring it home, he's not going to send anyone else into the field."

He waited. I said, "He'd shut the whole thing down?"

"The whole thing. I assume that from the vibrations you picked up you also realized that not only did he commit himself—and the Bureau—when he was with the prime minister, but he had to face the necessity of sending in an executive with, shall we say, none too sanguine a chance of staying alive. You'll forgive my disarming candor."

We were following the river now, north along Kremnevskaja, and I watched a garbage truck stuck in a snowdrift and trying to barge its way out like a trumpeting elephant, half lost in a cloud of diesel fumes.

"I know all that," I said in a moment. I felt I was moving—being pulled—toward something I wasn't going to like, wouldn't know how to handle.

"But you haven't thought about it," Ferris said, his voice sounding a little way off as my thoughts focused inward. "And you've got to do that, before we go any further."

I needed time, and took it. "I'm not quite sure what you mean. Before we push the mission any further?"

"Yes."

I wished he'd take his pale, unblinking eyes off me; I could feel them as I watched the river running past us, a coal black glitter with the reflection of the lamps afloat on the surface.

"Brief me," I said.

"It's not like that." Ferris waited, but I didn't say anything, still needed more time. "This is nothing I can brief you on."

"Oh for Christ's sake, how much has Croder told you?"

"Not much. I've only talked to him through signals, scrambled in Beijing."

"And?"

"He simply told me you'd accepted *Balalaika* and had asked for me to direct you in the field."

"So where did you pick up this—this other stuff?"

"From London."

"On the phone?"

"Yes. I sensed"—he lifted his pale hands, dropped them—"certain undercurrents."

And *this* is Ferris for you. At birth he was furnished with antennae, as sensitive as an insect's. It's why I always try to get him when there's a new mission on the board: he can show you the way through the labyrinth without even looking at the map.

"Who did you talk to in London?" I asked him.

"Who would you think?"

"Holmes?"

"Of course."

Had to be Holmes, yes, you could ask him things you couldn't ask anyone else, because you knew he wouldn't let it go any further; it would stop right there, locked in the security of his totally impregnable mind.

"And what did Holmes tell you?"

"He never really tells you anything, does he? You have to read between the ciphers." Ferris turned his head to watch the river for a while, and I left him to think, wasn't easy. Then he turned back and said, "I probably know the Chief of Signals rather better than you do, since the directors in the field are in closer touch with the controls. He comes across as Machiavelli on ice, doesn't he, hard as a diamond cut in the rough and all that. But deep under the shell he has a conscience, and it's bugging him now."

"You're talking about *Croder.*"

"Chief of Signals. But the problem here is that he started going too fast, gathered too much momentum when he came away from 10 Downing Street that night, and the result was that he suddenly found himself committing an executive to a probable early death. He—"

"I committed myself. He gave me every chance to say no."

"Oh, I'm quite sure. But he was offering you something he knew you couldn't resist." A beat, his eyes on me. "Wasn't he?"

"Look, it's not the first time I've agreed to a suicide run."

"Would you have committed yourself to *Balalaika* for Shatner? Or Flockhart?"

Two of the controls. "I don't know."

"You've got to face yourself. Then you will."

Jesus! I'd come to this rendezvous for debriefing, and here I was on a psychiatrist's couch. Ferris had never been like this before at the outset of a mission. *Nothing* had been like this before.

When I'd given it enough thought I said, "No. I wouldn't have done this one for any other control."

"Thank you. But you'll do it for Mr. Croder. That, too, is his problem. He's very much aware of your loyalty and your respect. You're not alone—he can make people do things for him they wouldn't do for anyone else."

"That's their decision. Our decision. Christ, you're right, it's too bloody hot in here." I tried to wind the window down, but the handle broke off so Ferris tried his, and the draft came cutting against our faces.

"Charlie," Ferris said, "turn the heater off for a bit."

"I get chilblains." But he reached for the switch.

Through the window the chiming of a clock sounded from somewhere in the Kremlin across the river, and in it I heard a note of inevitability, of life predestined.

"So give me the score," I told Ferris.

In a moment. "I wish I knew. I can't speak for Mr. Croder, nor can I ask him what's in his mind. All I can do is suggest a possibility, and you've got to see it as such. I think it's *possible* that at any given time Mr. Croder might act suddenly on the dictates of his conscience and instruct me to pull you out of *Balalaika* and send you home."

I listened to the clock, waiting for the last of the strokes, for the silence to come in, wary of it, not wanting time to move on. Then there was just the air freezing on our faces, and Ferris watching me.

"He can't do that," I said.

"He's your control."

"Tell him I've got access, for God's sake. Send a signal."

"I don't think I'd better, if you want to stay with the mission. The access you've got is to extreme hazard."

"But that's a given."

"I agree. But I don't think it'd take a great deal to tip the balance with Mr. Croder."

I watched a barge moving north along the river under the light of the quarter moon, leaving a white satin wake across the black velvet, a feather of smoke against the gold domes of the Kremlin. In Moscow the winter nights can be beautiful, and I didn't want to look away.

Waiting, Ferris, his pale eyes on me.

"If Croder pulls me out," I said at last, "there's nothing I can do."

"That's not quite true."

I felt pressed, hunted for the answer. "No other control would take it over. And no other executive."

Ferris wound the window up and the air was quiet again. "Put the heater back on, Charlie." Then he turned and lowered his voice. "Suppose *you* tell *me* what you'd do if the Chief of Signals pulled you out. And take your time."

We were turning south again now, along Varvarka, and in the distance across the square I could see a motorcade of four limousines on the move into the Kremlin, stark against the snow, funereal, three enormous Zils and—sign of the times—a Lincoln Continental, a piece of transport of which Boris Yeltsin was said to be fond. And suddenly I was listening to our voices, Croder's and mine, in the hollow confines of the church the night before.

And how was the prime minister?

In a towering rage. He told me in effect that while the US is pouring billions of dollars into the Yeltsin economy and the UK is doing its rather more limited best in the same direction, the Russian mafiya is threatening to destroy that same economy and bring the country to its knees.

St. Pyotr staring down from the wall of the chapel, his carved and painted eyes dispassionate.

We may remember that quite recently the head of Russia's Analytical Center for Social and Economic Policies warned Yeltsin that the growth in organized crime here could well overturn his government and force Russia, with her back to the wall and at gunpoint, to choose between anarchy and fascism under the leadership of some dangerous fanatic like Zhirinovsky— with twenty-eight thousand nuclear missiles at his command.

The black snow drifting past the colored windows as the shots came from the distance, a three-second burst, quite long enough to bring about what was intended.

A last echo came . . . *And bring the country to its knees . . .*

I watched the motorcade vanish through the lamp-lit gates into the Kremlin. Had that man, then, made his leap onto the tank for *nothing?*

Ferris, waiting—not, I knew, impatient, wanting me to take my time. But I'd done that now.

"If Croder pulled me out," I said, "I'd stay here in Moscow and go to ground and run *Balalaika* solo."

7
Caviar

I T WOULD DO, AT LEAST FOR THE TIME BEING.
"But you know the worst thing in all this?" The colonel fixed his bloodshot eyes on me. "The *worst* thing?"

I looked away to watch other people's faces, committing them to memory. In a moment I would ditch this man and move on. He didn't know Vasyl Sakkas.

The safe house would do, at least for the time being. The actual room was on the second floor. Ferris had given me the key to the only solid door left in the building, which was an abandoned ruin along Pushechnaya, the Street of the Cannon-makers near the Boulevard Ring, and I'd gone there alone to look at it after we'd shut down the rendezvous. It was nineteenth-century, had once been beautiful, if you care for Russo-Victorian, until the whole area had gone into decline and half this place had been gutted by fire and the other half left to rot with its paint peeling and its walls cracking and windows missing, smell of decay and despair.

"Do you know?"

This colonel was a bloody bore. "What? You mean the worst thing?"

"Yes."

"No, I don't."

"The caviar."

"I thought it was rather good." This was an official party launched by the Federal Counterintelligence Service, and Ferris had given me an invitation passed on from the British embassy, thought I might make some useful contacts.

"The caviar is *excellent,* yes," the colonel said. "But it is doomed!"

"Oh."

Make no mistake. When the Federal Counterintelligence Service throws a party, it's to make another attempt at cleaning up the image of the organization that hides beneath the sheepskin—the KGB—before the very eyes of foreign diplos from the major embassies, ranking journalists from the international press, local bankers, deputies, entrepreneurs, here to feast on the caviar and roast sturgeon and stuffed crab while the women in their miniskirts and minks and sables stalked the captains of industry and other selected prey with diamonds flashing on their wrists and fingers—though none of them were making a play for the Service brass, who had brought their shabbily overdressed wives for the occasion.

It was on the second floor, the room in the abandoned building, because the executive's refuge in any safe house is always there. The ground floor is too vulnerable to access, and the third floor is too far from the ground if he needs to get out fast. This room was on a corner and Legge had put two windows in and smeared them with grime, giving me the view of an abandoned soap factory from one of them and a side street from the other, this furnished with battered trash cans and a broken ladder and the rusting wreck of a Trabant halfway down, useful cover only if I managed to get that far should the street become a target zone.

"It is *doomed!*"

"The caviar?"

"But of course! Ninety percent of the sturgeon swim in the Caspian Sea, which has now been turned into a chemical waste dump by the shit coming down the Volga, not to mention the years of oil drilling near Baku." The colonel went on watching me for my reaction, the heat of his eyes on me as I took in the woman in the gold sequin dress who was passing behind him, an exquisite imitation Parisienne with the gloss of a porcelain Lladro; she prowled with grace through the packed banquet room, radiating

QUILLER BALALAIKA · 67

the confidence of a newly anointed mafiya moll: I was beginning to recognize them as they glowed like butterflies in their short-lived heyday before they made some kind of mistake or spoke out of turn and got beaten up and thrown back onto the street. There'd been women like this at the Baccarat Club, one of them sitting with a mobster, thick makeup over her bruises.

"And worse than that," the colonel said as I decided to move on, "the breakup of the Soviet Union"—moving with me, gripping my arm—"has brought Russia into competition with Azerbaijan, Iran, Turkmenistan and Kazakhstan for the fishing grounds, which are producing fortunes from the dwindling shoals of sturgeon that are still there!" He stopped me, and I waited. "Can you imagine, in two or three years, an evening like this, without *caviar?*"

"Terrible," I said.

"Can you imagine *life* without caviar?"

"Pretty shitty," I said. "Thank God for McDonald's."

I pried his hand away and moved for the buffet, taking it slowly, choosing the groups that looked interesting, that comprised the Service brass or had one or two of the mafiya dons in their midst, sleek in their silk suits, hair tonic gleaming, diamond rings on their fingers, some of them certainly former KGB officers who'd dropped out of the service to exchange the huge power of authority for the even greater power of megabucks. Six months ago it wouldn't have been possible to invite them here, but with Yeltsin staggering on the tightrope and Zhirinovsky in the ascendant, anything was possible today in Moscow, though I couldn't see any bodyguards here: Presumably our hosts had decided to draw the line at that.

A girl from the British embassy playing the little wallflower in traditional dress: a beige woolen cardigan and knee-length skirt with a single string of pearls and a circumspect perm, the pearls small but natural, not cultured, an innocuous-looking drink in her pale hand but with passion of her own kind latent in the soft blue eyes, I know her breed and am grateful that they walk the earth, my life being owed to one of them.

"And how is the queen?" I asked her, the accent broken but not thick—I've got my pride.

"The who?" In a tone of slight shock, since we hadn't been introduced.

"Your Queen Elizabeth."

"Oh." A gusty giggle. "I don't really know." She was eyeing my London-tailored blue serge, the two inches of linen at the wrist and the heavy gold links, the two diamond rings, courtesy of Legge, outfitter to the executive. Did she know the *mafiya* uniform? She didn't look scared, just alerted, intrigued: the Russian accent can be quite seductive.

"I admire her very much. We need a symbolic head of state like that in my country. Do you think she would accept the job if we asked her?"

Laughter like a peal of troika bells across the snow. "It's very nice of you, but I think she's rather busy."

"But of course. I was disappointed when your Prince Andrew declined Latvia's offer to reestablish the throne there for him and bring the country stability. There is no romance left for us today, do you not agree?"

"I don't really know."

"And how many DI6 agents do you have at your embassy at the present time?" I asked her and got her eyes wide open and stayed for a moment to admire them before I moved on to the group where an American was holding the attention of two Japanese diplomats and a woman loaded with Chanel No. 5 and her fifth vodka.

". . . Common knowledge in my department that these are still the same bastards that masterminded the whole *perestroika* policy to reestablish themselves in the security field and then set up the coup attempt on Gorbachev to entrench themselves deeper still."

"Then you don't believe," one of the Japanese asked him, "that real democracy is possible in Russia with the KGB still wielding influence behind the scenes?"

"Absolutely not. But even if we could nail these guys, who's going to nail the mob? Who's going to nail Zhirinovsky? You know what? There are so many goddamn roadblocks in the way of any real democracy coming to this country that I give Yeltsin another two months in power, and then we better *all* of us head for the shelters, because who the hell's going to finish up in charge of all those nukes?"

A good question, but I was more interested in the Federal Counterintelligence Service major standing over there near the massive copper samovar under the potted palm. He'd been sweeping a glass of vodka from the tray every time a waiter had gone past, and by this time might have his guard down.

"You people are doing a very good job," an FCS lieutenant-colonel told me as I began moving toward the other man.

"I'm glad to hear that."

"I mean it." A heavy face with several chins, eyes chipped off an iceberg, an ineradicable seven-o'clock shadow framing a greedy mouth, greedy, I thought, not so much for caviar or mille-feuille but for blood, for surrender, for the first scream as the high-voltage current hit the testicles under the blinding glare of the lamp: I'd seen, known, so many men like this one, had killed two, one of them in the street near Lubyanka, on that occasion for a lapse in manners. "You're doing a very good job indeed." His eyes serious, intent.

"We like to feel appreciated," I said.

"But of course you are. Continue to destroy the economy at this pace, and when the price of bread hits five thousand rubles a loaf the citizens will storm the streets to hang Yeltsin from a lamppost and we shall be called in to restore order and put Zhirinovsky into undisputed power. We can then stop calling ourselves the Federal Counterintelligence Service and resume our role in regulating the masses for their own protection as we did so diligently before. The nuclear missiles can be trained once more on Washington and the Western powers invited to acknowledge the new Russian Imperial reality." A hand on my arm—"Nor will the princes of commerce be forgotten for the part they will have played in the grand scheme of things. There'll be room enough in the hierarchy of the state for men of ambition and imagination, let me assure you."

"The prospects are overwhelming."

"I thought you would understand."

"I hope you'll find a good position for Sakkas."

The colonel inclined his head. "Please favor my left ear."

"I hope you'll find a good position for Vasyl Sakkas."

His eyes changed as he raised his head again, the light glancing across them as if they had no depth. "I think that might not be so easy."

"You know him?"

"Our paths hardly cross. But I know his reputation."

"And you don't see him as, say, chief of international trade in our new government?"

"Sakkas?" Eyeing me, wanting to know if I were serious.

"He's reported to be a gifted man in that field."

"I've no doubt." He looked away as a woman broke from the group near us, looked back to me. "I'll put it this way. Since so many of Vasyl Sakkas's competitors have met with such untimely deaths, I'm not sure his opponents in the Duma would sleep too well if he were offered a role in the affairs of state."

I shrugged. "Maybe you're—"

"Colonel Primakov! I've been looking for you everywhere!" A flash of iridescent eyes taking me in before the woman enveloped the colonel in an aura of Nuit de Folie and shimmering silk, the décolletage plunging to scented shadows, the nails gilded and long enough to draw blood in the instant if any male of the species were to take an uninvited liberty.

"If you'll excuse me," I said.

When I reached the major, he was still alone.

"Terrific party."

"Thank you. We try to make sure our guests enjoy themselves." His glass of vodka was tucked into an elbow against his chest for security.

"Berinov," I said. "Dmitri Berinov."

"Major Godorkin. You're not drinking?" He looked around for a waiter.

"I'm drying out for a while."

He considered this, his eyes tucked under the lids for shelter now, the drunk watching me, the man somewhere inside. "I see," he said in a moment.

I glanced around. "You didn't invite Sakkas here tonight?"

The eyes were suddenly tucked deeper. "Vasyl Sakkas?"

"Yes."

"Vasyl Sakkas doesn't 'ppear—appear in public. In any case I'm not pleased with him at the moment."

"Oh, really?"

"He ordered a hit on one of our people."

"When was this?"

"Two days ago. He should have tel—telephoned me before he did that." The tip of a palm frond was brushing his ear; he didn't notice.

"To warn you."

"What?"

"You could have"—I shrugged—"suggested an alternative."

His head began shaking slightly. "When Sakkas orders a hit, there's no poss—possible alternative. But I could have asked him to do it more discreetly. Instead of on the steps of our headquarters." He watched me as if from a distance. "He likes steps," he said. "A lot of his hits are made on steps. Judges, officials."

"You telephone him often?"

"*I* don't telephone *Sakkas*. But he knows my number. I was use—useful to him once."

"You've got an understanding."

"All I understand is that he must be treated with great caution."

"So I've heard. He's in Moscow now?"

"I don't know. No one ever knows where Sakkas is. But he was in Mos—Moscow two days ago. He always watches the hits."

"To make sure they're successful."

"No. They're always successful. He watches them because he likes it. People say—" He broke off as I tilted his glass straight for him; its rim had been catching under one of his medals. "What are you doing?"

"Don't worry about it. How often have you met Sakkas?"

"How—How often have I *met* him? No one ever *meets* Sakkas. Unless he wants them to."

"Likes his privacy."

"Yes. You know what those bastards did to me?" He was watching someone going past, head of gray hair, general's tabs.

"What did they do?"

"They passed me over for promotion again."

"Rather shortsighted."

"What? Of course. You know—you know how long I've been working in this bloody outfit?"

"Tell me."

"Nine years. Nine bloody years." He watched the general join a group near the buffet. "*His* fault, you see. Head of Personnel. Some—sometimes I wonder if I'm not in the wrong business." He looked back to me, his eyes taking time to focus. "You people do pretty well, don't you?"

"Mustn't grumble."

"You make mil—*millions*. I know that. Dollars. American bloody dollars."

"There are good times and bad. Tell me, where does Sakkas stay when he's in the capital?"

"You know what I make in this outfit? I make *peanuts!*"

"So why don't you come across?"

He watched me for a long time. "You deal in nickel, do you?"

"Sometimes."

"I know someone with a whole—whole trainload of nickel stuck at the Latvian frontier."

"He should offer the customs a bit more."

"If I left the service, I could help people like that."

"Help yourself, too."

"Of course. It's tem—tempting."

I got out my wallet and gave him my card. "Phone me anytime, Major. Perhaps we can work something out. But you'll have to steer clear of Sakkas if you start up in business. Where does he stay when he's in Moscow, by the way?"

"Steer *very* clear, yes. House—he's got a house in Sadovaja Samotecnaja ulica."

"On the Boulevard Ring."

"Yes."

"What number?"

"Don't know what number."

"A mansion, probably. An old mansion."

"Don't know."

"Would any of your colleagues know? What department—"

"No one—*no* one knows a thing like that." The sunken eyes were steady for a moment; I couldn't tell if he was alert enough to lie. "The big money," he said, "is in plutonium. You know that." It was either a jump in his train of thought or just a vodka-induced non sequitur. Was Sakkas, perhaps, in plutonium?

"When you can find it," I said.

"Not difficult. When that stuff is made in a fast-breeder reactor, they can turn out a kilo—kilogram more than the standards require for every hun—hundred changes of fuel." He watched me from under his heavy lids, didn't say any more, had lost his train of thought.

"And then?"

"What? Yes, and then the official amount is reg—registered in the books, and the surplus goes onto the black market. Some of the plants, they just throw the stuff over the wall, it's as sim—simple as that."

Then he dried up again, his head moving a little as someone came up behind me, and when I turned round I found myself looking straight into the eyes of the Cobra.

8
Moonlight

H E WOULDN'T WASTE ANY TIME.

"You assaulted two of my guards," he said. His eyes were fixed in a stare, as they'd been in the private room of the Baccarat Club last night. "I don't like that."

"You shouldn't have sent them after me. If you want the diamonds, you'll have to buy them."

Behind the stare, crystallizing it, giving it depth, was the rage again. "You assaulted the Cobra personally when you assaulted his guards."

This was new. I hadn't detected megalomania in him before. He was standing so still that he made a center of calm in the movement going on around him and behind him as the groups of people shifted, gestured, as the waiters weaved among them. There was quite a bit of the reptile about this man, but he wouldn't be aware of that, or he wouldn't have called himself the Cobra.

"Look, Vishinsky," I said, "I'm a businessman, and I deal with businessmen. I told you that at the club. If you want to play the robber baron that's entirely your choice and it's probably quite fun, but I'm not interested. I prefer working with men of intelligence."

Pushing him as far as I could to see what would happen, bring out his character, test his reactions, watching his eyes change, catching a hint of unease, which I understood quite well. There were no bodyguards in here: the Federal Counterintelligence Service people had presumably issued the invitations with that proviso, not wanting an army standing around to embarrass them in the presence of foreign diplomats. They would be outside the building, the guards, waiting for their employers, watching over the Mercedes and the Jaguars and the Lamborghinis. And this was worrying Vishinsky: at any other time he could have had me surrounded with muscle. It's the same situation when someone who relies on a gun finds he can't reach it in time: Suddenly he's lost, powerless. Legge would have to learn this, because it was a lesson that could one day cost him his life.

"You like provoking me, Berinov," Vishinsky said, his narrow head lifting an inch, the stare as steady as a beam of light playing on my face. "You like provoking the Cobra."

"Not really. I never waste energy, and frankly I've got better things to do. If you'll excuse me." I turned my back on him, looking past the drunken major to the massive gilt mirrors ranged along the wall.

Vishinsky wasn't wasting any time now, didn't want to show haste but moved deceptively fast among the guests toward the main doors, which were standing wide open because of the heat.

I waited until he was out of sight before I followed him, watching the top of his dark pomaded head as he went down the staircase to the lobby. There was a telephone on the mezzanine floor, and I used that.

I heard the line open as Ferris picked up on the second ring. He didn't speak.

"Red sector."

"Where?"

"The Hotel Fabergé"

"Do you need support?"

"No."

I shut down the signal and used the door to the fire stairs and climbed the eight floors of the building, taking my time. Vishinsky wouldn't bring any action into the hotel until the party was over, didn't need to. There would be three or four exits, possibly more, and by now there'd be at least one of his guards mounted on each of them, sealing the place off from the street. I didn't have any illusions: This was a trap.

You knew there was a chance he'd be here.

Very thin chance, yes. But there must be a hundred dons in this city, and only seven of them are here tonight. Weren't you counting?

I left the fire stairs and went into the corridor, looking for a vacant suite.

I don't like traps.

That's a shame.

Bloody little organism starting to panic.

You needn't have come here tonight.

I'm getting in their way, that's all. I've done it fifty times and the principle's perfectly sound: When you want to flush the opposition into the open, you just get in their way. You know that.

The door of the fifth suite along the passage was open and I went in there, found no one.

You could have asked for support.

Oh for Christ's sake shuddup.

The gradual emergence of sweat on the skin as the imagination tripped in and brought biochemical reactions, to be read as normal: A trap is a trap, and no animal is at peace in one.

Support was the last thing I wanted, anyway. Legge had said he could call on fourteen men in his group and Vishinsky had brought six guards into the Baccarat Club. There would have been no earthly point in staging a twenty-gun shoot-out in the street; my job was to infiltrate, not start a bloody war.

The Croder thing, though, was a worry.

The suite was ornate in the fin-de-siècle Russian style: an ormolu writing desk, two inlaid consoles, a Volkov print—*Girl with Red Bow*—ivory plush chairs. The windows looked down on the front of the hotel and I could see dark figures against the snow, their breath clouding under the lamplight. Later there would be more, if Vishinsky sent for increased support of his own.

The Croder thing was a worry because the executive had signaled a red sector to his director in the field, and it wouldn't stop there: Ferris would relay the information to London through the mast at Cheltenham, and the man at the board for *Balalaika* would reach for the chalk and when the Chief of Signals saw what he'd written, it could trigger his decision then and there. Ferris: *I think it's possible that at any given time Mr. Croder might act suddenly on the dictates of his conscience and instruct me to pull you out of* Balalaika *and send you home.*

We're usually at least halfway through the mission before we find ourselves in a red sector, but this time I'd got into one almost straight off the starting block. Croder wouldn't like that, would blame himself and pull me out before it was too late.

It might be too late already. This is—

Shuddup.

I moved for the door. Time was of the essence: We teach the neophytes at Norfolk that if you're in a red sector, you need to get out as fast as you can before the opposition brings in reinforcements and turns the trap into a siege. That was a Federal Counterintelligence Service party going on down there but the Fabergé was a regular commercial hotel and a mafiya boss of Vishinsky's caliber could tell the manager he wanted his guards to search the whole building, every vacant room, the elevators, the staircase, the corridors, the mezzanines: the only difference between the dons and the police squads in this city was that the dons didn't need to flash a badge.

Get out fast—but I hadn't got many options. Vishinsky would have ordered his people to cover every exit from this place and stay on the watch all night if they had to, all tomorrow, all the next day—he wouldn't give up, would, on the contrary, bring in more guards to mount the search, changing them in shifts until they'd found me. The Cobra was enraged, because I'd committed the unthinkable and laid a hand on his employees, and he wouldn't rest until I was pitched into the back of his Mercedes and driven into the forest and pushed against a tree with no blindfold, no ceremony, just the one short burst that would bring the rage down and leave him sated, redeemed.

With every exit covered, the only thing I could do was to get to higher ground, so I moved for the emergency staircase again and climbed the last flight. There was only one chance of getting out of here, and that was via the roof.

When I reached the top step I stood listening, hands on the rail as I watched the silent concrete vortex of the staircase below me for movement, shadows. Caught one almost at once, flowing across the wall down there and darkening, sharpening under the lamp and then softening as the man kept on climbing, the shadow-gun swinging, cradled in his arms. This was to be expected: the staircase was an obvious exit path and they'd cover it. I could hear his shoes now on the steps, softly, softly, not hurrying—he was simply patrolling the vertical perimeter of the search area, could lock onto me in the instant if he heard or saw me above or below him, rat-tat-tat and the echoes hammering, the smell of cordite, *finito*.

I moved and got the door open without making enough noise to travel down to him, got it shut again, inching it, my weight against the panel to stop the latch clicking, the air cold now against the face, the crescent of the moon clear below a cloud bank and spreading light across the snow-covered roof, usable, dangerous light according to how things went.

The snow crisp under my feet as I checked out the environment: Four squat chimneys stinking of soot, a cluster of metal ventilators, one with a cowl turning, some kind of wire antenna stretching halfway across the roof, the surface of the roof itself hidden by the snow, uncharted, perhaps treacherous if I went too near the parapets—this was nine floors up, call it a hundred feet from the ground for a building of this period with twelve-foot ceilings, not that it would make a dramatic difference if I fell nine floors or only six, five, *la même chose à la fin*, I'm not a bloody cat.

I didn't think the man on the staircase would come as far as the roof, or at least not yet, Vishinsky had last seen me in the ballroom on the second floor, would expect me to be there when he went back because I hadn't shown any signs of leaving, had made a point of it. He'd have the lower floors searched first, and it'd take him a little time to find the manager and give him the score.

So I had an immediately available but indeterminate time zone to work in before the man on the staircase thought of checking the roof—let's say ten minutes, and that was all I'd want. The thing to avoid was being seen at any distance from that door when—if—the guard pushed it open, because if I wasn't within reach of him, he'd simply level the thing and start pumping.

Light was flushing the building across the street from the entrance of the hotel. When I got to the parapet and looked down, I could see the two dark figures I'd seen before from the window of the vacant suite. The snow crunched under my feet as I crossed to the side of the hotel and looked down into the street and saw a single guard covering whatever doorway he'd found. Bouncing on his heels to keep the blood circulating, the muscles in tone, an athlete, one of the chorus line of mini-cobras.

Straighten up from the parapet and watch the door over there, the door to the staircase, don't *assume* too much, assumptions are dangerous, he can open it at any given time. Keep to cover, then, crossing the roof to the side street on the opposite face of the building, two men there, hands pushed into the pockets of their padded track suits, their breath white in the lamplight. Three sides of the building covered, then, so let us hope for more luck on the fourth.

Hands on the frozen parapet, a shadowed alleyway below, hardly even that, a four-foot gap between the buildings with not even room for a garbage can down there, no door, or there'd be a guard to cover it, no direct light from a window or anywhere else.

But there was a drainpipe.

Watch the door to the staircase.

A drainpipe, and this was what I'd been looking for. Not this one specifically, because sooner or later one of the guards would start patrolling the alleyway below; but there would be—should be—a pipe like this one running down from the roof of the next building.

What sort of red sector?

Croder, his voice coming out of the scrambler in Ferris's hotel room: He'd have got through by now, with only light traffic on the satellite into Moscow.

He didn't say.

Did he ask for support?

No, sir. He said he didn't want any.

No surprise in this for the Chief of Signals: He knows my views on support, especially at night when you need to identify people in a tricky field, and at *once.*

This was ten minutes ago?

Thirteen.

Silence on the line while Croder thought, while Ferris waited for him to say, "All right, if he breaks out of this I want you to abort the mission and send him home. Is that understood?"

Oh for Christ's sake, give me a bloody chance.

Watch, yes, the door. And think, reflect, my good friend, upon the situation, think again of clearing that four-foot gap between the buildings in these conditions: Frozen snow with only pale moonlight to work with, the shadows deceptive, the distance too great for any kind of confidence, the muscles sluggish because of the cold, the chances of success dauntingly thin, so look, yes, before you leap.

The problem was that I hadn't got any choice.

You shouldn't have—

Oh, piss *off.*

Vishinsky wouldn't do half the job. He would seal off this hotel—had already sealed it off—with every man he could muster, and they would be many when he called others in, as many as it would take to make absolutely certain that this single quarry would be flushed out, caught and cornered, spinning like a fox in the ring of clamoring hounds. After all, I had offended him, had displeased the Cobra.

Watch the door.

Ice cracked in the silence as the mass of the building shifted by a degree to its tectonic forces. Over the minutes, echoes came sharply from the walls of the buildings around it as the guests began leaving the party and getting into their cars and slamming the doors.

Certainties, then, consider the certainties. Vishinsky would never give up, would have me found and seized, and then would have me shot. This was certain. I couldn't stay here on the roof forever, even if no one came to search it. This too was certain. But if I could make that leap across the gap between the buildings without going down, without killing myself, I could use the drainpipe on the wall of the next building, and perhaps get to the ground, get to the ground and away. This at least was not certain, nor was death in the attempt.

Therefore make the attempt.

Voices from below, voices and laughter as one by one the revelers took their leave, the steam from their breath laced generously with vodka. Light flooded the walls of the buildings as the pinions bit into the starter bands and the cars moved off with their chains clinking across the snow, leaving me in the gathering silence with a sense of departure crucially more personal, and before too long: we have presentiments, my good friend, do we not, when we feel the party may be over now, and have no wish to go.

I crossed the roof toward the parapet, my shoes crackling on the snow as I passed close to the staircase door in the instant when it was pushed open and the guard looked out at me and swung up his gun.

9
Finito

H E SMELLED OF SWEAT, ATHLETE'S FOOT, and chewing gum. I would have liked to know his name. That's always important when death has to be dealt.

We were lying side by side on the brittle snow; his legs were drawn up. He was trying to find some kind of purchase for his splendid new Nikes, some way of kicking out and giving himself leverage. His breath rose in small clouds, and mine with it, as if we were brothers, which of course we were: All men are brothers.

When I'd moved in on him a minute ago, chopping down with a heel-palm against the muzzle of the AK-47, his finger hadn't had time to thrust itself into the trigger guard; the gun had not fired. It was lodged between us.

The door of the staircase was still open. Even if I could have moved, I wouldn't have closed it. If there were any more footsteps on the concrete stairs, I wanted to hear them. I couldn't move because we were in a double check, the fancy name for this situation, dreamed up by some chess-playing bloody poet in the Bureau. But I suppose—

Watch it.

He'd made an attempt at moving, this man, my brother, at first relaxing by infinite degrees so that I wouldn't notice, then blasting the motor nerves with signals; but I had noticed, and he didn't get his half-fist any farther than an inch or two, aimed at my throat. He'd been trained in close combat, which was not good news; on the other hand it made him more predictable, since I would know most—perhaps all—of his moves.

83

Sweat running on both of us: the muscular tension was enormous because neither wanted to let go, in other words, to get ourselves killed. To extend the fanciful idiom, that would be checkmate.

Earlier, thirty or forty seconds ago, he'd tried to reach the trigger of the assault rifle, in the hope of releasing a burst as a signal to the other guards. There was no chance at this stage of turning the muzzle on me—I've told you, these things are totally useless at close quarters.

I could feel his heartbeat. He could feel mine. They wouldn't slow for a long time, for minutes, until one of us was dead. We had a lot in common, as all brothers have; each of us was seeking—would soon seek more actively as fatigue set in and mistakes were made—the other's death.

Below in the street, a last car door slammed; I suppose one of the guests hadn't been in terribly good shape for driving, was now being escorted home. The staff would be clearing up the ballroom by now, the remains of the caviar and the boar's head, the roast goose, the dirty glasses, the single white glove dropped by one of the women, perhaps, a ballpoint pen or two, a business card, while in the—

No you fucking well don't.

He'd tried again, testing me.

While in the rest of the hotel Vishinsky would be conducting the search, the manager with him to placate any guests who were trying to sleep. They would take it floor by floor, starting on the ground and gradually coming higher. It hadn't occurred to this man lying here with me that the most he had to do was hold me off until there were footsteps on the stairs; if it had occurred to him, he wouldn't have tried those moves.

"What's your name?" I asked him, hardly enough breath to spare but as I say it's always important.

He didn't answer.

The cold air pressed against our faces, the chill of the sweat clammy, beginning to itch. I hadn't made a move yet because when I made it, I wanted it to succeed, to kill. There'd be no chance of letting him live: I had to get to the roof of the other building after I'd buried him under the snow.

I didn't know how much longer I had before another guard came up here to look around. Ten minutes? Five? None?

Watch the doorway.

He had calluses, this man, along the sword-edge, harder on the right hand. He liked chopping bricks, to show how strong he was—correction—to prove *to himself* how strong he was: these cocky superjocks always have the seed in them of self-doubt.

He made a move and I parried it but he was desperate and managed to bring an elbow-strike to graze my head and followed through with a knee-strike and I had to roll face down and try for his eyes but he got a hand free and found the trigger of the rifle and put out a short burst before I could do anything, blinding flash and the stink of cordite, the eyes having to accommodate now, the thought process having to reestablish itself after the shock of the percussion, time needed, milliseconds, before I could react and hook for his eyes to inflict pain, got it and found leverage enough to drive a half-fist into his throat with the necessary force to kill as he too rolled and found the trigger again but I was there first and broke his finger and now he began calling out or trying to, but the strike had broken the cartilage in his throat and internal hemorrhage was beginning and he couldn't manage any kind of sound that could raise the alarm.

Reassess time factor: Shots were heard at all hours of the night in this city and under the open sky, so there'd be no directional acoustics to guide the guards in the streets below—that short burst could have come from anywhere. But it would have sounded in the stairwell through the doorway, and I got the guard's wallet and put it away and pulled his padded jacket off because I'd checked my sable coat in the hotel lobby when I'd arrived tonight.

Liquid sounds now from my dying brother, *requiescat in pace,* the soft ululation of the blood blocking the windpipe as I got him into my arms to avoid leaving tracks, carried him across the roof, and laid him down and covered him with snow, kicking it loose and scooping it until my hands were raw and gradually his body took on the form of its own white crystalline grave. Then I left him and crossed to the emergency stairs and listened, heard nothing, closed the metal door and went to the parapet that faced the next building, didn't look down this time into the narrow gap, looked across to the parapet opposite, didn't think again of the conditions: *Frozen snow with only pale moonlight to work with, the shadows deceptive, the distance too great for any kind of confidence, the muscles sluggish because of the cold, the chances of success dauntingly thin.*

Needs must.

Yea, verily, but 'tis easily said.

I stood with my feet close to the parapet, the toes of my calfskin boots just touching it. This wouldn't be my point of departure: the parapet was ten inches high, twelve, a stumbling block. My point of departure would have to be the *top* of the parapet, giving my legs leverage, the instep hooked over the front angle of the stone as I pitched forward, kicking out to send me past the point of no return, balanced in the air above the gap and for a moment flying, wingless, borne on hope alone—hope? You must be joking, we mean desperation, don't we, because there's no bloody choice and if we don't do this we'll go down under the tree, *rat-tat-tat,* and onto the forest floor.

The ice crackled, its sound infinitely slight as the ancient building moved under its own weight and the earth's rotation and the change in temperature as midnight pressed down on the mercury one degree at a time. The ice melted under my feet: I could feel it. The ice was everywhere, here where I stood, over there on the other side of the further parapet, treacherous, uninviting.

The night's chill pressed at the face, burned on the fingers still aching from the work of the grave digging. Fear sat patiently at the threshold of the heart, awaiting admittance once the guard was down and the door swung back.

Rat-tat-tat and the rough bark of the tree grazing the neck as the body slumped, all we needed to give us the will to choose otherwise, so I scraped the frozen snow off the top of the parapet and stood with both feet on it and took in oxygen to fire the muscles and felt the rush of adrenaline and sighted across the gap and leaned into the skiing stance and waited until my weight carried me forward and felt the night close in to focus on this irrational act of *sauve qui peut* in the instant before I kicked out and thought of nothing more until the roof of the next building came slanting up and I flung my hands out to break the impact and brought my right shoulder into an aikido roll and followed it with another one and then a third as full consciousness came back after the gap in the mental process that had set in as I'd flown across the gap between the buildings, the high quarter-moon afloat in the void above me now, the sound of a car not far away in the street below, life becoming normal again, mundane.

"Yakub?"

I didn't move.

The voice was coming from the adjoining roof.

"Yakub, are you up here?"

Not in his entirety, no, just the chemical residue he left behind him under the makeshift tomb, don't go looking for him, don't start all *that*, the discovery and the sounding of the alarm and the hue and cry, for Christ's sake leave well alone, give me a break, don't stack these bloody odds, they're already as high as I can handle.

"Yakub?"

God's sake go away.

From where I lay I could just see the pale blur of his face as he left the doorway and looked around, swinging his Kalashnikov. I shut my eyes to hide the moon's reflected light in case he looked across here, would have liked *very* much to keep him in sight because I couldn't be presenting anything but the image of a man lying here on the melting snow, a man or a human body, perhaps Yakub's. But I had rolled into shadow, and that could give me a chance.

I lay in silence, listening for the movement of his boots, hearing the clink of the brass gun swivel as he turned, crunching over the frozen snow, the sound diminishing as it met the open doorway and ceased to echo.

Turning again—"Yakub?"

To reassure himself before he clanged the iron door shut and I lay for another minute, waiting until the thudding underneath me between the rib cage and the roof slowed to eighty, seventy-five, seventy and I rolled over and moved to the parapet where there should be a drainpipe, where there was indeed—look!—a drainpipe, tilting down in perspective against the wall of the building, thinning to a point where the alleyway lay under virgin snow and for the moment unpatrolled, a haven, if you will, if I could get there, nine floors below.

The guard across there had taken a quick look for Yakub but he was still missing and at any given time there'd be someone else coming up to make a thorough search of the roof—*Yakub? He was on the emergency staircase the last time I saw him, and as far as I know he hasn't come down*—and they'd find the tomb and kick the snow aside and *then* it would start, the alarm and the hue and cry, so I'd have to reach the alleyway before it happened, reach ground and get clear.

So I kicked the snow off the top of the parapet and swung my legs over before rational thought could get in my way, rational thought and primitive instinct—*I don't like this, you're going to kill yourself if*—

Possibly.

It's nine stories—

I'm glad you're learning to count at last.

It was solid, this drainpipe, square-section, cast iron, the way they made things in the nineteenth century, none of your thin tin tubing that wouldn't have given me a hope in hell, and between the pipe and the wall there was a gap an inch wide—not much, but adequate for fingerholds. And below, halfway down with any luck, there would be vines, thin tendrils at first and then larger, stronger, leafless and with the sap drained for the winter's hibernation, but that made no difference; it would provide me with a rope, a lifeline, so all is not lost, my good friend, providing the heart is sanguine and the will in charge.

And I was out of sight, had found cover.

Get Mr. Croder.

Cover of a sort, the iron pipe freezing the fingers, numbing them as I let my weight drop another six inches and found new purchase with my feet.

The executive's found cover, sir.

Six inches in one hundred feet.

He can't have.

Because the last signal was still there, chalked on the board for the mission: *Executive in red sector, no support requested.*

Before I could relay any new signal through Ferris, the red-sector designation would have to be wiped out with the chalk-powdered block, and they couldn't do that yet.

It's not terribly good cover, sir.

What the hell are you telling me?

It's a drainpipe, one hundred feet over a sheer drop.

And his hands, these hands, are frozen now, the bones providing claws and that was all: I could have done with Croder's steel grappling iron except that it would have made a noise, ringing through the hollows of the pipe, the sound transferred to the alleyway below.

For the first time I looked down, and saw no one, looked up again as the vertigo started like a worm in the cerebellum: one hundred feet, viewed from an angle of five degrees, looks like one thousand.

Let the weight go again, the toes of the calfskin boots scraping the wall, the claws that used to be hands and fingers shifting downward another six inches, hooking into the gap again and holding as I waited, controlling the breath, *I could use more adrenaline,* more heat, but for that to happen there would need to be the onset of panic as the claws slipped and one boot lost its purchase and the other one followed and the dead weight, the dying weight of the shadow executive for *Balalaika,* hung for a moment in the air and then dropped and gathered speed as the windstream played on the face and then tore at the cheekbones until the boots struck ground and the legs buckled, snapping at the knee joints, and by first light of the morning the director in the field would send the initial signal of the day: *No further report from the executive, red-sector call uncanceled. Request instructions.*

Croder, wakened from a moment of snatched sleep at two in the afternoon—*If he's still alive, pull him out and shut down the mission.*

If he's still alive, bullshit, of course I'll still be alive, drop another six inches, keep the iron rectangle between the feet for guidance, drop another six inches but the strain on the shoulders was beginning to nag, the shoulders and the biceps, what would you expect, drop another six but don't hurry, don't slip, ignore the absence of feeling now in the fingers, the claws, they're just obeying the motor nerves, clamp and wait and release and clamp again with the tenacity of a bloody crab, drop another six inches then and don't complain but the shoulders were on fire now and into my mind there came the question: Why wasn't the heat from them melting the snow? But there wasn't any snow on the wall, what was I—

Watch it—don't lose your marbles, this is hardly the time or the place.

Shook my head to clear it, just the strain, it was just the strain of the physical demand on the organism that was threatening to blank out rational thought, ignore and proceed and drop another six inches and look down, take another look down, oh Jesus, we weren't more than halfway through this desperate business and it was going to be a question of time now before the fingers, the claws lost their muscle tone and couldn't clamp any more, couldn't clamp and wait and release and clamp again, would simply come away from the pipe and send me backward into the air and down into the pit of oblivion, look up again and keep the eyes shut and wait for the vertigo to fade, think of nothing, or think of Yakub, the cooling cadaver whose padded coat I wore, smelling still of his sweat, are we then to meet, my good friend, my late adversary, is that the game now, are you waiting for me there, watching over the rites of passage this dangling crab thing is now embarked upon? Are we so soon to be united, my brother, in the death that shall transcend all means by which we shall dance in the shadowed hinterland of—

Watch it, for Christ's sake, *get the mind under control,* count five, then, and drop again, feel for the pipe below and drop again.

I think I was twenty feet from the ground, judging by the level of the window sills, when I realized there was no vine on this *bloody* wall, no fibrous lifeline I could use after all if I needed one, and it was now that I felt movement in the iron rectangle of the pipe as one of the big staples came away and the pipe quivered and I dropped again without intention this time and clawed for purchase as the adrenaline came flooding into my bloodstream and brought a flush to the skin as the pipe turned by degrees against the wall and another staple was ripped from its hole, loosened by my weight and movement and the erosion that had been going on for year after year and the—

Mother of God—

As the last section of pipe was torn from the wall it leaned across the gap over the alleyway and I went with it, dangling now like a monkey from a pole with my legs swinging in space and one hand losing its grip and the other clinging on until the whole section rolled and pitched me sideways and there was nothing but the air beneath me and I plummeted, hitting the wall and bouncing off with the sound of a huge bell ringing in my skull and the burst of star shells as I hit the ground and heard another sound, the quick thudding of feet, and as the dark came down I caught the pale blur of a face and the glint of a gun barrel slanting toward me and thought yes, *finis* this time, *finito.*

10
Play

T HE SMALL HEAD WAS HOODED, MAKING it look much larger, and the jaws were opening, the fangs curving back into the rippling pink throat. The eyes were black, reflecting the light and only half-concealing the anger of the predator disturbed.

It was swaying, the head, with a slow sinister rhythm, only inches from my face, so close that my eyes were losing focus. Then it stopped and drew back, preparing for the strike.

I rocked as icy water hit me and ran down to my chin.

"More."

Water again, bursting between my eyes, ice cubes bouncing like stones, the skin contracting to the chill. But I hardly noticed it, was worried about the snake, the hooded cobra.

"Again."

This time I closed my eyes in time, and when I opened them I saw that the thing's head had stopped swaying. I could see the whole of the gold silk pocket now, with the head emblazoned on it, then Vishinsky leaned back to watch me from his chair.

Vishinsky the Cobra, right, made sense, consciousness coming back.

Must, I must have smashed my head against the wall when I'd landed on the ground in the alleyway, last remembered image was the muzzle, the muzzle of the gun.

Some degree of concussion, then, or I'd lost blood when Yakub's bullet had grazed my skull on the roof. Memory clear enough, thank God for that.

"Again?"

"No."

Watching me, elegant in his gold silk dressing-gown, his eyes shimmering with fury.

No tree, then, behind me, no *rat-tat-tat*. But I could remember the car now, the inside of the car, the sharp athletic stink of sweat, I wish these bloody people would wash sometimes. Watching the play of street lights across the reflective surfaces of the car, I'd thought they were taking me to the forest. But later there'd been that impression of lightness as they'd carried me through a doorway and into an elevator with mirrored walls, heard the drone of the cables, then another blackout.

"Do you recognize me?"

Vishinsky.

I wasn't sure; I'd have to give it some thought. It might be better to fake it for a few minutes, the syncope, take a bit longer to pull out, give myself time to orientate.

"More water, boss?"

"No."

"I'm not sure," I told the man in the black-and-chromium chair.

"I am the Cobra."

Reminded me of the way he'd done this before, talked of himself in the third person, presenting, as a psychiatrist might put it, a degree of megalomania, might be useful, something to work with.

Head ached a bit, blood caked on the left side of the skull, I could feel it as I flexed the skin. Something blue underneath me, royal blue, a bath towel, I was sitting on a bath towel with my back to the wall. He didn't want to spoil the carpet, Vishinsky, with blood-stains, what infernal nerve, I was a guest here, if you want to stretch your imagination a bit.

"Oh," I said, "the Cobra. Yes, I remember now."

"Good." The tone cutting, soft with rage. I knew why, of course: they would have searched me for weapons, found Yakub's wallet.

Taste of blood in the mouth: perhaps my tongue had got between my teeth when I'd come unstuck in the alleyway. I didn't think there was any internal bleeding going on: there'd been no trauma to the lungs.

I looked around me and saw four bodyguards, all on their feet and watching me in a concerted focus of attention, star, I was the show, star of the show, head throbbing, take your time, we must take our time, there was no hurry to run through the final stages of my life in this particular reality before the man in the chair decided to bring it to a screaming halt because of what I'd done to Yakub, a modern suite, this, modern hotel, black glass and chrome surfaces with a whole console of communications equipment bristling with antennae over there near the long and sumptuously-stocked bar, a big Rousseau print, the jungle one, and a brushed-aluminum-framed painting of a cobra, rearing and hooded, above the fireplace where artificial logs were flickering unconvincingly, and look at that, a miniature guillotine, cute little basket and all—*fingers,* would that be the game, then, first the tips and then the rest of them, working down through the knuckles and the blood-crimson haze of the mind that refused to speak on its way to the only exit available, insanity? Because he had some questions for me, I knew that now: He'd had me taken alive.

Now 12:30 on the chic figureless clock on the wall over the bar, the witching hour well past and the morrow already here. And perfume in the air: a woman had been here, and not too long ago. He would have many of those, the Cobra.

"You killed one of my men." His tone almost hushed.

"What? That's right."

I managed to get him in focus again, felt a bit better now, not what you'd call operational, but able to think. That was going to help, if I wanted to get through the first hours of this new day still alive and mentally intact. Even all of the day.

"His wallet was found on you," the Cobra said softly.

"Yes?"

"Why did you take his wallet?"

"I wanted information."

"Information on what?"

"Whatever there was to find."

In a moment—"You've called yourself a 'businessman' on several occasions, Berinov. So I'm interested to know why a 'businessman' should be able to knock out three trained bodyguards and *almost* get out of a trap by going down the wall of a building in the dark."

Obviously, this was the first of the major questions he would ask me, and I'd worked out the answer already. "I was with the *Komitet*." The KGB.

"I see. Which department?"

"Department Four." Terrorist training and operations. "I liked the excitement, but of course I was younger then."

"Go on."

"Then I got interested in money when I found out how expensive women were, and how much they liked diamonds. The pay in the *Komitet* wasn't quite adequate."

He thought about that. "So how did you acquire your acumen as a 'businessman'?"

"Oh, look, it's not difficult to make money in Moscow these days—you know that. Or anywhere else, if you set a goal and go for it."

His sleek pomaded head tilted an inch. "That's very true. But it's difficult for me to believe that a former *Komitet* terrorist agent now doing business in the mafiya no longer carries a gun. It's inconsistent. Perhaps you can help me."

I gave a shrug. "The fact is that I find making money—big money, huge money—so attractive, that I've changed my self-image. Guns don't go with silk shirts and deerskin shoes and London-tailored suits. And if I get into trouble, I don't normally need a gun to help me to get out of it. Tonight I was simply out of luck."

Thin ice, terribly thin ice—I could hear it cracking.

"You were out of luck, yes," Vishinsky said. The fury still hadn't left his eyes: It was creating that glint of crystal in their depths. "And you'll be interested to know we've got something in common. I was also in the *Komitet*, working with Stasi in East Germany until the Wall came down." He allowed a pause. "I was sent there to train their people in advanced interrogation techniques."

I found my attention drawn to the cute little guillotine near the bar, but I didn't move my eyes or my head.

"So let me guess," I said. "You've got some questions for me tonight."

He nodded slowly. "The first one is, where are the diamonds?"

He couldn't leave them alone.

Suddenly I knew my direction, the only chance I had of seeing the dawn. This man was for sale. But I wasn't buying him in diamonds. "They're for Sakkas's mistress," I said. A prima ballerina, Croder had told me, and one of the most beautiful women in the whole of Russia.

"Antanova?"

"Yes." Mental freeze—it had been such a long shot.

"You know her?"

"I've seen her dance. I thought the diamonds might be a suitable introduction. Look, Vishinsky, if—"

The Cobra was leaning forward. "You had the idea of picking up Vasyl Sakkas's *mistress?*"

"They say she's stunning."

Vishinsky leaned back, his eyes glimmering: Perhaps he thought I was putting him on, didn't like it. "There are various ways of committing suicide. In any case, he never lets Natalya wear jewelry. To Sakkas she's cattle."

I waited, but he didn't say anything more, and I left it, took the heat off the subject in case I blew things. "Look," I said, "if you're short a couple of million dollars, I can steer you into something a lot more profitable than those little baubles, believe me. You know what they say—don't stop the parade to pick up a dime."

He went on watching me for a moment, then glanced upward at something beside me—someone standing against the wall, out of my vision field. Five guards, then, and noted. I think Vishinsky was on the point of ordering this one to beat me up until he got straight answers; then he seemed to change his mind and looked back at me.

"Go on," he said softly. I'd first heard this tone at the Baccarat Club; it meant that if I said something wrong, he would let me know.

"Let's call it five million," I said. "I'm talking about icons now, antiques. There's a very good market for that sort of thing in London and New York—for any kind of Russian art, especially from the Czarist period. It's very *in* now—miniatures, Fabergé eggs, gold snuffboxes, jewelry—and people here are busy searching out the sources—museums, banks, private collections, nowhere's safe. I was in London last week and I came back with fourteen million US dollars after only three days."

I waited, but Vishinsky didn't say anything. I didn't know if he was paying attention or even listening, and there was the uneasy feeling that the more rope I paid out the more he'd have to hang me with. But I couldn't stop now.

"If that interests you, I can give you introductions to some of the major collectors in the West, the most profitable sources of merchandise here and the most reliable courier services."

He took a long time, the Cobra.

"Why should you?"

I shrugged. "I'm putting a price on my head that I can pay."

"Explain that."

"It's pretty obvious. I muscled my way into your poker game at the club, and you didn't like that. I left two of your men in bad shape just afterwards and then I was forced to kill a third, and you don't like that either. I think you would have had me shot on sight tonight if you hadn't wanted the diamonds first, so you at least know the basics of good business, but that won't save my neck if you suddenly decide to order the kill to get rid of the anger that's in you."

Let the defense rest.

He watched me for a while, the crystalline light still playing deep in his eyes and replacing intelligence with raw emotion, so that I hadn't got a chance of knowing how I was making out.

"Yes," he said at last, "there's a great deal of anger in me, and killing you would give me much satisfaction. You have offended the Cobra."

"*Mea culpa.*"

Then he made one of his nonsequential leaps, and it worried me.

"Do you think this is a nice suite?"

I looked around. "Very nice."

"All the suites are like this one. There are seven floors. This is the Hotel Nikolai. I named it myself—I'm a monarchist at heart, you know."

"Really."

"I own the hotel."

"And how many others?"

He frowned. "This is the only one. I'm not in the hotel business."

"But that's very profitable too, Vishinsky. There are three hotels along the Boulevard Ring, fully furnished and going for a song. Fin de siècle, a lot of class, bronze, gilt, molded ceilings, tapestries. I could arrange for you to buy all three of them."

The shiny head tilting. "For how much?"

"Five million. They're worth fifty."

"How can you do that?"

"The owner is in my debt."

"For fifty million?"

"Much more. He owes me his life."

"I see. It will be very easy, of course, for me to check out this line you've been giving me."

"I'm expecting you to. I'm putting a generous price on my own life tonight. Don't miss this great opportunity."

Mistake—and I froze mentally. Vishinsky's head was tilting again. He wasn't familiar with that last phrase, because I'd given it a literal translation. To protect and maintain a foreign-national cover, you haven't only got to speak the language fluently, you've got to watch the idiom—I'd just used some American—and follow the customs, respect the etiquette, the taboos, adopt the characteristic attitudes to life: in France, philosophical; in the UK, polite, but a touch suspicious of strangers; in Germany, brisk and efficient; in

Russia, cynical to the bone. But I couldn't change the "great opportunity" thing now, would have to rely on Vishinsky's impression
that I did business in New York as well as London, knew my way
around there.

"You visit the United States?" Hadn't missed it.

"I spent six months there a few years ago. These days I'm there
every month or two. It depends on what I can dig up in the icon
mines here, and who wants to buy it in the Big Apple."

"The big—"

"New York. I'm not sure why they call it that."

"I see."

He was giving things a lot of thought again, and I let the silence
in and did some thinking of my own. If this man was going to play
ball I would ask for the use of a telephone and call Legge—*not
Ferris*—"Oh, this is Berinov. I want you to set up a few things for
me. I need a supply of some really good icons, rare ones, make it a
half dozen and throw in some jewelry—Fabergé if you can locate it
at short notice. I'll come round for them when you name the contact point—use the utmost discretion, as always."

Take it from there, leave it to Legge's imagination: perhaps he
could find some good reproductions, put up a show, give me the time
and the chance to get out of this place and meet him at the contact
point—heavily escorted, right, but once in the open streets again I
could use some imagination of my own, create a last-ditch chance
and go for it, shit or bust, life or death, I shall need your prayers, my
good friend, and I would ask you to be generous with them, even
stylish, indulge me, think of some Latin.

"I'm not sure," Vishinsky said at last, "if I should believe all
your—" and then the telephone rang and the nearest bodyguard
picked it up and listened. Vishinsky had stopped what he was
saying at once: The call was important and he'd been expecting it.

The guard brought him the phone. "Moskolets, Boss."

Vishinsky took it. "Well?"

I could hear the caller's voice faintly, couldn't catch the words,
but Vishinsky's eyes had changed. The fury in them was suddenly

explicit, blazing, and I was warned: This man was capable of anything, any act, however appalling, once he had enough rage to drive him.

"What?" Very softly.

I took a quick look at the guard standing behind him and saw the skin draw tight on his face and the fear come into his eyes.

"Why not?"—Vishinsky.

The time on the clock over the bar was now midnight plus thirty-seven, and I noted it simply because the scene in here was going to change and it might become important to remember when things had happened. I heard a sound, slight as the rustle of a dry leaf, from behind me as the man there shifted his feet, and the silence was so intense now that I heard him swallow.

Vishinsky was looking nowhere, at no one, his eyes set in a brilliant stare as he listened for another five seconds, ten, and then said— "Get here. *Get up here,*" and threw the phone for the guard to catch.

I leaned the back of my head against the wall to conserve the energy of my vertebrae, breathing a little deeper, tensing the major muscles and not finding any soreness critical enough to stop mobility, ultra-mobility if a chance came to do anything while Vishinsky was dealing with Moskolets, offering a diversion.

With five guards in here?

Christ, not you again.

To no one Vishinsky said in a different tone now, of a honed knife slitting snakeskin, "He didn't make the kill."

A soul saved, then, somewhere out there in the night, a banker or a judge on his late way home, or just some merchant tardy with his dues. But the Cobra was not pleased, and I thought of the guillotine again: perhaps he used it for purposes other than interrogation, for the teaching of lessons, *par exemple.*

"There were people around," he said, and I saw the guard near him flinch. *"There were people around,* so he thought it wasn't a good time to do it. *He thought it wasn't a good time."* He got out of his chair so fast that it was sent spinning as he stood staring at the guard. "What do you think of *that,* Vitali?"

"He should've made the kill, Boss."

"Of course he should have made the fucking kill!"

Metal vibrated somewhere on the bar, perhaps the handle of the ice bucket. I tensed the muscles again, relaxed them, took slow, deep breaths. Five guards, right, but they were all scared to death of this man and the degree of fear in them would diminish their muscle tone by half, more than half, and slow their reactions—decisively, if I could make any kind of move.

"You're out of your—"

Shuddup. I'm handling this.

Vishinsky had swung round again and was staring at me now, the rage so hot in his eyes that I could see he was trying to remember who I was, what I was doing here propped against the wall with blood caked on my head.

Then a buzzer sounded and he jerked his attention away, stood perfectly still in the middle of the room and watched one of the guards go to the door and look through the security lens before he opened it.

Moskolets came in quickly as if someone had pushed him, his thick body sloping ahead of his feet, a clot of caked snow coming off one of his boots. He saw Vishinsky and brought himself to a halt, his eyes tensed as if he were looking into strong light.

"Boss," he said, "I—"

"Get over there. Against the wall."

"Boss, I can explain—there were too many people in the—"

"Get over there."

The man ducked his head, pulling off his fur hat as he trotted across the room, turning when he reached the wall and standing there with the collar of his coat still turned up against the chill of the streets, one lapel bent back untidily, his thin hair pulled away from the bald patch by the action of taking off his hat, his face gray as he forced himself to look into the eyes of the Cobra, a hit man, Moskolets, older than the chorus boys in their monogrammed jumpsuits, a more experienced attendant, a specialist in the art of the distant kill, *rat-tat-tat,* wishing perhaps that he had his gun out now and ready to make the most important hit of his life, the one that would end the terror that was in him now.

In the silence I could hear tire chains clinking in the street below, even through the double-glazed and possibly bulletproof windows. Snow must be falling again, and this, too, was noted as a change in the environment. A red sector is a red sector, and the most trivial factors can suddenly become critical.

Vishinsky moved at last, going back to the chrome-and-vinyl chair and sitting down, and as he turned I saw his eyes had changed again, were almost expressionless as he looked across at the man standing against the wall.

"Explain, then," he said, singsong, as if to a child.

"Boss, there were five or six people—more than that—maybe seven or eight people, and two of them were—"

"Don't fiddle with your hat, Yuri."

The man looked down at his hands, stilling them, bringing his head up again with his face crumpling. This new role-playing—of parent and child—began to fascinate me as I was shown yet another side to Vishinsky's psychotic character: from a blaze of explicit rage he was capable of getting himself back under control, of driving his emotions inwards and holding them there with the potential of an unexploded bomb. And there was something appropriate in the parent-child relationship—the Russian word 'Sobri' was as close as the mafiyosa could get to the Al Capone title of 'Boss,' but it also had a suggestion of 'Father' about it, as in the French 'Patron.'

"Two of them were cops, Boss. You wouldn't have wanted me to make a hit in front of the cops, I knew that, I was sure of that." His small mouth hanging open, his breath fluttering, his eyes pleading now.

"Was it snowing, Yuri?"

"Snowing? Yes. Starting to come down quite a bit. The cops—"

"How was the street?"

"The street, Boss?"

"The surface. Try and understand what I'm saying, Yuri. And straighten your collar."

The man's hands fumbled with it, then he looked up again—was this better, was this pleasing to his *Sobri?* "The—the surface," he said, lost, then made a try. "The surface had got some snow on it. Not much, just a little." Was that the right answer?

"So you could have made an immediate getaway," Vishinsky said, his tone light, chiding, "as soon as you'd got the shots in. Isn't that right?"

"Boss, I—"

"Isn't that right?"

"With the cops there, I—"

"Vitali," Vishinsky said to the guard near him. "Bring me that imbecile's revolver."

"Boss," the man against the wall said, "Boss, I did what I thought was right—"

"Shut your mouth."

Moskolets unbuttoned his coat and the guard took his gun and brought it over to Vishinsky, presenting the butt with deference, his eyes uneasy. This had been enacted before, then, this little charade; it had its own traditional choreography, and every man in the room was familiar with it, and on edge.

Moskolets—"Boss, don't do this to me. Don't—"

"Shut up, you stupid son of a whore! *You know that fucking judge is going to be in court tomorrow, and he's got my brother up on a charge? Didn't you know that?"*

"Yes, Boss, but I—"

"Shut the *fuck up!"*

Vishinsky's hands were trembling as he hit the chamber of the gun open and shook five of the bullets out, scattering them onto the carpet and snapping the chamber back and giving the gun to the guard.

"Boss—" the voice of Moskolets, high-pitched now, a small boy's whimper—"Boss, I didn't mean to—"

"Vitali, give him the gun."

"Sure, Boss."

"Don't make me do it, for the sake of the holy Christ—"

"I'm giving you a chance, Moskolets. You do this or they take you to the forest, don't you understand? You spin that thing right and you can get out of here with your fucking skin. Don't you know *charity* when you see it?"

"Boss, please, Boss, for the sake—" his voice cracking.

But he took the gun, looked at it as if he'd never seen one before, silent now, his mouth shaking, his eyes wide, such are your typical hit men, put them on the wrong side of their favorite toy and this is what you see, call it a jellyfish, not good to look upon without a sour rush of contempt into the mouth.

"Play," Vishinsky cut across him. *"Play!"*

The guard Vitali stood away from the man quickly, perhaps bearing in mind how far a jet of blood will reach when an artery's hit, and there was a click as Moskolets pulled the trigger, another click as he pulled it again, wanting suddenly to get it over, know the worst, was that it?

I watched Vishinsky's face, the eyes of the cobra, as he stared at the roulette player, unblinking. Behind him the guard had his own eyes narrowed, his mouth compressed, his head jerking a degree as Vishinsky's voice came.

"Play, you fucking clod, come on, *three—fire!"*

Another click, the man's finger moving as if to the force of the other man's voice, the face of Moskolets now bright with sweat, his hand shaking as he kept the gun held to his temple, his eyes no longer registering anything as his mind passed beyond terror and beyond despair, dwelling in oblivion, already—

"*Play,* Moskolets, you—"

Crash of the gun and the guard jumped forward to catch the man as the blood bloomed crimson across the skull and the thick squat body jackknifed into Vitali's arms—

"Mind the carpet, don't get blood on the carpet!"

"Okay, Boss," cradling Moskolets's head against his jumpsuit as he lowered the body, two of the other guards moving in to help him.

"Get a bag." Vishinsky's voice quiet now as the cordite fumes curdled in the air below the lamp. "Put him into a bag and give me his gun."

"Sure, Boss."

One of them left the room, his feet quick, bouncing in their fancy Nikes across the carpet. Vishinsky didn't move, sat with his legs crossed and the revolver on his lap as he stared at the mottled face of Moskolets, his body propped against the wall, a guard holding the palm of his hand over the bloodied cavity in the skull.

It was a black bag the other man brought back, the standard model. I suppose it must have been tempting for the Cobra to have his escutcheon printed on it in gold—he must have kept a *supply* of these things for God's sake, *the Russian-style syndicates,* Croder had said, *make the Italian and Sicilian operators look like harmless amateurs,* yea, verily, in all sooth.

A dull musical note sounded, long-drawn-out and with a tone of finality in it as a guard pulled the zipper shut on the bag.

"Two of you, take him to the forest."

"Sure, Boss."

They lifted the body together, one at its shoulders and the other holding its feet. A third guard opened the door for them, closed it again, its sheet steel booming faintly like the echo of a prison gate. The fumes of the cordite hung on the air, bittersweet.

Vishinsky picked up one of the bullets from the carpet and slipped it into the chamber of the revolver and slapped it shut and threw the gun across to me.

"Now you," he said. "Play."

II
Spin

S WEAT OF A DEAD MAN'S HAND, chilling and intimate, on the butt of the gun as I caught it.

It was short-barrelled but heavy, a Taura .44 chambered to take a man-stopping shell, the scent of its last shot lacing the air.

It's no good pretending the Cobra was taking a risk. Yes, I could swing the chamber open and line up the cartridge and hit the thing shut and take aim and fire, drill him accurately between the frontal lobes, watch his surprise in the instant before the head snapped back under the impact. But the three remaining bodyguards would be on me like wolves. He knew that, and also that I hadn't the slightest interest in ending his life and then my own in some kind of personal Götterdämmerung.

I laid the gun on the floor.

"Pick it up," Vishinsky said softly.

"One day," I told him, "you're going to look back to the time when I came into your life and showed you the royal path to great riches. You need to think ahead a little. You need to realize that I don't hold my life cheaply, and I'm ready to pay."

He leaned forward an inch. "Pick up the gun."

I couldn't quite tell from his eyes whether the crystalline glitter was the lingering excitement of Moskolets's death or the anticipation of my own. But I could see that he was beyond linear thinking, oblivious to logic. He was all emotion now, with the forebrain shut down, the death of the hit man taking him into what we would call a feeding frenzy in a shark.

So I gave up the idea of appealing to his consciousness on the beta level and thought about the situation instead. With two of the guards absent burying the hit man, there were three left: too many. I would need to get control of four men within a time frame—call it a couple of seconds—far too narrow for success. And there was nowhere to run, no way out of here except for the heavy steel door: This was the seventh floor of the building, and the windows were sealed.

"Pick up the gun."

There might be a way of reaching Vishinsky through his emotions, but I doubted it. I didn't know him well enough to try probing his sensitivities.

I don't like this.

Shuddup.

So it was a question of choices. If I didn't give Vishinsky the death he craved in this way, he'd take it in another, here or in the forest. Or he'd tell his minions to drag me across the room to the guillotine and start work, or to smash me into pulp before the coup de grâce, whatever pleased him, whatever would sate his appetite.

"I'm giving you a chance," I heard him saying, his tone singsong again as if he were talking to a child, "just as I gave that imbecile Moskolets a chance. That's very generous."

"The risk's too big," I told him, but it meant nothing. As long as we could talk, express ideas, there might be something I could do.

"There's a risk, yes, but you've got to take it. You have no choice."

Perfectly true.

But you can't—

Oh for Christ's sake shuddup.

"You should leave room for logic, Vishinsky. You've heard of the goose and the golden eggs. If you let me live, I can—"

"Kaido," he said to the guard nearest me, "give him a little persuasion."

I heard the man moving, and this was the point when I knew I'd have to take the only way out. I picked up the gun.

"There, now," Vishinsky said, pleased.

The only way out was to rely on the odds. The Taura .44 was a six-shot but the odds weren't six to one; in fact, they were infinite. Rely on that.

"Six times and I miss and I'm free to go?"

"Yes. You have my word."

The air in the room was becoming still, pressing against the skin. The walls seemed to be contracting, an illusion triggered by the knowledge that I had no escape.

"I'd prefer to stand up," I told Vishinsky.

"Yes? I've no objection."

As I got onto my feet the guard nearest me closed in. I could smell the sweat on him. Either he thought I might try for some kind of action or he wanted to be near enough to catch me as I went down. I remembered Vishinsky—*Mind the carpet—don't get blood on the carpet!* A fastidious man.

"Play," he said now.

Spin the chamber, yes, buck the odds, go for a winner. But the sweat had begun creeping on the skin.

Trigger.

Click, and five to go.

Vishinsky was sitting back now, his long pale hands folded on the silk dressing gown, his eyes filled with that unholy light I'd seen before when he'd been watching Moskolets do this.

I could feel the wall at my back, pressing against my shoulder blades; in a way it gave me strength, a feeling of permanence. I watched Vishinsky. He watched the gun as I spun the chamber again and put the muzzle to my head.

This, or the forest. Take the chance.

Click, and four to go.

"Spin it," I heard Vishinsky saying, and realized that time had gone by as my senses drifted away from reality, desperate for escape.

"What?"

"Spin the chamber."

Yes. Concentrate. Four more. Wrong: not four. An infinite number of chances left; I *needed* only four.

That was fair odds and I spun the thing and put the muzzle to my temple and froze because even with infinite chances this could be the wrong spin.

There's something you're not thinking of.

I know. But I don't want—

Think about it. Don't deny it.

I spun the chamber.

All right, we'll get out of the denial phase. Of *course* this man won't give me freedom if I don't spin the cartridge into line and blow my head off, any more than he would have let Moskolets go. It'd destroy the climax for him, and he couldn't stand that, doesn't have to, it's his and I'm leading up to it for him, playing his game and making out I've got *one* chance in a *thousand* to win.

No way.

So what are you doing it for?

Good question, but there's an answer of a sort. To gain time.

I raised the gun.

There's no time for you to gain. Be realistic.

Something might happen. The phone could ring again, distract him, divert him to some other business. Or—

Whistling in the dark.

Perfectly true.

"Pull the trigger," I heard someone saying softly. Vishinsky.

Sweat crawling on me, on my face, didn't want him to see it, no choice, not too many choices left now, we're approaching the climax and he'll be stiff by this time under the gold silk dressing gown, God *damn* his eyes.

"What?"

To gain time.

"Pull the trigger."

Yes. But where is it now, the small bright polished killer? Lined up with the barrel, its pointed copper nose ready to meet the skin, the skull, the soft gray mass wherein there shines the last wavering light of hope? Or is it nestling in the next sheath of the chamber, biding its time?

He was leaning forward, Vishinsky, the reptilian eyes shimmering. Pull the trigger before he loses patience, or he'll—

Click.

I felt the breath trying to come out of me in an explosion but managed to control it, save face.

Or he'll just tell them to do it for me, shoot me down, bring on the climax, he wants it so badly now.

Three. Three more if we're going to play the game out, six chances, win or lose.

The walls still closing in, the focus of reality contracting, the air airless, the silence soundless as time passed, ungained.

Wait for him to move, Vishinsky, to show impatience.

I could hear the guard's breath, feel his aura. Kaido. Would he be at my head or my feet when they buried me? He was my brother, on the premise that all men are brothers, a premise difficult, God knows, to keep one's faith in when the chips are down. If—moving, Vishinsky, shifting in his chair—

I spun the chamber, put the gun to my temple and fired.

Click.

Silence crashed in.

He was still there, watching me, the Cobra. Or had it happened, was this illusion, the continuum across the brink of death, the leap into the new reality?

How do you know when it comes?

Two more.

I could feel the adrenaline coursing through the blood, hot with purpose, the muscles burning for release into action, the choices teeming in the mind—open the chamber and line the thing up and shoot Vishinsky, take on three athletic toughs in mortal combat? Let us be practical, my good friend. Make him a final offer, then, ten million US dollars for this wretched ferret in the field, would London pay that much if I could swing the deal? It might, but this man wouldn't go for it, all he wants now is his climax, he's far beyond conscious reach. Fling this gun away and go down in a sordid barroom brawl, take one of them with me if I can as a sop to pride? Surely we can do better than that.

"Spin the chamber." His voice coming from a long way off.

The light in here seemed brighter now, with the senses finely attuned to offer the organism every shred of data available that might help it survive: the light and the sound of the guard's breathing, the smell of his sweat, of mine, the pressure of the wall behind me, the sourness in the mouth.

I spun the thing and put the muzzle to my head and squeezed. *Click.*

The room rocked, steadied.

One. One more.

Think. Consider the choices again. Reflect.

There's no point. The choices are his, not mine. If I try *anything* at this stage, he'll lose the last of his control, order them to beat me to the point of death or take me to the guillotine for him to play with before the climax, then bring a body bag and remember the fingers, don't leave them lying there, throw them in and *don't* stain the carpet whatever you do.

One. One more. But when—

"Spin it."

His eyes brilliant with the light of joy.

Surely it must be there by now, taking its place in the scheme of things, ready to breach the skin, the bone, to shatter the seat of consciousness, to blow this beleaguered creature to Kingdom come.

I spun the chamber and raised the gun, felt the warmth of the muzzle against the skull.

I don't know how long it was before he spoke.

"This will be the sixth, won't it? Pull the trigger. Do it *now.*"

I thought I heard the echoes of his voice; in extremis, the mind conjures illusion.

Wait. Wait until his patience runs out.

The air pulsing, beating softly at the ears to the rhythm of the heart.

Wait.

"Fire, damn you, pull the trigger!"

Come then, dark of night, and gather shadows for thy shroud.

Click.

The room rocked again, steadied again. He was still there, the Cobra. Everything was still as it was. Sweat on my face, itching; life was real.

I threw the gun to Vishinsky and he caught it. His eyes had the light of hate in them as he stared at me. He could have told me to go on spinning the chamber, of course, go on firing until the gun kicked and they caught me as I dropped. But gamblers believe in the power of the fates: It's their whole rationale. So perhaps he thought that since the fates had spared me, they might show me other favors that could be dangerous if the game went on for too long. He'd played and he'd lost.

"Get get me a drink," he said softly. "Cognac."

Behind me as I moved for the bar I heard him slipping the rest of the shells back into the chamber of the gun and slapping it shut.

"You, Kaido?" he said.

"Sure, Boss."

"Then you can get another bag and take him to the forest."

12
Kick

I TOLD FERRIS, "GET LEGGE'S PEOPLE TO check on the Mercedes. It should still be in a side street near the Hotel Fabergé."

"Check on it?"

"It could go bang."

"I'll tell him. What did you come here in?"

"Nothing."

I ate some more goulash, hunger beginning. We were in an all-night greasy-spoon café, as far as I'd been able to walk from Vishinsky's hotel before I dropped.

I'd signaled Ferris from the phone booth outside and he'd got here a minute ago, so we had to deal with the essentials first. I didn't want some innocent policeman blowing himself up when he started investigating the abandoned Merc.

"Are you operational?" Ferris asked me. Another immediate essential.

"No."

He sat taking me in with his calm yellow eyes. He must have been distinctly edgy, over the last few hours. When the executive's in a red sector, his director in the field stays locked in his base with his nerves counting the roses on the wallpaper while London comes through on the scrambler every ten minutes to ask for an updated report.

"You need treatment?"

I said no. There was nothing broken. But it'd be a while before I could run flat out or jump a wall or take on more than one assailant at a time with any success, which was what operational meant. Perhaps tomorrow, if I could get any sleep in what remained of the night.

Ferris scraped the legs of his rickety aluminum chair on the tiled floor and went across to the counter and came back in a minute with a ragged cotton napkin and dropped it onto the table. I wrapped my left hand in it: The bleeding had started again.

"Any down?" Ferris asked me.

"Three."

He'd assumed I wouldn't be looking like this without somebody having become terminal somewhere along the line. There was Yakub, on the roof, and two of Vishinsky's bodyguards at the Hotel Nikolai.

"Self-defense," Ferris said.

"That's right." He'd have to report it to London.

I'd used a full *jokari*.

"You reached the board?" I asked Ferris. The board for *Balalaika*.

"Oh, yes. As soon as you signaled."

The stub of chalk would have gone squeaking across the slate: *Executive clear of red sector.* And Holmes would have gone over to pour himself some more coffee, celebrate, hallelujah.

"So you've no transport?" Ferris.

"What? No."

"You phoned from here?"

"Booth is outside."

I finished the gruel while he went and signaled Legge for another car for me to use.

At least, Koyama would have called it a *mawashi-geri*, a full-roundhouse kick. Qian would have called it a *tie-yu*, a hook kick. Actually it had been both, because when the roundhouse is drawn back to the fullest extent, it automatically forms a hook, with the foot at right angles to the leg.

When I'd heard Vishinsky telling the bodyguard what he wanted done, I was still approaching the bar to get him his cognac, and everything had slowed down. When we need more time, we are given it; any crisis will automatically trigger the mechanism.

At that instant the bar was still eight, nine feet away, and I had five or six seconds in which to think what to do. Something had to be done because as soon as I'd given Vishinsky his drink the bodyguard would drop me with a shot and they'd get the bag in here, *finis, finito.*

It was a full bar, ranging in proof from Dubonnet to straight vodka, twenty or thirty bottles in two rows. At the extreme right was a black-frosted bottle of Rémy-Martin, which was what Vishinsky would be waiting for. The height of the bar top was some three feet, the approximate height of a *jokari,* depending on the build of the *karateka* executing the kick, which assumes the horizontal the moment the leg is drawn back.

With four armed men in the room, I hadn't a chance of doing anything with my bare hands, and even a gun wouldn't have helped me. They never do. But all the same I would need a weapon, weapons, and here they were, lined up and immediately accessible. The *jokari* takes longer than any other kick to execute—as much as a full second—but it's also the strongest because of the buildup in momentum, and I thought there was a chance and went on walking toward the bar without breaking the pace, and when the distance had closed to an optimal two feet, I dragged in a breath to fire the muscles and felt the rush of the adrenaline and initiated the *jokari,* turning my head to look behind me as my body swung into the movement and seeing four of the bottles at the end of the rows nestling into the hook before I called on my whole complement of strength and brought the hook foward, loaded and flying in a curve toward the targets.

There wasn't any question of taking aim: it was inevitably a scattershot attack and I'd known that, but as the first of the bottles were hurled through the air I saw a man go down to one of them with blood springing from his face and then I was working hard for as many hooks as I had the strength for—three, four, five, the trunk swinging into a steady reciprocating rhythm and the hooks raking the top of the bar for more bottles, three of them reaching the window and crashing against the glass, their splinters glittering as a man found his gun and a shot puckered my sleeve before I lost track of the scene in detail, was aware only of the smashing glass and a man's scream and a fusillade of shots and Vishinsky yelling something about *get him* and the reek of cordite and alcohol as the kicks went on hooking, sweat in my eyes and blinding me and muscle-burn setting into my right thigh as I went on working, it was this or the forest, my choice, the breath sawing in and out of my lungs and a sudden freeze-frame glimpse of a guard lurching back as a bottle caught him on the front of the skull and smashed the bone, Vishinsky on the floor now with his gold dressing gown spread out around him and blotched with crimson while I kept the hooks coming, glass fluting through the air in a brilliant shower until hands reached for my legs and I chopped downward and broke a wrist, someone behind me and close and I used a spinning elbow strike and then fell, finding his face and using an eye-gouge and bringing a scream, silence coming in now, a kind of silence as I staggered up and saw Vishinsky groping for a fallen gun and smashed his hand with a heel strike and kicked the gun clear, stunned him with a front snap to the temple and saw him drop, heard movement and felt a hand clawing for me and snapped the fingers back and chose a heel-palm to finish him off and then stood clear and took in the scene, watching for danger.

But there was no movement now. Vishinsky and the guards were lying in a wasteland of smashed glass, blood pooling across the liquor-soaked carpet, a man's face upturned, one eye missing, another man's head cocked unnaturally beneath one of the walls, his hand still reaching for the gun he'd had smashed away from him. I moved from one to the next, checking for vital signs, then dropped like a dead weight as the reaction hit me, lay for minutes, starved for oxygen, lights flashing behind the eyes, a sense of having done something difficult, of being at least half-alive, until a degree of strength came back into the organism and I lurched onto my feet, going into the bathroom and washing the blood off my face and hands where the flying glass had cut into the flesh, then making my way out and down the fire escape and into the falling snow.

"Legge is worried about you," Ferris said when he came back and sat down.

"As long as he does what I want him to do, and otherwise keeps out of my way."

"He thinks you're trying to rush the mission."

"It's none of his bloody business."

I finished the goulash, felt better.

"Well, hello, boys."

Rouge as thick as mud, navy blue eye shadow, a broken tooth— what d'you expect in a greasy spoon?

"Don't let me get in your way," I told Ferris.

"But my *dear*," she said and touched my arm skittishly, and she went off on her rounds.

"How's London?" I asked him.

"We'll come to that. Debrief?"

Damn his eyes, I didn't want to wait to hear how things were in London, they didn't sound too *bloody* good. But he wouldn't tell me until he was ready—you know Ferris.

So I went into the debriefing from the point where I'd run into Vishinsky at the party to the *jokari* bit forty-five minutes ago. Ferris didn't interrupt, made a couple of notes on his scratch pad, that was all, and this worried me, too.

"That's it?" he asked me.

"I think so." If there was anything I'd forgotten it'd come to me later, with any luck. Just at the moment I was trying to get the wall back into focus: the concussion thing hadn't improved during the fuss at Vishinsky's hotel, and I needed *sleep*, for the love of God.

"What sort of shape was Vishinsky in when you left him?"

"Not bad. Had to put him out."

"How liable is he to try tracking you and settling the score?"

"He'll do his best, I'd say. He's a psychopathic megalomaniac and takes offense easily."

"But you left a cold trail."

I swung my head up and looked at him, said nothing.

"You *think* you did," he said evenly, "but you've still got some lingering concussion."

Point taken. No one in Vishinsky's suite could have trailed me but someone else could have seen me leaving the building at two in the morning looking like a zombie and decided to check me out—it was Vishinsky's hotel, and he might have peeps stationed in the environment.

"I wasn't so far gone," I told Ferris carefully, "that I couldn't see a tracker. If I hadn't got here clean this place would be full of ticks by now, and look, I've got to say this, do you *really* think I'd signal my director in the field for a rendezvous if I thought there was the *slightest* risk?"

The DIF, by the nature of his calling, must stay strictly out of the action, whatever's happening in the field, and part of the shadow executive's job is to protect him from any risk of exposure. This is sacrosanct, and with good reason: The shadow needs to know that he can *always* rely on getting signals to London, getting support in the field, getting everything he needs—sometimes desperately—to help him through the mission. The director in the field is his communications channel, his universal provider, counselor, and nurse. Without him, nothing can work.

"Just checking," Ferris said, his eyes still on me. That, too, is part of his job: to assess what condition the executive is in after there's been some action, to query whether he might have picked up a tick, to decide whether his charge is fit enough to continue the mission, and if not, send him home.

"Understood. As long as we—"

Headlights swept the steamed-up window and Ferris scraped his chair back and went over to the door, taking a look before he went outside.

The food counter began sloping at five or ten degrees and the heavy-faced *babushka* behind it swayed to one side until I got my head back straight and reestablished focus.

"Mercedes," Ferris said when he came back. "Not the same model, but it's this year's—all right?"

"I'll take it."

"Some more goulash?"

"No."

A couple of seconds went by and then Ferris said, "About London."

I didn't want to hear. I tell you I did *not* want to hear about bloody *London*. You know why?

"You're being recalled."

That was why. I'd seen it coming, of course. I'd worked with Ferris long enough to catch his vibes, and ever since he'd come in here I'd been listening to the knell of doom in the far distance of my mind.

"Bullshit," I said.

There was a crust of bread on the table I hadn't eaten and I began breaking it up, pulling it apart, still moist, doughy, smelling of the oven, and I remember doing this, I suppose, because in the last few seconds *Balalaika* had started to run clean off the track. *But that was all.* It hadn't crashed. I wasn't going to let that happen.

"Mr. Croder," Ferris said evenly, "sends you his congratulations, of course."

On getting clear of the red sector alive. "How nice," I said.

"As I told you before, he may not be sleeping too well, having sent you into this one rather impulsively, to save his face vis-à-vis the prime minister."

Ferris had never spoken like this before: Croder, Chief of Signals and arguably the most effective control in the whole of the Bureau, is regarded with infinite respect, and his personal motivation is never called into question.

"Tell him to take a couple of Oblivons," I said.

Ferris tilted his chair back, his lean body sloping like a board as he watched me obliquely. "Strictly *entre nous*, he may be considering his resignation."

I stopped fiddling with the crust. *"Croder?"*

"His ego," Ferris said, "is almost as bad as yours, and just now his pride's hurt, I believe terminally."

In a moment I said, "There's something he hasn't considered, in his excess of overweening pride."

Ferris waited, turning his head an inch, and I saw the cockroach darting along the bottom of the wall, bloody place was teeming with them.

"So tell me," he said.

"I can save his face for him. All he's got to do is leave me in the field, and there's a very good chance I can bring this thing off, then he can go back to the PM and shine like an archangel in his eyes. It'd give me a *lot* of satisfaction to do that for a man like Croder. And for Christ's sake, leave those bloody things alone." He likes putting his foot on them, hearing them crack open. You know that.

Someone came in and Ferris swung his head, a shift worker, leaning a shovel against the wall, snow on its blade.

"Even if you weren't being recalled," Ferris said as he looked back at me, "you're not going to be physically operational for another week, and they can't keep this one on the board forever."

"I'll be back in shape in a couple of days. For God's sake, give me a chance, I'm not superhuman."

"Even though you may think you are."

"And a merry Christmas to you, too."

He got up and went over to the wall and I tried to tune out the little cracking noises and when he came back he said, "The problem, of course, is that these are the instructions I've received from Control."

In brief there was nothing he could do. When Control instructs the director in the field it's with the voice of God, and this is well understood.

"Have you booked the flight?" I asked him.

"Control only told me tonight, when I reported you out of the red sector. Don't worry, I'll give you plenty of time to rest up first, where you won't be disturbed."

In a moment I said, "That's deuced civil of you, but there's another problem. It's my decision to stay in the field, and neither you nor Control can do anything about that."

I didn't throw down the ace because I didn't know how much it was worth. During the night's business I'd seen the chance, thin if you like, of getting closer to the target for the mission: Vasyl Sakkas. And that was all I needed to run with.

"You make it difficult for me," Ferris said.

"That's a shame."

"I can't, as you well know, ignore my instructions. This is—"

"Oh for Christ's sake"—blowing up now and high time—"the Chief of Signals *himself* comes to Moscow to offer me a decidedly tricky mission, and I agree to take it as far as I can go because it's a challenge and I'm under his personal control and I gain access on the second day out and move into some action that leaves me a touch groggy and *then* I'm recalled to London because he suddenly gets cold feet. I *don't* intend—"

"Rather more than a touch groggy—you were very nearly terminal. And the Chief—"

"How many times have I come close to getting wiped out in any given mission, for God's sake, it's part of the job, you know that—"

"There's never been a mission quite so predictably lethal—"

"Then Croder shouldn't have challenged me—"

"And that is precisely what he's come to realize now—"

"A bit late—"

"Actually no, because you're still alive and that's the condition he wants to see you in when you reach London—I'm not interested in shipping a coffin out of Moscow. And let me remind you that as your director in the field, I'm responsible for giving you whatever instructions I think fit, and you're responsible for carrying them out."

Pulling rank. He'd never done that before, and I was warned. By nature Ferris is the coolest of cats, and he never raises his voice or drives his executives into a corner; but now he was really putting things on the line and I wasn't so stupid as not to listen. But I'd already made up my mind, so the only thing left was to try ducking the fallout.

"Be that as it may, I'm going to ground," I said.

And left it. You've heard, my good friend, of throwing down the gauntlet. That is the sound it makes.

The man who'd brought the shovel in from the street was going across from the counter to the table with his tin tray loaded with potato pancakes and a mug of *vasti,* and the tart moved in on principle, though her expression was not sanguine. Headlights swept the window again and Ferris watched the shadows swinging across the wall and didn't speak until they'd faded. This was noted, though I said nothing.

I gave him his time. For the executive to go to ground means that he vanishes from the face of the earth, usually with the full understanding on the part of his director in the field that he needs to do this because the situation suddenly demands it—there's been some action and the mission's running hot and the hunt is up and the opposition's closing in and the shadow has no choice but to get out of harm's way. But to go to ground against his DIF's instructions is to burn his boats and leave the ashes strewn across the field—and risk the ultimate sanction: the end of his career.

"If you do that," Ferris said at last, and carefully, "you would be aborting the mission."

"Protecting it," I told him.

"Without your being operational in the field, there'd be no mission."

"I *am* the mission."

Ignoring this—"If you go to ground, the Chief of Signals will shut down the board for *Balalaika.* You'll have no director in the field and no support."

He knew I realized this but he wanted to spell it out for the sake of formality. I had indeed made things difficult for him, and he also would need to duck the fallout when he got back to London: *I warned the executive of the consequences,* and so forth.

"Point taken," I said, and in my mind's eye saw the lights going out above the board for *Balalaika* in the signals room, the dusting block erasing the first reports in from the field and leaving the slate blank as Holmes stood staring at Croder with disbelief in his eyes and those bloody people upstairs put it on record: *Mission abandoned, executive's decision.*

"Have you any kind of a lead?" Ferris was asking. This was typical: His intuition had cleared a gap.

"Conceivably."

"How useful?"

"It's pretty thin."

"But it's there."

"Yes."

"And you want to follow it up?"

"Intend."

"It concerns the target?"

"Sakkas."

The cockroaches were out again after his recent assault, but now he wasn't interested.

"Do you think it might get you closer to the target?"

"There's a chance."

In a moment—"Obviously, if you felt like clueing me in, I might want to signal Control. And he might change his mind."

"It's too slight," I said. "It's just someone's name, out of the blue. Croder wouldn't go for it."

"Suppose"—Ferris picked up one of the crumbs from the table in his thin pale fingers and rolled it into powder—"suppose *I* thought of going for it?"

"What would you do?"

"There are quite a few things I could do. I could delay signaling London with your decision to go to ground."

"You'd take that much responsibility?"

"It's vested in me as your DIF."

He'd never sounded so formal. I asked him, "What else could you do?"

He looked away. "Would you go to the safe house?"

"No. Somewhere else." It could expose him to risk because he knew where it was, the place Legge had fixed up for me. A safe house, once blown, is the most dangerous place in the field. Besides which, Legge himself knew where it was, and he was liable to get in my way: he already thought I was "rushing the mission," none of his bloody business; I don't like a pushy chief of support—they too can be dangerous.

"If you holed up somewhere else," Ferris said slowly, "then Mr. Croder might instruct me to mount a search for you, so that I could send you home after all. Then in the meantime, if this lead of yours paid off, you could signal me and I'd report it to London. That could change Mr. Croder's mind, too."

Read it like this: He was prepared to stay in the field in case I needed him, provided he could do it on formal instructions and the pretext that he was mounting a search through my support group. That could put *Balalaika* right back on track, keep my communications open, and provide me with support if things started running hot. But I knew that Croder, despite his conscience, could throw me to the dogs once he was told I'd gone to ground: My DIF had been given instructions to get me home, and if I chose to risk death on the streets of Moscow, then it wouldn't be Croder's responsibility.

I told Ferris: "I can't see him leaving you out here with no executive and no mission."

"There's a chance."

"All right. Try."

The flat of his hand came down softly on the table and he let out a breath. "Let us pray, then, for *Balalaika*." It was the closest, in my experience, for Ferris to show the slightest emotion.

"Amen."

But I didn't think there was going to be any dancing in the streets. No control of Croder's stature would take kindly to his executive going to ground on his own decision: It was the ultimate offense, implying distrust and indiscipline.

"I'll give you three days," Ferris said. "Unless, of course, the Chief extends that."

"I'll signal you."

Headlights swung across the window again and he watched the

wall. Then the lights were doused and a car door slammed and a man came in, stomping the snow off his boots.

"D'you need anything more to eat?" Ferris asked me.

"No."

"Then we'll go." He nodded to the man as we made for the door and he followed us out. "This is Dr. Westridge from the UK embassy."

Jolly and red-faced, despite the hour. "And this is the patient?"

"Yes."

"Let's get into my car," Westridge said. "There's all my gear in there."

"Look," I said, "I'm perfectly—"

Ferris cut across me. "Just for the moment, you're under my instructions, so get in."

Westridge got his bag and opened it. "Been in the wars a bit, have we?"

"Not really." God protect me from jolly and red-faced men at three-thirty in the morning. "I need some sleep, that's all."

"Don't we all! Let's have your wrist."

Three days. That was generous of Ferris. I could check out my one frail lead in less than twenty-four hours. "What's that?" I asked Westridge.

He pushed the air out of the syringe. "Tetanus. Sleeve up, which arm is to be?"

We took it from there, the knee-jerk reaction, flashlight in my eyes, tongue out, blood pressure, "Still feel a bit shaky, do we?"

"Just need sleep."

"No giddiness when you stand up? Headache?"

"I feel like shit."

A breezy chuckle—"Well *that's* putting it in a nutshell! Now hold your hand still. You'll just feel a little prick, that's all." I didn't say anything, didn't feel like jokes. "Tell me when the numbness sets in," he said.

Snow drifted across the windscreen. "Is that it?" I asked Ferris.

"What?" He swung his head to look. "Yes."

Mercedes SL-4 E, black, two-door, Moscow plates. "Got a phone?"

Ferris looked at me and said nothing, looked away. Point taken: Did I *really* think he'd fix me up with transport that didn't have a telephone? He's always good at the touché, however long it takes.

"Gone dead," I told Westridge.

"That's the stuff. Now hold still. What did you cut your hand on?"

"Glass."

"Clean glass?"

"Some alcohol around."

"Good, I've always said Chivas Regal's the best antiseptic. Barroom brawl, was it?" A gusty laugh. "Lucky you didn't get into anything worse than that, in this fair city. You hear about Seidov, the banker?"

"Car bomb," Ferris said, "I believe."

"Second in a week, and he was the *head* of the Moskva Trust." The curved needle went in again. "Known for his defiance of the mafiyosa, it just isn't worth it, pay them and cut your losses. Hurt?"

"What?"

"Still numb, is it?"

"Yes."

He got out some Band-Aids. "Any more cuts anywhere, grazes, bruises, joints feel limber?"

"I'm fine." Got him in focus again.

"That's the stuff! Now go and get some shut-eye, do you the world of good."

When we got out of his car, Ferris asked me, "You all right to drive?"

"Yes."

"Follow you up?"

"There's no need. Look," I said as Westridge left us standing in a cloud of exhaust gas, "how will I know if Croder drops me cold and calls you in?"

Ferris looked at me, his eyes amber now under the streetlight.

"You'll know when you signal me and there's no answer."

13
Marius

SHE DANCED PRETTILY, ANTANOVA.
I watched her through the pearl-framed opera glasses, alone in the box on the second tier. Her *glissades* were enchanting, but she lacked the strength for the *grands jetés*, her balance wavering a little. In any case it was her face I was interested in.

They're for Sakkas's mistress, I'd told Vishinsky in the hotel. The diamonds.

Antanova?

Yes.

One name to conjure with, in all Moscow. The floor of my new safe house had been littered with ballet programs when I'd left there; I'd got them this morning from the Tourist Bureau.

In any case—Vishinsky—*he never lets Natalya wear jewelry. To Sakkas she's cattle.*

Out of the seven major ballet companies, I'd found twelve Antanovas, nine of them in the corps de ballet, three of them soloists, one of them with the first name of Natalya, appearing in *Giselle* at the Metropolitan.

An *entrechat cinque*, prettily done. The theater was overheated, and women with bare shoulders and diamanté necklaces were fanning themselves. The performance had been running for an hour.

I'd arrived thirty minutes before curtain-up, taking off my overcoat and leaving it in the Mercedes, going across to the stage door in the overalls I was wearing underneath.

"I'm here to fix Antanova's car," I told the stage door-keeper. "Which one is it?"

"What?"

Hard of hearing, a drip on his nose, his hands chilblained. I told him again.

"There are two Antanovas in the company."

"Natalya."

"The BMW."

"There are three BMW's out there."

"The gunmetal gray coupe."

"Are you sure?" This was important.

He stared at me, rheumy-eyed, as if I were mental. "I know *all* their cars." He picked up his newspaper again, shaking it out.

Snow was whirling under the lights as I went back to the Mercedes; it had been coming down harder in the past hour; the forecast had warned of a blizzard moving in before midnight. I peeled off the overalls, pulling my dinner jacket straight and checking the tie, putting on the overcoat and walking down the pavement for half a block to the first taxi in the rank, giving the driver a $50 bill and telling him what I wanted him to do.

"I'm going to lose a fare when the audience turns out, this snow and all," he said.

I was ready for this and gave him another $50. "Do it right, or I'll skin your hide."

"I don't think there'll be any problem."

I didn't let the thought worry me, as I sat watching the exquisite Antanova, that the whole of the mission could now depend on whether that driver out there did *exactly* what I'd told him to do. Go anywhere near the stage door or remain in sight, and he'd blow *Balalaika.*

Another *glissade,* this one enough to catch the breath. If Natalya Antanova was working to become a prima ballerina, what was she doing with a man like Sakkas?

I didn't hurry when the curtain came down; she'd take a little time getting the greasepaint off. People were bunching on the pavement outside the vestibule as the limousines and taxis came rolling in, forming a double lane. My driver wasn't among them.

I was sitting in the Mercedes when the first of the dancers came through the stage door, seeing the snow and hunching forward as they crossed to their cars. With their fur collars raised to shield their faces, I wouldn't have recognized Antanova, had to wait until she reached her BMW and saw the taxi blocking it in and turned to look around for the driver.

I got out and went across to her. "It's broken down," I said.

She almost whirled on me, her eyes wide. "How do you know?"

"The driver told me. He's gone to find a mechanic, if he can."

Her expression half-believing as she stood staring at me, the snow falling on her shoulders; I thought it probable that she only half-believed anything, was running scared, like Mitzi Piatilova.

"How long will he be?" she asked me.

"On a night like this, I doubt if he'll be able to fetch a mechanic out, anyway. Let me offer you a lift."

"No, I—" she swung away to look at the warmly lit stage door while I wondered if she'd go in there to use the telephone and call someone to pick her up, two seconds, three, the waiting difficult for me because if she did that, the whole scenario would be wrecked at the outset. The snow spiraled, black against the lights, the wind chill cutting the face.

Swinging back to me, taking in my expensive coat, the sable hat. "Which way are you going?"

"The Boulevard Ring." Sakkas wouldn't rule his empire from the suburbs.

"Which is your car?" she asked me.

"That one. You'll freeze, standing out here."

An expensive Mercedes seemed as reassuring to her as the coat, and she nodded and went over to it and I stopped myself in time from opening the door for her. It would be surprising—dangerous in terms of a tight cover—in a Muscovite, especially to a woman who was regarded as cattle.

"Your performance is beautiful to watch," I said as we turned north.

"Thank you."

The face elfin, sculpted almost in miniature, the cheekbones perfect, the eyes large, luminous, the mouth tender, traces of rouge still glowing on one cheek, clownlike, where she'd missed it in the dressing-room mirror, a single curl of chestnut hair hanging loose below her ear, no jewelry. One of the most beautiful women in Russia, Croder had said, yes.

"How long have you been dancing?"

"Since I was three years old." But with with no interest in her tone, even though her work must be her life, or whatever life Vasyl Sakkas allowed her. Perhaps she had worries on her mind tonight, wasn't always so scared of strangers.

The snow was hitting the windshield with enough force to smother it, and I switched on the wipers and slowed until the glass cleared.

"I need the address," I told Antanova.

"Number 1183. It's one of the big houses, lying back."

I gave it a moment. "How is Vasyl?"

At the edge of my vision field I saw her head jerk to look at me. "You know him?"

"I remember the address."

Still watching me—"He's in St. Petersburg."

Throp, throp, the wipers. Steam was rising against the windshield as the lights of a car swept across it and the clinking of chains loudened suddenly, snow drumming in a wave against the side of the Mercedes as the other vehicle swerved across the ruts.

"When's he coming back?" I asked Antanova.

"Tonight." She was facing her front now, worried about an accident.

"I would have liked to talk to him."

"Vasyl? You'd need an appointment, and screening. Or do you know him well?"

"We've done business. And excuse me—my name's Berinov, Dmitri. I'm in jewelry, chiefly export."

We passed 1175, the snow blinding in the beams, the dim outlines of the houses ghostly on either side of the street, some of their numbers legible in the backlight.

"In any case, he won't be in Moscow until the early hours." Then she was silent for a time, and when I glanced at her I saw she was crying, her face buried in her furs, the tears glistening in the half-light.

In a moment I asked her, "Can I help?"

She said nothing, shook her head vigorously, even desperately. Perhaps the worry on her mind tonight, then, was Sakkas's return to Moscow. He would have missed her, and was not a gentle man. I pushed the thought away.

Then 1181, and as I began slowing, headlights on full beam stabbed suddenly from the distance, and I dragged down the visor.

"The next house?" I asked Antanova.

She was shielding her eyes against the glare. "I don't want to go in," she told me, the tone raw, a soft cry muted by her hands.

"All right."

But the headlights were closing on us very fast now and I said sharply—"Get down."

"It's one of—"

"Get down low."

She dropped forward, holding her face in her hands, and I waited for the shots because this could be a hit set up for someone else, someone who was expected to arrive at No. 1183 at precisely this time, someone Sakkas wanted out of his way.

I kept on a straight course, accelerating a little and hearing the chains searching for traction; if I made a U-turn and tried to get out as fast as I could, there'd be shots anyway: Mere suspicion would be a good enough excuse in the mind of the mafiya.

"Stay down," I told Antanova as the headlights came blazing through the snow directly at the Mercedes and then swung and went past and I felt the gross impact of the shots as the brain gave way to illusion, then there was only the white tunnel of our own lights ahead of us through the blizzard and I told Antanova she could straighten up.

"It was one of Vasil's security units?"

She nodded, tightening her seat belt, staring ahead.

"How many are there?"

"Several cars." Blowing into a small embroidered handkerchief. "They're always in the street."

"And behind the house?"

"Of course. Everywhere." Her face turned to watch me—"You didn't notice them before?"

"When I came to the house? It was in daylight, and he'd sent a car for me." Security units standing off and guards, for certain, at the gates: Sakkas territory, keep out. I'd memorized the number of the house, but it was clear enough now that I'd have no hope of surveilling it, even by night.

"You want to stay with friends?" I asked Antanova.

"Friends? No. I must go back there soon."

"You want to drive around for a while?"

"No. Take me to the Entr'acte. Turning to me—"Do you have time?"

"All the time you need. That's a club?"

"Yes."

"Where is it?"

She gave me the directions and I turned away from the Ring and headed south; in blizzard conditions it would take fifteen minutes, twenty.

"You can leave me there and I'll get someone to take me to the house later." Didn't say "home."

"Vasyl's coming in by air?"

"Yes."

"They'll have canceled the flight, of course."

"He'll be in his own 747."

"Even so, he can't land until this clears and they've opened up the runways again."

"But I must go back there soon, anyway, or they'll report me."

"His guards?"

"His aides."

She wasn't withholding anything, even from a stranger; either she assumed I knew what the relationship was or she just didn't care, just needed to talk, to share her misery.

"Tell me exactly when you've got to be back there." For her safety's sake, I didn't want her to be late.

"By midnight."

The clock on the instrument panel showed 10:31.

"That's your curfew?"

In a moment, disliking the word. "It's when I need to be back. You should turn left at the next intersection. If you like, you can drop me off at the taxi rank outside the Romanov Palace."

"No, I'll see you to the club. Are you warm enough?"

"Yes."

Not strictly true, even though the heater was switched to full fan; she was frozen, crouched beside me with her small body rigid, frozen with cold, frozen with fear as the snow drove against the windshield in blinding gusts and the illuminated clock flicked to 10:32, another minute nearer midnight.

"So why don't you leave him?"

"I can't."

She said it impatiently, as if I should have known. Did she expect everybody to know everything about her life with Sakkas? Did he parade her through the clubs of Moscow as his beautiful, talented white slave? It was an important question because all I knew about him was that he liked his privacy, was a reserved, remote, and ruthless entrepreneur operating from his winter fortress in the capital of the new Russia, unassailable because of his ability to control the very center of Moscow's crime network. Most of this was in the briefing; some of it I'd picked up on my way into the mission, a lean dog hungry for scraps. But I'd found no kind of Achilles' heel in the man, though now I thought it might lie here, in his relationship with Natalya Antanova, and this could give me something to work on, even a chance of closing in on him.

"Why can't you leave him?"

She looked down, then up again, but not at me, looking around her in the half-dark: the only light was from candles burning in

Tiffany glass bowls on the little tables, so that the scene was a kaleidoscope of fragmented images—the bright outlines of bottles, the sheen of bare shoulders, the glimmer of eyes in shadowed faces, some of them turned to watch Antanova. They seemed to be mostly artists here, gathered together with friends after curtain-down to bemoan their performances and seek the comfort of immediate rebuttal—but darling, you were marvelous!

Natalya's eyes on me now. "I can't leave Vasyl because he would have my brother killed."

The man in the corner near the bar was one of the people watching her; I'd locked on to him when he'd come in here, less than a minute after we had. He could be an admirer, like the others, or could be simply standing there with one foot hooked over the bar stool enjoying his lust at a distance. Or he could be one of Sakkas's henchmen.

"Tell me about your brother."

She countered this. "How long have you known Vasyl?"

"Only a few weeks. We just did one brief deal."

"You will do other deals with him?"

"No."

"Why not?"

"He doesn't leave much room for profit. And of course one can't protest." I gave it a beat. "He hasn't got my confidence, and I certainly don't have his. You can speak freely."

Her dark eyes were glistening. "There are so few things I can do freely, and that is why I've told you as much as I have, even—" she shrugged, and the delicate silver bells on the fringe of her stole shivered with sound.

"Even though I'm a stranger."

"Yes."

"Don't let it worry you."

Taking a breath she said, "My brother—his name is Marius—was with Vasyl almost from the time he came out here from England. You know Vasyl is a British national?"

"So I gathered."

"My brother was already in the mafiya, and introduced him to all the right people. He—"

"The right people in the mafiya, or the government?"

"Both. Vasyl impressed him enormously, as he does everyone, and in a short time Marius was offered what he called the 'honor' of becoming his chief aide. I didn't know Vasyl then; I knew only that Marius was getting in deep with the organization and making enormous money." With a shrug—"It didn't worry me; Moscow was changing overnight, the streets filling with Mercedes and Lincolns and Ferraris, new clubs opening up, Western clothes and cosmetics and music flooding in. But then the killings began, and the ordinary people of the city were given an idea of how ugly the mafiya was, behind all the opulent extravaganza. And I started worrying about my brother." Taking another deep breath—"And then about a year ago, last winter, he introduced me to Vasyl Sakkas at a very exclusive party."

In the silence I said, "Not your favorite day to remember. Natalya, don't look directly at the man standing at the end of the bar with his foot on the stool. Just glance across him when you next look around." With her eyes still on mine, she said, "Very well. No, it was not my favorite day. Even before we parted company that night I knew that Vasyl hadn't just fallen for me—he wanted to *possess* me. At first I think I was flattered, even proud. I knew from what my brother had told me that Vasyl Sakkas was a powerful man, one of the most powerful men in Moscow." Looking around her—"He came to watch me dance, with an enormous entourage of bodyguards, and escorted me home to my cramped little apartment in Povaskaya-ulica. He gave me sables, diamonds, and a brand-new BMW. It's all right, I know that man—he's just one of my followers, that's all. He never comes up or pesters me."

"Fair enough," I said.

"And then I was invited to Vasyl's house for the first time, to dine with him alone. And you know what happened? I woke up two days later in his enormous baroque bed, still groggy from whatever drug I'd been given, though the truth didn't occur to me right away. There were three private nurses looking after me, and a doctor came twice a day to question them about my 'progress.' They said it was some kind of food poisoning, because two of the staff were also taken ill. And you know? I believed it. So did my brother Marius."

"And what did your brother Marius feel about your having woken up in Vasyl's bed?"

With a shrug—"He knows I have affairs. I think maybe he was rather pleased that his boss favored me, and that I was responding."

"But were you? I don't want to—"

"No. I refused, the first time Vasyl made a serious pass. I think maybe I wanted to hold him off just to see what it felt like, to show a man as powerful as he was that he couldn't buy me—at least, not instantly. Maybe it was that, I don't know. But it must have angered him, even though he never shows anger."

"No?"

"Just cruelty."

Two men came in, blunt-faced, hoods, letting the door slam shut on its spring, walking to the bar in step, hands in the pockets of their coats as they stared straight ahead of them.

"When did you start thinking it hadn't been food poisoning?" I asked Natalya.

Her mouth twisting with bitterness—"Pretty soon. He made me stay in bed until the doctor said I could get up, and then—"

"For a few days? A week?"

"Maybe a week. By that time it was driving me crazy that I couldn't go to the theater—I was already a soloist. I told Vasyl they could fire me; work isn't that easy to find, even at my level. He didn't listen. Then I saw the whole picture."

A bald man in a velvet smoking jacket and gold-rimmed glasses came out of the room behind the bar and nodded, motioning the two hoods inside.

"The whole picture," I said.

"Yes—I could go back to my work, but I would live in Vasyl's house now, permanently. I would be there when he wanted me, when I wasn't performing. I would be his kept woman. His white slave, if you like."

"He didn't put it like that."

"Of course not. Vasyl says very little, but nobody ever mistakes what he means."

"How did your brother feel about this?"

"May I have another drink?"

"The same?"

"Yes."

I got our girl over and ordered more Canada Dry.

"I think Marius saw it as a very good situation developing all round. I seemed to accept Vasyl, and Vasyl seemed to be bringing me into a totally new lifestyle, like a waif out of the snow. I didn't want to worry my brother at that stage; I knew I was trapped into something I couldn't escape, so I decided to make the best of it, just keep on with my work and cope with the other half of my life as it came." Hands flat on the table suddenly, her eyes becoming intense—"Although that's not putting it well. The *whole* of my life is my work; it always has been. So maybe that was why I found it easier to accept the other things. I don't know."

The door behind the bar opened and the two hoods came out, one of them tucking an envelope into the double-breasted coat. The man in the gold-rimmed glasses asked the bartender for a drink as the hoods walked in step to the door and a Hare Krishna acolyte came in, snow on his saffron robes and tonsured head. One of the hoods made a quick movement and the acolyte doubled over with a cry of pain as they went on out, one of them laughing, letting the door slam.

"When did the cruelty begin?" I asked Natalya.

"Soon afterwards. I don't want to talk about that."

"Did your brother know?"

"Not at first. He found out last summer. We were by the

swimming pool at Vasyl's country dacha. I'd forgotten to put makeup over a bruise, and he asked me how I'd got it. I told him."

When the drinks arrived, we stirred the ice and I asked her, "Why did you suddenly decide—"

"To tell him? Maybe I just didn't think anything of it, you see, by then. As long as Vasyl didn't hurt me enough to stop me dancing, I let it go. But—"

"How did Marius react?"

"He was appalled. And then furious, so much so that I had to warn him not to let Vasyl know I'd told him what was going on."

"He took some persuading?"

"We argued half the night. Vasyl was away for two days, at the coast." The candlelight on the ice threw spangles of color across her face as she stirred her drink. "Marius is nine years older than me, and he's always been the 'big brother,' protecting me from things when there was any trouble."

"He finally agreed to say nothing to Vasyl?"

"Yes. I made him."

"Not easy for him."

"No."

"But his attitude to Vasyl, from then on, must have been cooler."

Hands flat on the table again—"Look, Marius was a trusted lieutenant—actually, a whole lot more than that: by this time he was managing most of Vasyl's empire because my brother is a very astute businessman, and very discreet. Maybe his attitude was different, but if Vasyl noticed, he wouldn't have questioned it. Maybe he thought my brother knew everything already, but anyway he wouldn't have cared. Vasyl cares about *no one*. That's why he has no friends. Only enemies."

"Their business relationship went on just the same?"

"Of course. Marius was enormously important to his boss, much too important to lose—or he was at that time."

"At that time?"

"Three months later. Three months ago, it's the same thing."

"Marius isn't managing things now?"

"No."

"Where is he?"

Natalya looked down, her body going slack suddenly. "He's in a forced-labor camp in Siberia, for life."

14
Shadow

IGHTS FLASHING, SENDING WAVES OF COLOR through the snow as the emergency lights circled on the roofs of the police cars. The chains bit as I hit the brakes. It was the third crash scene we'd come across since we'd left the Entr'acte Club.

An illuminated baton made motions, and I put the window down and looked into a raw face buried under a hood smothered in snow. *"This street's blocked!* Take the next left, then right, then left again. *Get a move on!"* The baton swung in practiced arcs. Sirens were fading in behind us and the lights of two ambulances flooded the street as I made the turn.

I glanced down at Natalya. We hadn't spoken since we'd got into the car, and I'd left her to her tears. She said at last, "Of course it was my fault."

"What was?"

"Marius being sent to the camp. He couldn't help trying to protect me, you see, at first in small ways, and it began to annoy Vasyl. And there was the other thing: For a long time my brother had been worried about the killings."

"The ones Sakkas ordered?"

"Yes." She pulled her legs up and rested her chin on her knees, and I reached across and checked the seatbelt for tension. "There were so many."

"Did he start objecting to them?"

"After a time, yes. I once heard voices raised, and my brother saying he was getting sick of it, that business was business, there was no need to kill people. You know? It really worried him."

"So Sakkas broke off the relationship?"

A short, bitter laugh—"You could put it like that. What actually happened was that the Ministry of the Interior sent a squad to arrest my brother as he was coming out of a café on the Ring one night. The next day there were charges brought and he was summarily convicted of murdering a judge and sentenced to a life term at the camp in Gulanka. These days the Ministry can do things like that under the emergency legislation, with so much crime to deal with. It happens a lot—they herd the convicted prisoners out on trains."

"You've been to a lawyer?"

"Of course, secretly. But I've no money, and it's so dangerous to do *anything* against Vasyl."

A huge black Zil came at us through the blizzard with its lights blinding and I swung the Mercedes across the pavement and clouted a garbage can and ripped away the front fender and got a shout from the limo. Then it was gone like a shark in white water.

When I'd straightened course, I said, "You told me your brother knows everything about Sakkas's 'empire.'"

"Of course—he ran it. I'm talking about an international network, worldwide, with offices and warehouses right across Europe and even in America. Last year Vasyl made more than one billion dollars. My brother also knows every one of his major contacts in the government and the Russian army, all of them very high up and all of them paid either to keep their mouths shut or steer 'business' his way. Marius has the whole picture, and Vasyl would have had him shot if it weren't for me."

It didn't sound right. "You mean out of his feelings for you?"

Natalya swung her head to stare at me and her voice was harsh. "His feelings for *me?* He doesn't know what feelings are. But he wants to keep me with him, to show off to the other mafiyosa—they vie with each other over their possessions."

"So Marius is a hostage."

"Of course. That is why I'm trapped."

"Did you ever try to leave Sakkas, before your brother was sent to the camp?"

"Twice. But Vasyl is uncanny, you know? His goons found me within hours, even though I kept away from my friends."

I didn't ask her what the punishment was when the goons brought her back, didn't want to know. If she tried it again, it would be infinitely worse: Sakkas would have her brother's body sent from the camp to Moscow for her to identify, while he savored her grief. I was beginning to know him.

I turned left along the Boulevard Ring, going east, looking for a plush hotel. "I'm going to put you into a taxi," I told Natalya. "Is that all right?"

"Of course."

If I dropped her off at the house, I could get shot at, afterward, or tracked through the streets. "I've got the number of the stage door at the theater," I told her. "I might need to contact you again."

"That would be dangerous. If one of his goons saw us tonight—"

"They didn't," I said.

With a shrug—"Then we were lucky. They're everywhere."

I slid the Mercedes alongside the first taxi in the rank outside the Moscow Waldorf. "If I can do anything to help your brother, I'll let you know."

She looked at me. "No one can help him. No one."

Perfectly right, he was in Baikshu, for Christ's sake, in northern Siberia. But for what it was worth I would tell Ferris, see if he could do anything through London.

"All I can hope for," she said bleakly, "is that one day, somehow, he might escape."

"Let's pray for that."

She unclipped her seat belt, turning to face me. With formality— "Thank you for your hospitality. And it was kind of you to take so much interest."

"You should talk more to your friends."

"They all know my story. I needed a stranger to listen."

I got out and spoke to the driver, giving him a $50 bill. "Take good care of her, my friend, on a night like this."

Natalya slipped off her right glove and I kissed her hand and closed the door of the taxi and watched it away, the rear lights slewing in the snow as the Zhiguli bounced across the ruts.

I was halfway to my hotel when I picked up the shadow.

There had been three vehicles behind me from the moment when I'd watched Natalya's taxi driving away to the present time, but now the scene had changed: Two of them had peeled off and the third was still behind me, but now it had pulled back a little and its lights were doused.

Present time: 11:43.

I switched off the dashboard displays and let the my eyes refocus. I didn't think the other car was a tracker. I thought it might be a hit team checking on me before it moved in for the strike or decided I was the wrong target. *He'll be leaving his office before midnight and going east on Pogrovskij Boulevard. Take him before he reaches his apartment.* A banker or some brave chief executive holding out against the pressure to buy protection, or perhaps simply a rival mafiyoso who had started getting in the way.

The snow was coming almost straight down from the sky now, making a curtain instead of a maelstrom. The main force of the wind had dropped in the past hour, and the big flakes drifted until the slipstream of the Mercedes caught them and whirled them behind in the mirrors.

It couldn't be a tracker because I'd checked three times on my way from Sakkas's house this evening, doubling and making loops and watching the mirrors. There had been *no one* behind me when I'd pulled up near the Entr'acte Club, no one of any interest.

I made another loop now, gunning up as far as the ice permitted, using the drifts to sling the rear end straight when we lost traction, a plume of snow flying upwards from the front tire where the fender had been ripped away.

QUILLER BALALAIKA · 147

Shadow.

Still there and quite large, another 300 SL perhaps. All I could make out was its general shape as it passed under the streetlights, their reflection flashing for an instant across the bodywork before it became dark again, almost invisible. The driver was trained, could hang on to the target without any trouble. But he couldn't be tracking me specifically, because—

A shrinking of the scalp, the nerves firing and the brain suddenly alerted as it ranged over the possibility that I'd made a mistake at some point after I'd left Sakkas's house. Correction, yes: *at some time after I'd arrived at the Entr'acte Club with Natalya.* And we can do that. We can make mistakes, even the most experienced executives, *especially* the most experienced, because familiarity with the field can make us cocky, overconfident. And we're talking now, tonight, suddenly, aren't we, about one of the most basic and effective methods of concealing anything.

Or anyone.

Hide them in plain sight.

It's all right—Natalya—*I know that man—he's just one of my followers, that's all. He never comes up or pesters me.*

Of course not. He was a Sakkas man.

Take another loop and do it faster this time, don't worry about ripping some more fenders off, go for it, get the chains dug in and use that wall to break down the swing and get me round, first left, first right, first right, with the lights flooding the narrow streets and bouncing off windows, the drumming of the engine bringing echoes from the buildings as the rear wheels sent waves of snow in our wake so that I lost sight of the tracker, could see only whiteness in the mirrors, take *another* loop and blow the chains off if we have to, push this *bloody* thing to the limits of the conditions and swing ... bounce ... swing in a series of tangents, one of the chains snapping and its loose end hitting against the fender with the beat of a mad drummer until I was back in the main street and gunning up for the next intersection in a final attempt to break clear, watching the mirrors.

Watching the shadow.

Time off for review: There would be two of them—at least two—in the car behind, and they would be armed with assault rifles, the weapon à la mode for Moscow. I had sent them the distinct message that I didn't want them on my tail, but it had been a calculated risk: I might have got clear with all that busy driving just now. If I stopped, all I could do would be to sit and wait for them to make their approach on foot. I would *not* get out of the car, on the principle we teach the neophytes at Norfolk: *Never leave shelter if you've got any.* There could be a chance, however remote, of gunning up again while they were making their approach on foot, though if there were more than two of them they'd leave a driver behind in case I tried exactly that. If they didn't leave one there and I made the try, they would both start pumping a long-sustained burst, one at the tires and one at me, unless I could get the chains to bite soon enough and make distance. Those were the options.

I don't like this.

Shut up.

For the moment just keep driving, normal speed for the conditions, fifty kph, sixty, as the snow spreads lace over the headlights and the adrenaline begins flowing out of the glands.

You're in a trap. You—

Oh for God's sake shuddup.

Take a left, head for the short, narrow streets where there was no late-night traffic to get in the way and where I might get a chance to make a right angle and douse the lights and reach the next turn before they closed in.

Never forget, I would tell them, the neophytes, the technique of hiding things or yourself in plain sight. Never forget that the opposition might also do it at any given time—*I ran into this one in Moscow last year, and* . . . if I were there again in Norfolk to tell them at all, if I didn't end the night as just another corpse found in a Mercedes with the driver's-side window gaping to the fusillade of shot and the head blown away, but then we mustn't be morbid, my good friend, we must remain, must we not, stout of heart.

Take a right, judge the distance, gun up and hit the next street, douse the lights and keep going, the snow coming up in dark waves across the mirrors, take more *chances,* don't pussyfoot this bloody thing through, the loose chain hammering, filling the streets like cannon fire, *keep going, keep—*

Then I was hitting the brakes and swinging left and right as the antilock system broke the momentum and the Mercedes reared on one side as we met up with a packed snowdrift and I avoided a roll by letting the wheel go slack to give some equilibrium to the front end, then we were halted, so close to the other car, the *second* one that was blocking the street, that I could see faces through the windshield.

The tracker had used his phone, that was all, and called in a backup; I should have known he might. But this was academic: There would've been nothing I could do.

The scene very bright now, dazzling: both cars had their headlights on and mine was trapped in the middle, throwing its oblique shadow against the walls and across the ruts in the ice. There was just the sound of engines running as the snow came floating down, big, heavy flakes from a swollen sky.

I waited.

Voices came in, I think from one of their radio phones. These weren't the callow, athletic jocks the Cobra ran; these were professionals, calling in a backup and contacting base and shutting me in without a chance in a thousand. These were Sakkas men.

Acid in the mouth as the adrenaline hit performance levels in the bloodstream; sweat coming out; a feeling a lightness, of poise, the muscles craving release, taut as a bowstring.

A door clicked open and faint backlit shadows formed on the walls as two of them came on foot from the car behind, their boots crunching over the snow. No one got out of the car in front: they would stay where they were, riding shotgun.

I put the window down.

"Show me your papers," one of them said. The other man was keeping back, his AK-47 aimed at my head.

Showed him.

"Import-Export. What does that mean?" He was interested in my expensive astrakhan coat and Barguzin sable hat, my expensive 300E, wanted to know if I was in the mob, was perhaps a rival to his boss and therefore expendable.

"I ship things in and ship other things out."

"What sort of things?" Hadn't given my papers back.

"Nickel, furs, jewelry, gold, whatever's available."

He had a pale, doughy face with an eagle's nose and heavy eyebrows, a man of forty, perhaps more, cynical, seasoned, nobody's fool. His eyes hooked themselves onto mine and stayed there until he was through with his thinking.

"Get out."

"I'd like my papers back."

"Get out." Didn't raise his voice.

I snapped the door open and stood on the snow, feeling it sink under my weight.

"Open your coat." He frisked me with methodical expertise, his breath clouding in the glare of the lights. "Get into the car behind."

"Look, I want to know—"

"Get into the car behind." The other man swung his gun as emphasis.

"Who the hell are you people? Are you from the RAOC?"

The man with the gun stepped up smartly and drove the muzzle into my back and I tilted my pelvis forward an inch to diminish the shock. Then two of us crunched across the snow to the car, the gun prodding. I couldn't hear the other man's footsteps.

"Get in."

I opened the rear door. There wasn't in fact a driver at the wheel, just this one man in the immediate environment, and a scenario for the instant future flashed across my mind, but the plot didn't stand up: I could deal with one man, especially with an assault rifle because they're even more useless than handguns at short range—you can't swing that much weight one-tenth as fast as you can smash a hammerfist to the wrist. But the other car was there and facing this way and they'd shoot for the legs when I started running.

Smell of new hide and a good cologne, Jesus, these were just his *security* people. I looked through the windshield but couldn't see much against the glare. The other man, the one with the eyebrows, must have gone to talk to the crew of the backup car.

A clock was chiming in the silence with deep, authoritative tones, an ancient custodian of the night, of man's affairs, announcing the witching hour. I listened to it with a Buddhist's attention, finding in it a reminder of how steady one must be, how unhurried, if one were to survive the blows of unkind fate.

How is Mr. Sakkas?

Rehearsed it a couple of times but decided against saying it aloud. On the one hand, it could be useful to pretend an acquaintanceship, as I'd done with Natalya Antanov; on the other hand, it could make things worse because I'd have to follow it up, tell them how I'd met him, what sort of deal it had been. People of this caliber would have computers filled with a massive amount of information at their base, and they could access them from here. *Berinov? There's no entry of any deal with any Berinov on that date, or any other.*

Better to play it straight, as an innocent caught in the cogs.

The other man was coming back as the car behind him pulled out and went rocking past us over the churned surface, its chains jingling like the harness of a troika through the snow. He climbed into the rear and slammed the door and got out a heavy Korean DP51 9mm Parabellum with a double-stacked magazine holding thirteen shells as he sat back in the corner to face me. White, manicured hands, perfectly still.

"Where were you tonight?"

He had the patient, almost bored voice I'd heard before so many times in the interrogation cells. This could be a former KGB officer: His attitude bore the stamp. Later he might start yelling in the traditional style, then cooing again to confuse me, but I didn't think it would come to that because he wouldn't have the time, or need it. My story wouldn't merit intense grilling: He'd have to take it at face value.

He knew where I was tonight.

"I went to the ballet. *Giselle.* Look, you've obviously mistaken me for somebody—"

"What did you do after the ballet?"

"I went to a club. The Entr'acte. I'd had the luck to meet Antanova, the soloist." Went through it for him, the taxi, so forth. And waited for the question.

"Do you know who Antanova is?"

Not that question. What had happened to the other one? *Did you go straight from the theater to the club?* So at least I was right about one thing: They hadn't tracked me from the Sakkas house tonight.

"I've just told you, she's one of the soloists in the—"

"You've just told me, yes. I know." But I hadn't given him the answer he'd been probing for: *She's Vasyl Sakkas's mistress.* "What did you discuss at the club?"

"Ballet, of course, Her performance tonight. It was an honor for me to talk to her at all."

"What else do you know about her?"

Still probing.

"She said she was only three when she was first given—"

"What else, aside from her career?"

In a moment. "I can't think of anything, frankly. It's all they can talk about, those people, and it was all I wanted to listen to. Tonight she gave one of the—"

"Yes, she is very talented." Switch—"When we began following your car, why did you try to evade us?"

"I was a bit scared, if you want to know."

"Why?"

"There are so many people getting killed. It's all in the papers—a car comes up from behind, especially at night, and before you know anything's wrong—"

"You have been followed before?"

"Well, no, but—"

"Did Antanova name any of her friends?"

"What? No."

"Acquaintances?"

"No. I've told you, she just—"

The telephone sounded and the driver pressed for Receive, didn't pick up the handset because there was an open mike system.

"Igor."

"We've found no Berinov, Dmitri, doing any major import-export business in Moscow. The only two businesses under that name are a car dealership and a brothel."

"And the Mercedes?"

"It's rented from Galactica Lease and Rental, on the Garden Ring."

"Okay." The driver pressed for End.

"So what do you say?" the man beside me asked.

"I work mainly out of St. Petersburg and Tashkent. My suppliers—"

"The business card reads Moscow."

"It always sounds better. More central."

"Why do you rent your Mercedes?"

"Convenience. I'm abroad a lot. Galactica looks after it for me till I get back."

"She didn't seem depressed? Antanova?"

Definitely KGB, kept switching the subject, watching for my reaction.

"Antanova? No, I don't think so. A bit tired, maybe, after the show. I suppose that's understandable."

"So when you left the club, you drove her home?"

"Not all the way. She—"

"Why not?"

"I was expected back, and it was already—"

"So how did she get home?"

"I put her into a taxi."

"Even though you said you were honored to talk to her, and no doubt found her very attractive."

"I needed sleep." I looked at my watch. "I'm on a plane for New York in the morning, if they've got a runway cleared."

Then there were suddenly no more questions. He settled farther back in the corner, keeping the gun aimed and not moving his head or his eyes beyond ten degrees or so from my body. The safety catch was off and his finger was inside the trigger guard: The bullet would be in me before I could even prepare for the strike.

In the silence I sat listening to the soft hum of the heater fan.

The driver's eyes were in the mirror, watching the other man, waiting, I thought, for orders. The heavy snowflakes were steadily deepening the blanket on the hood of the car, jeweling it with a rainbow scintillation; some of them eddied, touching the windshield and melting there, to leave water trails. A vision of Christmas flashed through my mind, robins and holly and candles on the tree in the firelight, reality seeking shelter.

Then the man beside me was speaking again in a monotone, watching my face now, his eyes moving from one of mine to the other. "I don't like your story. It has many gaps, many inconsistencies, many . . . improvisations. I have listened to stories like yours before. I think—"

"But look, I've answered every—"

"I think you may be dangerous to certain associates of mine, and so we will remove the danger." Flicking his eyes to the mirror, meeting Igor's. "You know where to go."

15
Orion

I T WAS BEAUTIFUL IN THE FOREST.

There was more light now from the sky, and its reflection on the ground gave an unearthly radiance among the trees, their tall black trunks standing in orderly ranks and supporting the weight of the snow on the branches above them.

The headlights of the Mercedes cut through this ensorcelling scene with an obtrusive brilliance, throwing shadows carved out of night. The silence, at this moment, was absolute. Igor, the driver, had switched off the engine and was standing off a little with the assault rifle just below the horizontal. He'd got out of the car first, of course, to cover me. The other man was also standing in the snow, his boots deep in it; but he was closer, waiting for me to join him, the thirteen-shot Parabellum cradled in his right hand.

Mr. Croder would not be pleased.

Flakes of snow were still floating from the sky and making the silence visual, to be listened to with the eyes. One can't watch a falling snowflake and imagine sound.

I got out of the car.

He'd ordered me home, after all, Mr. Croder, and if I'd reached London in a more or less presentable condition they could at least have put that much into the records: *Executive recalled, will be able to resume duties.* When the AK-47 went through its *rat-tat-tat* routine a few minutes from now, the records would look less favorable for the Chief of Signals: *Executive missing in the field, untraceable.* It's every control's responsibility to bring his ferret back alive, and if he can keep on doing that it means we can think of him as an okay guy. But there would be nothing in Croder's records to show that his executive had, in fact, ignored his instructions and stuck his neck into a noose and paid the ultimate price, and that would be upsetting for him, and I hoped he wouldn't flay Ferris alive for letting it happen.

A mass of snow unshipped itself from a branch not far from where Igor was standing, leaving a cascade of jewels to stream through the headlight beams. Igor didn't move, or turn his head.

"Walk," the other man told me, and shifted his gun upward an inch.

I looked at him in silence. On the drive here from the city I'd thought out some compromises in terms of my behavior. I had to continue playing the luckless innocent, victim of mistaken identity, because I couldn't switch now. But an innocent citizen would be going through a kicking-and-screaming fit by this time, *Please, please, I've got a wife and kids,* asking to be dragged out of the car by his collar and pushed headlong to his execution, *You can't do this to an innocent citizen,* lurching among the trees with his body heaving with sobs, so forth. This would have clouded the issue with melodrama and these people might have simply opened fire to bring down the curtain.

So I was playing it a touch more subtly, still an innocent but appalled, bewildered, numbed, speechless, and therefore nonthreatening, easy to handle, just in case there was a chance.

"Walk," the man said again.

"Walk where?" No longer capable of coherent thought.

"Into the trees. Follow the headlight beam."

I began walking.

But there was of course *no* chance left of survival, *none,* and when this happens the psychochemistry of the doomed organism is interesting: Fatalism, moving in to occupy the mind, leaves the subconscious to sort over any options that might be left, and this was happening as I made my way through the snow, my shadow stark in front of me.

They must surely send, then, this time, a rose for Moira, as a signal to let her know what had happened. This had been agreed, though she'd told me not to worry, I'd always come back.

Meanwhile follow the shadow, my shadow, and keep conscious thought aware only of the crunching of my calfskin boots through the snow and beyond it the vast silence of the night, of the universe, leaving the gossamer-fine attentions of the subconscious to address my karma and conjure if they could a ray of light.

"Over there."

His voice fainter, that of a character lost among the trees in the midwinter night's dream.

"Over where?"

"Stand against that tree. Face this way."

To my aid, Oberon, if you are there.

The conscious mind fanciful, freewheeling, stand back to the tree, this tree, this one?

The headlights dazzling; all I could see were two short figures against the snow, the one with the AK and the other one, closer, their faces blurred. I didn't think he would take an interest, the closer one, because of any avarice, but simply because of its power in the mind of man as I pulled it out of my pocket and held it up to assert its brilliance in the light, the universal power of the diamond.

The snow drifted down between us, black against the glare.

Burning bright at the edge of my vision field as I went on holding it at arm's length, turning it, tilting it to make it flash.

Time drew out, leaning across the silence, forgetting to count.

"What is that?"

"A diamond."

He turned to look behind him, make sure that Igor was well positioned, then turned back and began walking towards me.

A kaleidoscope of colors freckled the snow on the ground as shards of light were sent arrowing from the gem.

Suddenly he was standing in front of me, a black silhouette against the headlights, his left hand held out, the Parabellum in the other hand, in the aim. I gave him the diamond.

There was of course no question of buying my life with this thing. It was already his, and in a moment he would put it into his pocket and turn and move to a safe distance and raise his hand to Igor. The diamond could only have been used as I'd used it in the Baccarat Club, as a come-hither.

"Magnificent," he said, the freckles of colored light on his face now as he turned the facets.

I didn't answer.

Watch his hand, the left one. When it begins moving to put the diamond away, take the final chance, for here is the moment of truth.

Time slammed shut as he moved his hand and I used an open hammer-strike downward onto his gun wrist and heard it snap in the instant before the gun fired off-target and I made the next strike to kill, a half-fist into the throat with the knuckles burying deep into the cartilage, and as he started dropping I locked the inside of my elbows under his armpits and slid my hands found his neck and wrapped them across and lifted his body above the snow and pushed him forward as Igor gave a shout, ignore, and the dance began.

Blood on my fingers: internal hemorrhage had started underneath the smashed cartilage and his mouth was running crimson. We made for Igor, the cadaver and I, because I would have to deal with him in whatever way I could when we got close enough. All I had now was a shield against the AK-47 and since its back was to Igor he couldn't see what had happened, thought his partner was still alive and in the line of fire.

Dancing like two bears through the snow, the weight of the dead man more than I'd thought it would be, my face beside his and our heads bumping together, smell of his blood as his rib cage flexed and his lungs sent bubbling sounds from his throat, dancing together into the glare of the light and hearing another shout, ignore, sweat running now and the breathing labored as we lurched with his legs dangling and his eyes staring across my shoulder as I shifted the weight, his appalling weight, *dance*, you son of a *bitch*, the night's not over yet.

"*Stop! Stop right where you are!*"

Waving the rifle up and down but he couldn't do anything with it unless he tried a face shot which was all he could see as a target but my head was pressed against my dancing partner's as we lumbered toward him and I wouldn't think he'd risk it, wouldn't *think* but didn't *know,* and if he did take a chance my brains would be spread all over the trunk of that tree and I hated the thought of a messy end, *dance,* you son of a *whore,* but oh Jesus Christ he was heavy now and the triceps were beginning to burn and I didn't know how long—

"*Stop!*"

Ignore, of course. I was waiting for him to do *one* thing and that would end the matter, waiting for him to make *one* mistake and I knew what it was and he might not, *might* not, so let us pray, sweat running into the eyes and half-blinding them in the glare, he was to the right of us now, Igor, slightly to the right so I watched his shadow on the snow, black as night now in the headlights because we were closer, a *lot* closer and the breath was sawing in and out of my lungs and my head was beginning to pulse, waves of dark and light washing across my eyes, music, it would have been a help if we could have done this to music, matched our rhythm to it, say Bach or Vivaldi, something measured, a stately minuet, close now, we were getting *very* close and I thought there could be a chance, a remote possibility of hallelujah, but we mustn't hatch our chick—count our hatch—watch it for God's sake you *must* not lose it now—

"*Stop right there or I'll fire!*"

Bullshit, you'll fire the moment you can see a clear target but I'm not leaving shelter and if you try getting round on my blind side I can turn my shield much faster than you can move and you know that. Keep up the rhythm, keep up the rhythm under this appalling weight, the muscles running with liquid fire now and the lungs gaping under the ribs as the sweat poured on my face and I began counting—*one* and forward again, come on you bastard, *two* and forward again and stop that awful bubbling noise, *three* and forward again and then *Igor made his mistake* and as he sprang to the side and swung the gun up I hurled the cadaver down and across the barrel with the last of my strength and the shots hammered into the trees and I moved in for the kill with my muscles light, released from their burden, and before Igor had time to bring the gun up for the final burst I was into him with a series of three interconnected strikes, driving the nose bone upward into the brain and coming down with a claw hand to blind him if there were still sight left and then thrusting a half-fist into the throat, its force rising from the heel through the hip and into the shoulder as I felt the tracheal sinews flex and snap as he reeled and fell with my body on top of him, blood springing in the glare of the lights, the snow cool against my face as I bit into it, the parched husk of my mouth receiving its bounty as suddenly the night came down in waves, washing over the spirit, let us rest, my brother, let us lie for a while in this vale of sweet oblivion.

16
Lifeline

I SIGNALED FERRIS JUST BEFORE TEN the next morning to debrief. He didn't pick up until the seventh ring and it worried me: He'd said that if there was no answer it would mean he'd been recalled from the field.

I needed him here.

"Yes?"

"Debrief?" He would have the scrambler on.

"Where?"

"We don't need to meet," I said.

"Why not?" Debriefing isn't done much over the telephone.

"You'd be at risk."

In a moment, "You know the score."

"Yes. All right, two men down."

"Self-defense?"

"Yes."

"What happened?"

"They drove me into the forest last night."

Another pause. "Who were they?"

"Sakkas men."

Hence the risk to Ferris if we met anywhere in broad daylight. *He's uncanny*, Natalya had told me, talking of Sakkas. Conceivably one or more of the Cobra's gym team could see me somewhere in the streets and move in; with Sakkas the risk was much higher: he could have landed in Moscow by now and the moment he heard that two of his men were missing he'd send out half his army to investigate. Last night's snatch had been reported to his communications base, and even my cover name was in their computer.

"You've made contact with the target?"

"No."

I could hear the snowplows working down in the streets. They'd been there since first thing, making their rounds. Overhead the sky was dull pewter, brooding, more like a winter twilight two hours before noon.

"Do you expect to?" Ferris asked me.

Feeling his way carefully, his yellow eyes slightly oblique as he listened. I would have liked a rendezvous, yes, if it weren't for the risk. At this of all times, I wanted Ferris here in Moscow, keeping the lifeline secure while I was away. During the remnants of the night I'd woken several times as my dreams, sometimes spinning like a vortex, sometimes leading me to consider in a waking state a plan of action, had left me with some decision-making by first light, and this had been done.

"No," I said. Did I expect to make contact with the target.

"Have you made any progress?"

"No." I knew the question had come from London. *Progress,* it was all they could bloody well think about. If I made any progress, I'd tell them, wouldn't I? Head felt like a drum this morning, taut, vibrating, not terribly surprising I suppose. I hoped it would feel normal again soon: I had to be operational as soon as I could manage it, you get trapped on the street by bad luck and you're feeling like a zombie and it's *finito,* I don't need to tell you that.

"Have you any leads?" I was letting Ferris put the questions: This was debriefing.

"Yes."

"How promising are they?"

"Not very."

"But you'll follow them up?"

"Yes."

"We should really have a rendezvous."

"No, I want to get on with things."

In a moment. "What can I report to London?"

I'd given this some thought, because inevitably he would ask. "Nothing."

"But you're committed to following up your leads?"

"Mentally. I'll need to work things out."

In a moment Ferris said carefully, "I could give it to Control personally, for his ears only. It needn't go on the board."

Didn't want to get the signals room in an uproar. Sometimes an executive in the field will go native if he's pushed far enough by the mission, imagine his whole career will depend on one last trick and believe he can snatch success out of the red-hot coals, and then Control will start screaming at him through the mast at Cheltenham, trying to bring him down before he blows the whole of the mission into kingdom come.

I wasn't going to do that.

"Look," I said, "I've decided on a slightly tricky move, and it might come off and it might not. If it does, I'm going to give you the target for the mission and bring *Balalaika* home. If it doesn't, you won't hear from me again. Try telling Croder that, but stand well back."

"By the sound of things," Ferris said in a moment, "he wouldn't allow it."

"Damn right."

"And nor should I."

"You've got no choice."

Rumbling of the plows below like the roaring of a riptide, ominous, getting on my nerves. When you're committed to moving right into a red sector with your eyes wide open you're prey to the visitation of auguries and portents. Ignore.

"You should know," I heard Ferris saying, "that I was ordered back to London at five o'clock this morning. I was packing when you signaled."

In a moment I said, "I need you here."

Waited.

"I'd like to stay on, if only to rake the ashes for what I can find."

I'd never heard him be so graphic. He was worried, that was all. *Ferris* was worried. Then help me, God. "It could be interesting," I said.

"Unfortunately I've got instructions from Control."

"Twist his arm."

"On what grounds? When you've got *nothing* to report."

"Perfectly true." It doesn't help, either, while you're listening to the roaring of the riptide, to hear that your director in the field is striking camp.

"Just give me one good argument," Ferris said. "Just one."

It was tempting to make a rendezvous and give him the whole picture, but it wouldn't work. He'd tell me I hadn't got a chance of pulling this one off, that for the first time I was letting the mission run me totally out of control: I was groggy from getting clear of two red sectors and couldn't be expected to think rationally, and the thing to do was to let him take me home while I was still alive, fight again another day, so forth, and all this in his most silken tones, stroking my ego and gently calming it down, getting inside my defenses as only he could do, without leaving an entry wound.

"I haven't got any argument you could use to Control," I said at last. "Go home."

"I'm afraid those are already my instructions."

"No regrets, then. But do something before you leave. Get Legge to pick up the Mercedes." I told him where I'd left it. "If it's not there, then the opposition's commandeered it."

"How did you get back from the forest?"

"In their car. They didn't want it anymore."

The thought was cheap, sour, and Ferris heard the note.

"Are you operational?" he asked me.

"Actually, no. That doctor, by the way—where can I find him?"

"What's the problem?"

"I pulled the stitches, that's all."

"He's near the UK embassy." He gave me the address. "I'll meet you there." Didn't want to leave his executive less than operational in the field, would try very hard, if I let him see me, to get me home.

"You'd be wasting your time," I told him. "Give my love to Blighty."

I shut down the signal and, in the silence of the room, heard the lifeline snap.

Mitzi Piatilova came out of the RAOC office alone again, taking a chance crossing the icy street and tossing her head back and laughing as a driver yelled at her.

I followed her into the fast-food café and got behind her in the line and whispered, "This is on me. Go for the caviar."

She turned, recognized me, couldn't think of my name.

"Dmitri," I said.

"Well, hi! What are you doing here?"

"I hoped I could join you."

"Sure!" Remembered the thousand dollars she'd earned the last time.

At the table she dropped her coat onto a chair and pulled her black sweater tight, her eyes bright in the haze of tobacco smoke. "Did your friend get off that charge? What was his name?"

I looked around. "Boris. Yes. Thanks to the Cobra."

Her eyes went deep. "When was this?"

"On Monday. Four days ago."

"You know he's dead, do you?"

"Vishinsky?"

"Yes."

"I hadn't heard."

"The police had a call on Tuesday and went into his hotel and found his suite looking like a slaughterhouse."

"That's the mob for you."

"I guess. So how's business?"

"Very good. Except that someone's getting in my way."

She stilled, looked down, up again. "You need something done about him?"

"Yes and no. But I'm not looking for a hit."

"Why not?"

"It doesn't always have to be the answer. I'm a businessman at heart."

"So what do you need from me?"

I told her.

17
Gulanka

"WHERE IS YOUR POLICE ESCORT?"

I grunted, shaking my head, pointing to my ears, then to my mouth.

The receiving officer gave a frown, squeezing the whole of his enormous face into it, as mystified as if I'd let forth with a torrent of Italian.

"What do you mean, you clod?" In a cloud of vodka.

I shook my head again, pointing.

He stared at me, then stared down at my papers again, his hands shaking, the split in his thumbnail impacted with grime.

The train stood waiting, a black, rusting barrier against the west, the rails beneath it shining, the mounds of trash between them covered with snow, an acrid reek of excrement drifting from where the contents of a lavatory had been dumped. Overhead the sky was dark, swollen with more snow to come, the only light in it electric, charged with unpent force.

The clock on the platform wall showed noon.

The officer shook my papers out again with a huge raw hand, a forefinger stabbing at the name near the top. *Berinov, Dmitri Vladimirovich.* Then he thumped me in the chest. "*You?*"

I nodded. I'd asked Mitzi to have the papers made out bearing the forged signatures of a magistrate and a clerk of the court, plus the official stamps and frankings. I'd filled in my own name later, in capitals. The charge on which Berinov, Dmitri Vladimirovich had been convicted was specified as murder.

"Where is your *escort?*" the officer asked me again, pointing to one of the policemen standing against the train with his rifle slung.

I looked confused. I'd chosen the deaf-and-dumb act to avoid too many questions. This was nothing more than a cattle drive going on, which I'd expected, but bureaucracy would nevertheless be in charge of things, and papers were papers. He was extraordinarily worried, this huge redheaded man, that I hadn't been correctly presented to him by an escort detailed by the bailiff of the court. It was like watching table manners in a buffalo.

"*Clod!*" He picked up his pen and dipped it into the encrusted inkwell, scratching his signature at the bottom of the sheet. His desk was a packing crate, once having contained—according to the stenciling—sewer fittings from No. 3 Sanitation Equipment Factory, Smolensk. "Over there!"

I tapped the papers and looked inquiringly.

"What? No, I keep these. *Over there!*"

Two of the police guards came forward to lead me across to the huddle of prisoners near the front of the train, and I heard the metallic echo of the last of so many doors slamming behind me. I'd listened to them all morning, the first time when I'd left the hotel in the railway worker's clothes Legge had originally provided, complete with a heavy moth-eaten astrakhan hat and pigskin boots, the coat cut out of thick woolen felt, proof against even a Siberian wind-chill. The second time I'd heard a door slam was when I'd got into the taxi, telling the driver to take me to Gorkogo Station in the southeast part of the city. The third time was of course when I'd arrived here and sat for half an hour on one of the benches outside, going over the whole thing again and reviewing the few, ineffective alternatives and coming up with the same answer, always the same answer: this was the *only* chance I'd got of bringing *Balalaika* home.

Then I'd picked up my duffel bag and walked into the station, and that door had slammed, too, and my nerves had flickered like iced lightning through the system as I reached the point of no return.

"Got a cigarette?"

A thin man beside me as we stood packed together, tears on his face from the cold, a five-day stubble.

"I don't smoke."

He turned away.

Gulanka, it said on the weathered board near the rear of the train, the letters scoured by time and the whipping slipstream.

Once he's in there, Mitzi had told me, *you won't see him again. No one ever gets out of Gulanka.*

Wire mesh, half a mile of it, stretched like a shimmering net across the rocks and bearing a frieze of curved blades glinting like scimitars in the glare of the floodlights, beyond them a cliff, a massif of sheer rock rising to five hundred feet against the arctic night sky, gates swinging open on shrieking hinges, their timbers shaking as the huge locomotive rumbled between them, steam clouding under the lights, and now an outcry from a pack of dogs straining at the leashes of the handlers, their wolflike shapes rearing alongside the carriages, the guards behind them in ranks, rifles slung, and finally whistles blowing, an outbreak of shouted orders, doors slamming back.

We marched—were marched—on the double, our packs of belongings bumping, our boots slipping on the frozen ground, our steaming breath whipped away by the wind coming off the Arctic Ocean.

On each side, mounds of split rock, bare facets of it showing through snowdrifts; mining rigs, tools, cranes, crates, trolleys on a single line heaped with shining ore, a timber yard stacked with beams, poles, props, weatherboarding; and then the huts, running in blocks halfway to the massif, their windows dark.

"Over there!"

Boots shuffled, shoulders bumped against the walls; the noisy heaving of lungs as we stood getting our breath back after the running march.

"Don't bunch! One a time, can't you fucking listen?"

Another flash from the camera on the other side of the office.

A man dropped, hitting his head against the corner of a desk, his fur hat coming off to show wisps of graying hair.

"Get him out of here!"

"You, next!" He fished for my papers as I stood forward. "Berinov, Dmitri Vladimirovich—is that you?"

"Yes."

"Yes, *Officer!*"

"Yes, Officer."

His eyes bulbous in the shadow of his peaked cap, the veins broken into a bloodied web across his face, a bottle of vodka on his desk, half empty. "What work did you do?"

"I was a shipping clerk, Officer."

"So you can read and write?"

"Yes, Officer."

My papers were shaking between his hands as he went on scanning them. "What else? What other work did you do?"

"A little merchandising."

His head jerked up. "You were in the mob?"

"On the fringe."

"You make much money?"

"I was comfortable."

A sudden roar of laughter, spittle shining on his stubbled chin. "*Were* you now! Then you'll find a slight fucking difference here, my friend. How much did you bring with you?"

"The regulation amount."

"You sure?"

"Yes, Officer." We'd been body-searched twice, coming through.

He looked down again. "We've got no use for a clerk here right now. If we need another one I'll send for you." He scrawled something in red across the papers. "Meantime, see how you like the mines."

"Can I ask a question?"

"You can try."

"There's a friend of mine here, Marius Antanov. Can you tell me which hut he's in?"

"That's none of your business. It's confidential information, and we respect privacy in this place, you understand that? No names, no details. Now get over there."

"You! Come on, then!"

A guard pushed me between ragged yellow tapes.

"Hold still!"

The camera flashed.

"All right, get over there. *Boris!* One more for Hut 9—you got room?"

"No, but I'll take him. He can sleep on the floor."

My watch had stopped, but I judged it to be three or four hours after midnight. Sleep had been difficult: For the first time in five days, the floor was no longer rocking. Rumbling through the Urals and then north and east across the steppes and into the mountains of the Siberian uplands, our main concern had been to keep from freezing: there'd been a dozen cases of frostbite as we'd been herded through the inspection rooms. On the train, to fall asleep had been dangerous unless your body temperature was adequate; survival depended on a minimum of circulation.

This hadn't changed very much: a draft was still slicing across the floor from under the door to the urinals outside, but I'd found some newspaper and blocked at least half of it. The silence was also hard to get used to after the noise of the train, and I lay awake for another hour, listening to the distant voice of warning that hadn't given me any peace since we'd arrived at the camp.

It was the first time I'd taken an uncalculated risk during a mission, and now I knew why the idea had always frightened me: with a calculated risk, when you know most of the data, most of the hazards and the chances of escape, you can keep a modicum of control over the operation. Without that, you're plunging into the labyrinth blind, and may God have mercy on you.

It was something I'd been certain I would never do, however hot a mission was running, however urgent the need, the one thing that as a seasoned professional I would never allow myself to take, because of its deadly threat to survival.

The uncalculated risk.

Mea culpa. But stay, be gentle with me, my good friend, grant me your charity, for madness of whatever kind can come upon any man at any time.

Sleep came at last from the shadowed silence of the night, broken only by the distant howling of the wolves across the snow.

18
Bones

"WHAT'S YOUR NAME?"

I stowed my spare mittens in the empty orange crate along with the rest of my stuff. The crate was my locker, nailed to the wall above the bunk.

I looked round. "Berinov."

"Berinov." He said it slowly, giving it a sarcastic twist, as if I'd said it was Napoleon. "That the only name you got?"

He was a big man with a sloping forehead and eyes buried in puckered flesh, a hare lip distorting his mouth. Other men were gathered in the hut, getting what warmth they could out of the dying stove. It was evening, and a time for rest.

"It's the only name I'm giving you," I told the big man.

"And why's that, now?"

There was a hook on the wall by the crate, made from a bent rod, but we never took off our coats until we were ready for bed. They'd taken the one I'd worn here at the check-in yesterday and given me a regulation issue with broad stripes on it; it wasn't lined but it was thick, and kept out most of the cold.

"Whoreson," the big man said. "I asked you a question."

Some of the men were turning to watch. They'd seen this before, had been victims of it themselves, probably, the old sweat and the new-recruit routine. This was my second day in Gulanka.

"You're in my bunk space," I told him. "You can leave."

"I'm in your *what?*"

I went to move past him to get nearer the stove, but he stopped me with a push of his hand. "You telling me what I can do?" Feigning total disbelief, not a terribly good actor. He smelled of sweat and stale beer. "What's *your* name?" I asked him.

"None of your fucking business, whoreson."

"All right, then let's call you Mickey Mouse. You've only got one little problem, Mickey. You're full of shit." I wanted to put a stop to this before I got bored, and there was only one way to do it.

"Say it again?" Cocking his head as if he really hadn't heard.

"I said you're full of shit."

His eyes glinted and he pulled back his right elbow with his fist bunched and I looked around the whole of the exposed target area and decided on a sword-hand to the right carotid artery because he was leaving plenty of time for it, and as he dropped I drove a finger into the spatulate nerve and got a scream that filled the hut, drove it in again and got another one and stopped right there because I didn't want him to start vomiting; there's always the risk with this strike because of the pain.

"Holy Christ," someone said from near the stove, his voice hushed. I assumed nobody had put the big man down before.

He was rolling on the boards, hands clutching his jawbone with his eyes squeezed shut.

"Mickey," I said, "you're in my way there." He didn't answer, quite possibly couldn't, so I took a light kick at the median nerve in his arm to wake him up. "Mickey, you've got three seconds. Crawl if you have to, but get out. *One.*"

He was moaning now but I knew he could hear.

Some of the dogs were voicing outside, having heard the screams. "*Two.*"

I hoped one of the guards didn't come in.

"*Three.*"

But he'd got the message, was crawling now, his big callused hands reaching ahead of him and dragging his body after. He could at least have *tried* to get up, for God's sake, at least put on a show.

I watched to make sure he kept moving, then went over to the stove, where two or three of the men gave me room.

"Christ," one of them said, "You know who he is?"
"Of course. Mickey Mouse."

"Could you teach me that?"

I swung the pick again, brought down stones, working my way along the vein.

"Could I teach you what?"

He was young, not more than twenty, light in his body, hunched, defensive; I'd noticed the way he walked, head down, glancing from side to side as if he expected trouble.

"What you did to Gradov."

"Who's he?"

"The big guy in the hut."

"Oh. What's your name, son?"

"Babichev."

"Christian name."

"Max."

He'd stopped work, was giving me the whole of his attention, and I glanced along the pit at the guard. "Keep working, Max," I said, and swung my pick again and caught the glint of nickel.

"Yeah." He saw the change in the vein too. "You've struck," he said.

"Looks like it. Why do you want me to teach you things like that?"

"I get picked on. You know?" He turned his face to me, his cheeks pinched from the weather, the cold, the misery, his eyes in a permanent flinch. "There's no women here."

"You haven't tried protecting yourself?"

He swung his pick. "You don't understand. I'm not a big guy."

"But you've got muscle."

"Oh, sure. Yeah, I've tried hitting, a bit, but they like that, they like me to struggle, you know? They come at me two at a time, see, sometimes more. You don't know what it's like."

I got the pans from the trolley and we started hammering the iron wedges into the vein. "All right," I said, "I'll give you one or two of the basics. But it's not something you can pick up in five minutes."

With a quick shivering laugh—"Okay, but we've got more than five minutes to spare in this place, right? Rest of our lives."

By the third day, I knew more about Gulanka.

The twelve-foot-high reinforced steel fencing with its inward-curving scimitar frieze was bolted to the rock face of the massif with half-inch-thick iron strips; the rock face itself was sheer, and floodlit by night. The thirty war-trained pit-bull guard dogs could be unleashed within a second by their handlers from quick-action snap cleats, and they understood the command to kill; they were fed the minimum rations to keep them hunting fit, and their staple diet was fresh red meat from the goats that were farmed at the side of the camp. The gates under the enormous archway where the trains came in were manned routinely by dogs and sentries, but were impenetrable anyway and fitted with foot-long, one-inch-diameter bolts. When a train came through with supplies or prisoners and took away nickel and waste, the guards were trebled and armed with Chinese assault rifles, and every inmate of the camp was confined to quarters until the train had left and the gates were bolted again.

At night the main thousand-watt floodlights were supplied with current from three huge stationary diesels that ran from six in the morning until midnight, when the floods were switched off, to leave marker lights along walkways and around the buildings. A shifting roster of fifty guards was on duty through the clock. Most buildings outside the hut area were out of bounds, but inmates could walk along the fence if they wanted to and look through it.

Most of the supplies for keeping seven hundred men alive came in by train from Khatanga, on the river from the estuary opening into the Arctic Ocean, but in the short summers there were a few crops raised in the camp, mostly corn and potatoes.

No prisoners were ever released from Gulanka: They were

brought here, without exception, to serve a life sentence. When they died—rarely past middle age—their bodies were sent by train to their relatives, if they could afford the one-million-ruble fee for this service. Mostly they were buried here outside the wire, with nothing to mark their grave. There were two priests at the camp, one Catholic and one Russian Orthodox, but they were drunk half the time, shacked up with a wood-burning stove and free rations of vodka and magazines sent from Moscow.

The rest, for most of the year, was snow. It was borne in from the coast on gale-force winds, to drift and pile against the fence and between the wooden hutments, sometimes bringing the crews out of the mines to clear emergency gangways through it. In summer the sun was seen on good days, and you could take off your coats and hoods and scarves and mittens, and sometimes even bare your arms to feel the warmth.

In winter, which lasted from September to May, wood smoke hung across the camp in a permanent fog except when the winds cleared it for a day or two. Half the inmates suffered from lung trouble, and emphysema was commonplace, the leading cause of death.

Outside the camp there were only the mountains and the snows, with at night the vast silence concealing and then revealing, as the wind shifted, the voicing of the wolves.

"They feed them meat," Igor told me. "It's to keep them near the camp."

"You mean people escape?"

He cast his milky eye at me, his huge knife stopping its work on the pit prop. Today the snow was too heavy to allow crews to reach the mines, and we'd been detailed to the timber shop. Igor was one of the few aging inmates I'd seen here, but he wasn't given light duties: He was as gnarled as an oak with a voice coming out of a barrel, and for this I respected him as a survivor.

"Escape? Well, yes, but none too often. Last year there was a character who tried it, croaked a guard one night and put on his uniform next day and went out with a mining crew and buried himself in the snow till evening—you can keep warm that way if you're well wrapped up. Then the same night we heard the wolves howling, a real chorus this time, and a search party went out and found a few scraps of this poor bugger left on the bones." He worked his knife again. "There's a big pack out there, twenty or thirty of 'em with a huge dominant male. You think the wire's something to get through? Try getting through the wolves. That's why they feed them, so they're never far away."

I finished a pole and started on another one. The wood was seasoned, pine-scented, the slivers coming away clean under the knife. The guard was at the other end of the shed near the door, out of earshot if we kept our voices low.

"Have there been any other attempts?"

"To escape?"

"Yes."

"Some. people get wire fever, in this place. They'll run at the fence sometimes, yelling their heads off. Those are the new ones in, been here only weeks. Could catch up with you—you never know what you'll do, the first weeks, never know *yourself* till Gulanka gets to you. Them as gets the fever gets put under special guard for a time, because it's after that they try and escape. You interested in escaping? Say no and you'll be lying in your teeth." He swung his head to check on the guard, then looked back at me. "What would you say's the easiest way of getting out of this place?"

"The train."

"Right. It's kind of obvious, ain't it? We had a character try that one. He'd been a rich man, back in the city, in the mob, name was Nyazov, I knew him well, he was in my hut." The "city" was Moscow. Everyone talked about the "city," a shining paradise at the end of the railroad line. "He bribed the guard who was taking roll call. Tell you something—before they let a train come through those gates, we're all confined to quarters and then roll's called, and if only one of us out of six or seven hundred doesn't answer his name—isn't *seen* to answer his name—the hunt's up, and until he's found they won't open them gates. You know Colonel Kalentsov? The commandant? He's been in charge here for twenty years, and takes pride in the fact that in the last twenty years *no* one's ever got out of Gulanka." With a shrug—"He's not a bad skipper, though, never touches the vodka, never—"

"What happened to the man who tried to get out on the train?"

Igor's milky eye was on me again. "I'll tell you. Like I say, he bribed the guard so he wasn't down as missing. Then he got a civvy coat from somewhere and walked down to the gates with a whole bunch of official-looking papers in his hand. All the rolls had reported every man present in his hut, so they let the train come in. Well this character Nyazov was going up and down handing out these papers—I saw one of them afterwards, they was just copies of a new daily-routine order he'd filched from the orderly room." He kicked his pine shavings together and dumped them into the bin. "Then the train got up steam and started rolling, and you know what this character did? He knew it'd be stupid to just cimb on board, so he waited till he thought no one was looking and made a dive underneath. Idea was, I reckon, to hang on to the struts and find space enough to wedge himself in for the ride."

He'd stopped work again for a minute, and the guard gave him a shout. *"Get a move on, then!"*

"Fuck yourself," Igor said under his breath, and struck down again with the huge blade to make a perfect slice. "But he came unstuck, poor old Nyazov, couldn't hang on for more than a couple o' minutes, lost his grip. They heard him scream, one o' the guards told me afterwards, when he went down under the wheels. They brought the two halves of his body back into camp, shoved 'em in a box and took 'em out there to the graveyard. Next morning at general roll call, we got all the details from the commandant, told us to take it as a warning of what happens when people try and escape. Of course he'd been out of his bloody mind, Nyazov, because it was November and even if he'd managed to hang on under that train for more than a few miles he'd have been found some fine day stiff as a bloody icicle, still there. Those trains go seventy mile an hour, so what d'you think the wind chill factor is when the temperature's fifty below for a start? Out of his bloody mind." The big blade bit, sliced and came away, leaving a perfect taper. "You want to know the only way to get out of Gulanka? It's easy, and there's some who's done it. Get yourself a bit of rope and sling it over a beam and kick the box away."

"Okay, this is a sword-hand. Palm flat, fingers tight together, thumb in line with the first finger, *not* tucked in, or you'll diminish the muscle tension."

He watched me, Max, his eyes intent in the dim light. We were in the washhouse, the last to leave. Smell of soap, urine, tobacco smoke, the night smell, the morning smell.

"You right-handed?"

"Yeah."

"Okay, the strike's like this and the usual target's the neck. It's to stun, if you hit the carotid artery right. That's here. You'll kill only if you use terrific force at that point—the sword-hand's not normally used for killing. You cold?"

"Bit."

He was always cold; most of it was fear. "Swing your arms, but keep watching. "This is the hammer-fist. You can use it for a downward block or target the head with it, or the elbow or the groin or the knee, depending on the situation. The trouble with the sword-hand and the hammer-fist is that you need to pull back first to get the momentum, and that takes a lot of time, at least two seconds, and if your opponent's quick he'll get in first. But don't underestimate them as weapons—they can do significant damage."

A wind was rising from the north, from the Arctic, coming over the top of the massif and curving down across the camp, rustling paper, rattling the doors. Another blizzard, Igor had told us; last night had been nothing.

"Getting warmer?"

"Bit."

"Keep swinging. This is the half-fist, and it doesn't look like much but it's used mainly for killing. It's effective because the knuckles make a blade and you can drive the strike from the hip without having to waste time pulling back first—you're in there before your opponent knows it. Stop swinging a minute and try it. No, fingers tight, really *tight*, lots of tension at the instant when you go in, thumb tucked against the first fingertip—no, *tight*, that's it. You can practice the hand position whenever you get the chance—last thing at night in bed's a good time. Train the muscles—they're not used to it."

"The hand set?"

"The shape you form with it. This is the hand set for the half-fist we're forming now. Okay, but tighter than that, *tighter*. Right, now this is the killing area, the best target for the half-fist, takes two seconds to kill once you're good enough. But if you mean to kill, *don't* pull the strike, *go* for it. And try and make sure you've got witnesses who can say it was in self-defense."

"That would kill Gradov?" His young eyes awed.

The man with the harelip. "Once your muscles are up to strength, yes. But that's going to take you a few months, a whole lot of secret training."

On a slow breath—"Gradov."

"Anyone. But look, you don't have to kill people to make them understand you're not just a pushover. Cool them down with a strike or two and leave them to think about it."

Snowflakes were mottling the black windowpane, and the wind began keening under the door.

"Will you show me—"

"Not tonight. Maybe tomorrow. But you can start practicing right away, in bed. Get those muscles into condition—that's half the battle." I put an arm round him. "How long have you been taking this kind of thing, Max?"

"This kind of—oh. Two years. Ever since I got here."

"Well look, I know it's tough to say, but give it another two months, maybe three. The most dangerous thing you can do is to start hitting back before you've got the strength and the moves down right—they'll stop you in your tracks and things'll be even worse for you. Now come on, before we freeze to death in here."

Later, after midnight when the main floodlights were switched off, I left the hut and made my way between the snowbanks, taking my time, taking an hour, more, watching for the sentries as they sheltered under the eaves, finding detours to avoid them and to avoid the marker lights as the new snow whirled past my face on the strengthening wind. Then I reached the target building.

It was a standard cylinder lock and I pushed the key in, my own version made out of a sardine-can opener bent at right angles and flattened at one end, felt for the tumblers, testing their resistance, finding the right pressure, turning the key and forcing them back and turning the handle next, cracking open the door.

Because there was one thing I had to do, primordially, despite the guards and the sentries and the machine-gun posts and the wire and the wolves.

Keep *Balalaika* running.

19
Flashlight

BEHIND THE COUNTER THE SO-CALLED ORDERLY room was a mess, box files made of cardboard at all angles across the floor and piled up the wall, three empty vodka bottles still where they'd been dropped among the cigarette cartons, five or six pairs of snow boots crowded near the door at the rear with a thick rawhide whip lying across them, the tip of its lash frayed from long use and the bone handle worn to an ivory brilliance, teasing the nerves unpleasantly.

It was cold in here, but that was all: not freezing, you could feel your fingers, there'd be some embers still warm in the potbellied stove. I kept the small plastic lamp held low—there were no curtains. The lamp had been on a bicycle once, Max had told me, was part dynamo, and he'd managed to keep it hidden when he'd arrived at Gulanka and the guards had gone through his belongings; every day he secretly spun the wheel of the dynamo to keep the lamp charged; the only source of light we were allowed here was a box of matches.

Antanov, Marius.

The tricky thing was going to be leaving the files as I found them: They didn't seem to be in any particular order. A to K, for instance, was on one of the labels, but this box dealt with guard duties. The A to K file next to it dealt with the inmates of Hut 5, Arkady to Bakar, no Antanov between them. There were, I would have said, thirty or forty files.

Midnight plus fifty on the wall clock, no means of knowing if a sentry came round to check, or if so, how often. The orderly room was the nerve center of the camp, and therefore for me, now, a distinct red sector.

Mr. Croder? Another red sector signal for Balalaika's *just come through from Moscow.*

Joking, of course: it was eight days since Ferris had been ordered out of the field, and by now the lights would be switched off over the board. Either that or a new mission would already be set up there with data coming in from the director in Algeria or Baghdad or Beijing, while Mr. Croder shut himself up in his tempered-steel shell to consider whether or not to resign, how much guilt to feel for the little ferret he'd left running in circles through the snow, or whether he could hold out a spider's-thread hope for an eleventh-hour last-ditch breakthrough for the mission, knowing as he did the blind tenacity of said ferret when the jaws of adversity gaped from the shadows of the labyrinth.

It wasn't my concern now. London could go straight to hell.

MOSKVA. Deliveries by train from the "city" last week: three tons of canned food, twelve pairs of new boots, a field telephone, two radios, three dozen towels, two hundred feet of one-inch rope and a hundred feet of half-inch cord, ten handcuffs, ten chain shackles, four pinewood coffins, six crates of vodka.

I'd seen two men going into the dinner hall yesterday with their feet shackled and their heads shaven and no winter jackets on, simply trousers and T-shirts; they'd been blue with the cold. In a place like this there'd be a whole variety of punishments.

The wind was moaning under the door, powdering the bare boards with snow. Somewhere above the storm layer was a full moon two diameters high from the horizon, and from the window the light was eerie and the snowflakes black, silhouetted against the eastern sky.

Voices and I switched off the lamp and froze.

Voices or the wind, or voices *in* the wind.

A beam of light was on the move out there, probing along one of the pathways that had been cleared earlier, two dark figures behind it with their faces backlit. Turning left, turning right, coming back, the beam sweeping the door of a hut—the commandant's HQ—and moving on again and again coming back along a parallel path, coming this way as I lowered myself behind a cabinet, waiting, the voices out there torn by the wind but louder now.

And what, if those men came in here, would there be to say? Some instant rehearsal was in order.

I was looking for a friend of mine in the files.

Who let you in here?

Nobody.

You've got no permission to be here?

No.

You mean you broke in?

I picked the lock.

Isn't that breaking in?

I suppose so. But—

My God, are you in trouble! Hold your hands behind your back.

Click.

The beam of the lamp flooding the window now, then the cracks of the door, flickering across the powdering of snow on the floor and gilding it.

Waited.

"I told him I wasn't going to do another fucking guard duty for him till he'd paid me for the last time."

"Maybe he's out of cash."

"*Shit,* then that's *his* problem, not mine."

The clump of their boots on the pathway, the sound fading.

Inside the organism the pulse rate higher, throbbing at the temples, and I gave it a couple of minutes to come down. It wasn't the idea of having to answer a few questions that worried me, or the handcuffs, or the thought of the rawhide whip. *This* was the worry: if I left here tonight without finding Antanov in the files, there'd never be another chance.

Time, then, is distinctly of the essence. I cannot *afford* to be caught in here before I've finished. Hold one thing and one thing only within the third eye.

Marius Antanov is the key to *Balalaika*.

Hut 19. Abel, Aker, Avonik.

In half an hour I spun the dynamo wheel, running it along the edge of the wooden counter for three minutes, switching on the lamp again, finding it brighter.

01:17. I was among the boxes piled against the wall now, taking the top one down, remembering the angle at which it had been set there.

INCIDENTS. 1994 to 1996. Escape attempts: details. Death due to escape attempts: Inside camp. Details. Outside camp (wolves.) Punishments Awarded for 1) Disobedience, 2) Breach of Lights Out, 3) Attacks on other inmates, 4) Attacks on Guards. Details. Punishments: 1) Snow Clearing for 20 Hours with 2 15-minute breaks, hard Rations. 2)Flagellation (12 Strokes.) 3) Shackles, head shaven, 6 Days. 4) Solitary Confinement, 3 to 30 Days.

The wind moaned under the door.

01:48. Hut 15. Blank.

02:13. Hut 17. Blank.

02:39. Hut 19. Blank.

03:21. Hut 22.

The last one.

Berechov, Bulgarin, no "A"s. No Antanov down as Present, no Antanov down as Absent, Missing or Deceased.

What actually happened—Natalya—*was that the Ministry of the Interior sent a squad to arrest my brother as he was coming out of a cafe on the Ring one night. The next day there were charges brought and he was summarily convicted of murdering a judge and sentenced to a life term at Gulanka.*

I hadn't misheard her. Gulanka was one of the three most notorious penal settlements in Siberia, allocated specifically for life terms with no remote possibility of release.

So Antanov had been sent somewhere else? To one of the other two? Mother of God.

I should have checked.

I should have asked Mitzli Piatilova to confirm it for me at her office. If I'd had a director in the field, I would have had the time to think, to make careful plans, to structure the moves. But I'd got off the blocks too *bloody* fast, wanting to make a breakthrough and signal London and get Ferris back to help me put smoke out and head Sakkas off before he could send his army in, tie up the whole mission and bring *Balalaika* home to the cheering of the crowds and the dancing in the streets before it was too late to do anything as a lone-wolf executive with no local direction and no support group and no signals, no instructions through Cheltenham, running a mission with its head cut off, *finis, finto,* the end of the line.

Mea culpa.

Moaning under the door, the high wind from the Arctic sweeping the ice and tumbling the silvered crests across the ocean under the lowering moon, to reach the coast and the land and the massif out there, hurling a wave of snow across the camp and with such force now that the flakes hit the window audibly as I stood motionless. Of what import is the life, of what import is the fate of this one puny creature trapped in the maelstrom of such a night, pinned by his predicament and unable even to move as he comes to know, is brought to know the truth, to hear the death knell of his grandiose ambitions?

Not much.

Yet we must strive, must we not, my good friend, to play the game and at whatever cost? What else can we do when we're thrown the bloody ball?

Gulanka. She had said *Gulanka,* and quite clearly.

So if they'd sent Marius Antanov to one of the other camps it had been done without her knowledge, perhaps deliberately, so that he would never receive her letters, her parcels of comfort, her love, her encouragement. That would be something a man like Sakkas would think of, would arrange. Or there'd simply been some official decision reached behind the scenes: Gulanka was already running beyond its specified capacity, Igor had told me yesterday, and the crowding had brought complaints from some of the staff. And again, Natalya Antanova hadn't known, hadn't been informed by the authorities—why should she be? Her brother had been thrown on the trash heap in northern Siberia and was of no further account.

So face the facts.

To find which camp Antanov had actually been sent to, I would have to get out of this one first and reach Moscow and see Mitzi and start all over again. Easy to say. *You want to know the only way to get out of Gulanka?* Igor, his big knife whittling at the prop. *Get yourself a bit of rope and sling it over a beam and kick the box away.*

The hut flexed to the wind, and somewhere on the roof a loose patch of tarred fabric flapped, fretting at the nerves as I stood motionless still, thinking, letting the subconscious play in what peace it could find while I held patient, waiting for the final readout.

Conscious business: Watch the window; the sentries would be back in this area before long now, or possibly new ones, after an unscheduled changing of the guard because of the blizzard. Rehearse again what I would say if anyone came in here, embellish on it. Remember that whatever the risk of standing for any length of time outside to lock the door again with the makeshift key, take it: it *must* be found locked, in case I ran foul of a sentry on my way back to the hut and they started putting two and two together in the morning.

Patient, be patient, let the infinitely subtle processes of the subconscious consult the higher self and look for answers, while in the forebrain the thoughts circled under the garish light of logic. . . . Even if I tried to get out of this place there were the guards, the guns, the dogs, the wire, the wolves . . . *there's a big pack out there, thirty or forty of 'em with a huge dominant male. You think the wire's something to get through? Try getting through the wolves.* And even if I could—

Readout.

Not a breakthrough, but let's look it over. Conceivably, yes, Marius Antanov could have been sent to Gulanka under an alias, perhaps to sever his link with Sakkas. So I should now search the files again for a name I didn't even know?

No. Look at the photographs.

And start now: there are six or seven hundred of them.

03:32.

And don't just look at them, study them carefully. She had an elfin face, Natalya, finely sculpted and delicate. I wouldn't expect to find that in her brother, though there could be the same bone structure, the same overall slightness of feature. Or his genes could be paternal-dominant or he could even be a throwback to an earlier generation and look totally different, his face square, heavyset.

04:49. Three hundred of the photographs scrutinized, two noted as possibles.

05:35. The storm buffeted the hut, screaming now through the overhead cables outside.

Six hundred faces, with two more possibles, and forget the sinking of the heart as the cold hard facts nagged at the mind: it was a total shot in the dark to think that Antanov was here in the camp under a different name, and if he were, the chances of his looking anything like his sister were slight in the extreme; you can tell people more easily by their walk, the way they turn their head, the movement of their hands, their speech patterns; the camera is notoriously inaccurate, limited by the light factor and only two dimensions.

06:12. Six hundred and seventy-one, with a total of twelve possibles, the embers in the stove long since dead and the hands numbed and the feet frozen, the blood sugar low by this time and my estimation of the chances of success close to zero.

I slid the last of the files back into its correct position as voices sounded again in the alleyways outside and a beam of light began playing across the doors of the huts. A new guard would have come on at 06:00 if they conformed to recognized routine, and I sighted through the window again from cover.

I couldn't recognize them in their fur hats, but one of them was stopping at the door of the commandant's office to try the handle and my boot kicked the corner of the counter as I came through the gap very fast but the sound wouldn't have carried outside. The key was in my hand as the two sentries—a change of guard, yes, the last ones hadn't checked the door handles—came along the pathway with the beam of light swinging through the snow.

Faster.

The tumblers obstinate, the crude key slipping across their surfaces, the voices outside louder now, the beam of light brighter, the wind screaming through the overhead cables, *faster,* the tumblers as firm as rocks, if that guard had checked the commandant's office door he'd be certain to check *this* one, tilt the key the other way, *tilt* it and try again, it doesn't follow that a homemade lock pick will work from both sides but keep on trying, tilt it *this* way again, the voices louder still, shouting against the wind as the beam swung across the window and then flooded the gap below the door, take the last chance then and abandon the lock and get behind the counter, got *right* down as the handle rattled and the door swung open and the sentries came in through a gust of driving snow, slamming the door against it and coming across to the counter.

"Leave 'em a note, Rudi, door found unlocked, 06:17. The skipper's going to piss all over poor old Sasha but we've got to report it, bloody hell, this is the *orderly* room, *anyone* could just walk right in."

"God's truth."

I could hear him tearing a sheet off a pad and raking among some pens, his breathing noisy as he took his time forming the words he wanted. Crouched on the floor in the shadows, I could see the top of his hat, the snow melting into diamond drops on the fur. If he raised his head too far, my own would come into his line of vision—an inch too far, two inches, not more than that.

"Unlocked," he asked, "or left open?"

"What? Unlocked. Door wasn't open, was it? There's a difference. Door'd been open, this place would'a been covered in snow by now."

A brief laugh. "God's truth. Unlocked, then."

"Right."

I couldn't move down any lower than I was, couldn't turn my

head farther into the shadows, had to wait it out, listening to the guard's breathing and thinking of the whip, the shackles, the solitary cell.

"Come on, Rudi!"

"Writing ain't my best thing—you know that."

"Let's have a look." His boots clumping over the boards. "'Found' has got a 'd,' for Christ sake, it's not 'foun'. Put a 'd.' Look."

"Oh."

"That's it. Now come on, we're holding up the fucking parade."

For an instant I saw his eyes, Rudi's, but he wasn't looking down but turning away, dropping the pen onto the counter. Then their boots marched across to the door and one of their rifles swung and hit the frame as they went out into the howling wind and I heard the bunch of keys jingling outside as I slowed the breath, let the muscles go, reestablishing the norms in the system.

I gave them ten minutes to clear the area and then got the door unlocked again and worked on it from the outside before I left, took short detours between the huts on the way back to my own, tramping through the deep new snowfall with the names of the twelve apostles of *Balalaika* lodged in my head.

20
Midnight

"MARIUS ANTANOV?"

"Who, me? No."

"Do you know anyone calling himself that?"

"Antanov? Not in this hut, no."

"YES, THAT'S GOOD, YOU'VE GOT THE move down all right. But with all these strikes you've got to use the whole of your body. Try the heel palm again."

"To the chin?"

"The chin or the nose, I don't mind. The strike to the chin could kill by breaking the spinal vertebrae, given enough power, but with half as much force, the one to the nose will drive the bone into the brain, and that's instant death."

He made the strike, and well enough, but with no strength yet, of course.

"All right, now start it from the ball of the rear foot and build up the momentum through the calf and the thigh and the hip and the shoulder and *then* the arm and the hand. Swing the *whole* body into the move. And if the target's the nose, don't aim at that. Aim at the area *behind* the nose, up into the inside of the skull, bury the strike right *through* the target into the brain, smash your way *through.*"

He made three strikes, trebling their power.

"Right. Practice it that way. In every strike, go for the target accurately but *imagine* going *through* it. Make yourself a punching bag, stuff a sack full of garbage or rotten potatoes, whatever you can find. Give me three more."

He swung in fast, driving from the foot. "That's it. One day you'll be good, Max."

"God," he said, his breath clouding on the air, his young eyes bright, seeing hope. "This is strong stuff!"

"You bet."

He bent over with his hands on his knees, getting his breath; at this altitude it was hard to come by. The storm was over, had died before noon, and the camp rang with snow shovels.

"Give me three more," I said in a minute. "Half-fist to the larynx this time, and *go* for it."

"Marius Antanov?"

"Talking to me?"

"Yes."

He shook his head, wiping the sweat from his eyes. We were in the mine. "Akunin, Danata."

"You know anyone calling himself Marius Antanov?"

"Nope. There's an Antanov in Hut 14, but his name's Boris."

Seven to go, by the end of the day.

By midnight, six.

The air was still as I stood for a last few minutes outside the hut. The night was clear, with the star fields strewn across the vastness of space in a shower of silver dust, Sirius ablaze in the southeast, Mars a glowing ruby overhead.

Thou shalt elect a thing, and it shall be bestowed upon thee, and light shall shine upon thy ways.

Then let me find him. Let him be here, somewhere. That's all I ask.

Swing the pick, swing it hard, yea, even heartily, see it cleave the rock.

There have been times in my life, in my career—which is my life—when I've known that I've placed myself outside reality, committed myself to achieving the unachievable. It's very dangerous, but on these occasions there is no choice.

Swing, hit, cleave, watch the rock come away, watch for the glint, the vein, the nickel.

"You're working too hard," Igor said from beside me. "Save your energy."

"What for?"

"The rest of your life."

Swing lustily, feel the muscles play, sustain the morale.

"What are you going to find here, Igor, for the rest of your life?"

"My life."

At the times of which I was just speaking, you can come very close to despair, and that's the most dangerous thing of all, except panic. You can take your time over despair, but panic is quick-acting, deadly. I've never given in to panic, but yes, I've come close to despair.

Five of the apostles left, and the day to get through, the evening to be spent in making my calls on the five remaining huts, continuing the search, keeping the flame burning, shielding it from the likelihood, the extreme likelihood that I would never find the Holy Grail, would never bring *Balalaika* home.

Would never reach home at all.

I would know before midnight.

"That's very good," I told Max.

"You're not just saying that?"

"I wouldn't be so irresponsible. Overconfidence could get you killed."

He was out of breath again, and I decided to call it a day. We were working in the gap between the garbage dumps and the wire on the west side, where a degree or two of warmth lingered from the winter sun that had come out in the wake of the blizzard, flushing the snows with a pale roseate light.

"When will I be ready?" Max asked.

"Two more months. Go off half-cocked and God help you." I threw a sword-hand across his face, and he was painfully slow. "You've got to work on your reaction time, too. Drop things and catch them before they hit the ground. Listen to people talking, and the next time you hear the word 'maybe' or 'always' or whatever you choose, squeeze a fist—instantly. It'll take some doing—you don't want to be jumpy, you want to be *fast.*"

"Is there anything I can do to repay you for all this?" he asked me with an appealing diffidence on our way back to the hut.

"I'm doing it for my own satisfaction. But if I think of anything, yes, I'll let you know."

"Is your name Marius Antanov?"

"No. You've got the wrong man."

Three now.

Three.

The huts full of steaming men, the ringing of the shovels over for the day, the pathways cleared, a feeling of good work done, someone singing in the wash rooms, *singing,* in this place, *My life,* Igor had said, I took his point.

The gruel filthy in its tin bowl, but we spooned it up with gusto, blowing on it, searching for the end of a carrot, a lump of potato, a few black beans.

I thought of something that Max could do for me, yes. Perhaps tomorrow, whatever news midnight would bring.

"Marius Antanov?"

He looked at me, the eyes suddenly wary in the thin, sculpted face.

"And who are you?"

21
Key

"HOW IS SHE?"

"Worried about you, of course," I said.

"I suppose so." He sat shivering on the ragged matting, hunched in his striped overcoat. He felt the cold.

We were in the gymnasium, if you want to call it that, a bigger hut than the others with no stove, just a few moth-eaten mats strewn around and a rickety vaulting-horse and some parallel bars made of gnarled pit props, no punching bag—any kind of combat training was strictly prohibited in Gulanka. Place reeked of sweat, as you can imagine.

It was the evening end-of-work hour, what we called free time.

"Natalya didn't send her love because she didn't know I was coming here."

He moved his head. "How much warning did you get?"

Justice was summary in the capital these days.

"I came here on my own account, chose my own time."

There was a pause. Marius listened attentively, then considered before he spoke. He was the kind of man, I thought, who would have been good at running the Sakkas empire, cool, intelligent, creative. In Gulanka he worked in the commandant's office as a bookkeeper, he'd told me, his talents not totally wasted.

"You came here on your own account," he said. "And what does that mean?"

"I fiddled my way onto the train, with false papers."

"To Gulanka." Listening very hard now.

"Yes."

"Why?"

"To look for you."

Watching me with his pale attentive eyes. "For me."

"I'm taking you back to Moscow. I assume you've no objection."

He blinked, which he didn't do often. He was a bit like Ferris, a cool cat, raised an eyebrow when he felt moved, instead of the roof.

"Taking me back to Moscow," he said. "And how long have you been here?"

"Four or five days."

"Not long enough to learn anything about Gulanka."

"I learn fast. But do me a favor. Imagine for a moment that I could in fact get you back to the city."

Two beats. "I should tell you it's entirely academic, but very well."

"What would you want to do in Moscow, after you'd seen your sister?"

He thought for a long time now, turning his head away, turning it back. Then quietly, "Destroy Sakkas."

I caught something in his eyes for the first time, a brightness, hatred, I thought, an intense hatred.

"Destroy," I said. "You mean kill?"

"Not immediately. Bring him down first. Destroy everything he has, first. Then kill, or have killed: I'd bring in a professional, to make certain I didn't bungle things. That's something I would very much like not to bungle."

The door at the other end of the gym came open with a bang and someone came in, the snow under the lamps outside casting a wash of light across the rafters. He shot us a look, slammed the door and shook off his overcoat, dropping onto a mat and stretching out.

"This is because of what he did to your sister?"

"For the most part. And for what he did to me."

"I didn't come here just to give you the chance of destroying Sakkas, though I wouldn't object. I need your services in return."

In a moment, "My services. And what are they?"

"I'll tell you when we reach Moscow."

Watching me with steady concentration. "Who are you?"

"I work for a European government, but as a freelance."

"I see." He was too intelligent to ask which government, or what post; if I'd wanted him to know, I would have told him.

"Let me ask you something. Have you done much training?"

He looked at me. "Training?"

"In athletics. Or just—you know—jogging, aerobics, that kind of thing. How fit are you?"

"Oh, all right I suppose. I used to jog every day in Gorky Park."

"How long for?"

"Maybe half an hour."

"Do anything with the arms?"

"Arms?" He was thinking suddenly of assault rifles. "Oh, lifted a few weights when I had the time."

"Push-ups?"

"Too boring."

"They are, aren't they." I left it. It was too late to tell him to start a crash program now: he'd get muscle-bound.

"You're pretty fit yourself," he said in a moment. "I heard what you did to that man Gradov."

"He was easy meat, run to fat." I watched the man on the mat over there, doing some leg-raises now, his breath steaming under the bleak yellow lights. "How's the commandant these days?"

No surprise in the eyes: he fielded unexpected questions well. "He's a very angry man."

"Why?"

"Someone tried to bribe one of the guards."

"The CO doesn't like that?"

"He hates it. He considers himself an honorable man, and feels demeaned if anyone attempts to buy him. We get mafiya types sent here—looking at me obliquely—and some of them are millionaires, of course. The first thing they try to do is get the CO to let them escape, at pretty well any price he cares to name. Wrong again—he's proud of his record in keeping his prisoners captive, since those are his orders."

"So I've heard."

"I expect so." His thinking runs right down through the ranks. One or two guards take bribes, probably, but they must know how dangerous it is. The punishment's always the same—a public flogging in the gym here, over that vaulting horse. It's not pretty. So if you thought you could simply buy our tickets to Moscow, I advise you to forget it."

"I didn't."

"I'm so glad. Your back would have taken six months to heal."

The man who'd come in here to train was on the parallel bars now, grunting in time with his swings. In the next three days I'd be working on those myself, would need the vital difference between a muscle that held and a muscle that ripped.

"You work for a government agency. But not at a desk, I imagine."

He was thinking of the Gradov thing again, I suppose. "I'm pretty active," I said. "But look, I want to know, first, whether you're ready to get out of Gulanka. I can look after you through the entire operation, but there'll be risks, some of them unpredictable." I was watching him now, watching his pale eyes, their depths, needing to see the truth there, whatever he might put into words.

In a moment he said, "You've got the kind of madness in you that seems to have worked, historically. There are legends, aren't there, that pass on—"

"I'm not sure what you mean by madness."

"Oh. No offense, but you tell me you can get me out of a place like this, where no one's escaped for twenty years, since the present CO took over. I mean—"

"I see, yes. But my mind is perfectly sound, so I haven't been concentrating on the difficulties, only on the solutions. You'll have to make a mental switch yourself there, in the next three days—that's our countdown period. But for now I need your answer to one question, and it's critical. You tell me you want to destroy Sakkas if I can get you to Moscow, and—as I've said—there are unpredictable risks. So here's the question, and I want you to take your time: Exactly how *much* are you prepared to risk? What's the ultimate?"

I watched his eyes, the way they changed, grew darker, until in a moment or two he felt he was ready.

"Death," he said, "if you put it like that."

I saw Max again soon after midnight. He came to me at the rendezvous we'd arranged, in the gap between the garbage dumps and the wire on the west side.

"Last one," he said, and thrust the sacking bundle into my hands. "Took some getting."

"I hung around."

"You're a good friend."

"It's an honor."

He watched me in the light of the three-quarter moon, his young face pinched, his eyes bright, waiting for me to say something more, giving me the impression that whatever I said, he'd listen to it, and take it to heart. Anything, anything, so that one fine day he could vanquish the monster of all his nightmares, break his pride, shatter his reputation, obliterate his face. Annihilate Gradov, in front of a hut full of men. God knew what I'd started.

But I suppose it was the boy's readiness to listen to me, whatever I might say, that prompted me to wrap the whole thing up for him, because I wouldn't be seeing him the next day: I would be too busy.

"Listen, we've got to get our sleep." We were extending the mine in the morning, twenty minutes for breakfast, only half an hour for the midday break. "But first I want to add a bit to what we've been doing in training."

"Okay." The wind was rising a little, and he pulled the collar of his overcoat tighter.

"Although this doesn't apply only to training. It applies to whatever you want to do in life, whatever you've *got* to do. It's the ultimate key to success, and it's the only one, so when you've found it, don't lose it." It was coming out like an avuncular homily, but I couldn't help that. At the core it was sound, and that was what mattered.

The boy's eyes were brighter still as he locked them onto mine in the moonlight. "Okay," on a shiver of breath.

"We create our own reality, Max. You've seen those bumper stickers in Moscow on the back of some of the trucks—*Shit happens*. And those people are dead right—that's what happens to them, because that's what they expect—they get what they're looking for, what they've created for themselves."

I waited, hearing the snuffling beyond the wire, watching the colored glint of eyes across the snow. We could see them on most nights when the weather was clear.

"On the other side of the coin there are the miracles. I'll bring it down to size for you, in terms of training. When you make a strike, any kind of strike, you look first to the physical needs—drive from the ball of the foot, bring the force in through the hips, attend to the bodywork. But there are two final requirements in making the strike a success. The first is psychological: As you commit yourself to the target, there's just the one thought you've got to hold in your mind, to the exclusion of all others. *Get there.*"

Max nodded with little jerks of his head. "Okay. *Get there.*"

"Right." I noticed my voice sounded as if it were coming from a distance now, from well outside the aura, or perhaps it wasn't my voice, but someone else's, because things were going on that didn't really concern Max, things that would concern me later, tomorrow, when the moon would be full and the choice taken and the bridges burned.

"The final requirement," I said, "is drawn from the field of the spiritual. It's not a thought, but a feeling. *Be there.*"

The wind rose again, fluting among the eaves of the huts, dying away.

"Okay," Max said. *"Be there.* Okay."

I don't think he'd really got it; it was a lot to ask of a man his age. But maybe he'd work on it, lying in his bunk in the quiet of the night.

"Right," I said, and thought of the towering dark where tomorrow night the moon would be floating, of the towering odds against success, which could only be defeated if I could manage, during the torments of the trial by ordeal, not to lose the key.

22

Zero

B Y EARLY AFTERNOON A LIGHT SNOW had started, borne by an errant wind from the hills to the east of the camp. By 09:00, with dark down for the past six hours, it had thickened a little, enough to hide the big floodlit gates from the main hutment area.

I watched the snow continuously. Later it would become one of the critical factors involved.

By 11:45 I was standing in the lee of the gymnasium, shielded by the eaves on the west side. I had been there for ten minutes, making detours to cover my tracks in the new snowfall, and to avoid the sentries. The rear of the camp was never patrolled: it was a dead zone, the only foot traffic leading to and away from the gymnasium itself on the south side.

At 11:53 I heard a sound.

The timing was also critical. My watch was still out of kilter, and Igor had given me one he said he'd picked up from a prisoner in return for a favor. I think it was his own. Igor knew what I'd been setting up for the last three days, simply because I trusted him to know. Like Marius, he'd told me I was mad. But he and Max had both let me have their goat-meat ration during the evening meals. Max knew nothing, of course, had seen nothing even in my eyes. The idea would have fired him up, and he could have given me away without intention.

A faint clinking of metal, from somewhere close by. The moon was still behind the mountains to the east, but I could see well enough in the peripheral glow from the tall arched floodlights.

"Deadline." A whisper from the shadows.

"Zero." We synchronized watches. "You've got all your stuff?"

"Of course." He sounded impatient. Since I'd told him three days ago what we were going to do, he'd been like that, his tone sometimes letting me know he wasn't an idiot, could be relied on, wouldn't screw things up. It was fear, that was all, and understandable.

I'd told him only what we would be doing, and how to prepare himself, what to collect, conceal, and bring with him tonight. I hadn't given him all the actual phases, details, minutiae; there'd been no point. He'd been told the essentials, and told to go over them in his mind day and night until mentally he was letter-perfect. I'd challenged him on some of them and he'd got them right every time, but there was this impatient tone that came out sometimes, and I'd learned it wasn't only his expression of fear. Marius had been running the Sakkas empire for three years, and had been used to a high order of respect and instant obedience from his aides and underlings, wasn't used to anyone but Sakkas himself dictating to him. I'd gone with this as best I could, deferring to him when possible; but it worried me that he might turn arrogant later, when I would need to be in total and absolute charge.

The snow was coming in flurries now and still thickening. That was all right, but if it increased to blizzard strength it could become deadly.

I checked Igor's watch at 11:50 in the faint light. I'd timed zero for 11:55 because the main floodlights would normally be switched off at midnight and I wanted the initial phase to trip in before that, to cause confusion.

"Marius," I said, "it's fifty yards from here, and we'll have to pick our way over the new snow. Don't worry too much about making a noise—it'll be quite well covered. Just get there as fast as you can."

"Understood." There was a tightness in his tone now, and that was good: I wanted the adrenaline to run.

I helped him shrug out of his heavy striped overcoat, and he helped me with mine; then we buried them under the snow. Underneath we wore black bomber jackets, stolen at three o'clock last night from the reception hut where incoming prisoners were issued with new gear.

Another sound came in now: boots crunching from south of us, toward the center of the camp.

"Flatten yourself against the wall," I whispered to Marius, "then freeze."

I watched the shadow as it lengthened across the snow, a man's figure, the bulk of an assault rifle projecting from it. Rattle of a door handle as he tried the gym. The last two nights there'd been no sentries coming this far: I'd checked. Perhaps tonight it was the punctilious guard, the only one who tried the door handles.

If he comes any farther to check the rear end of the hut, strike to kill, don't risk anything now, it's too close to zero.

I could see the steam from his breath at the corner of the gym, lit from beyond him, then the sudden glint on the barrel of the rifle as he came into sight, his head turned in this direction, the beam of his flashlight swinging, the flurries of snow whirling between us, hiding me, revealing me. Hiding me enough? Revealing me too much? I couldn't turn my face away, needed to watch him, to prepare the strike.

To the other side of me there was nothing but the wall of the massif with its rocky outcrops, so perhaps I was blending in with it because the guard was still swinging his torch, over me and away again, the backglare from the snow half-blinding him as I stood with my eyes narrowed to slits, their lashes putting him surrealistically behind bars as I watched him.

If he keeps on coming we shall need great speed: go into the toraki-kuo *within two seconds before he can bring up the gun.*

To kill.

But he was turning now, the snow in his face, in his eyes, and his boots crunched away down the path from the gymnasium.

I checked my watch immediately: it was one minute to zero.

"He's gone?"

"What? Yes. Relax."

I heard Marius let a breath out.

"We're beginning the countdown," I told him, "with less than a minute to go. You feeling okay?"

"Of course."

Bloody arrogance.

Last one, Max had said as he thrust the burlap bundle into my hands. The last one of six. He didn't know what I wanted them for, didn't know when I was going to use them.

Thirty seconds.

"Thirty seconds," I told Marius.

He didn't answer.

A flush of silver light was creeping across the snow from the east. It would be moonrise, but we couldn't watch it from here, from the west side of the gym.

The tin alarm clock had been less easy to get hold of. The prisoners hung on to any possession they could call their own; it made them feel like people of property. I'd had to trade my extra pair of boots for the clock.

Fifteen.

I told Marius, but again he didn't answer. What could he say, after all? Good luck? Of course we'd need good luck, every vestige of it that God almighty could spare us, and you don't think I'm praying, do you? You think I never pray.

Ten.

Nine.

Eight.

The snowflakes whirled, pretty as cherry blossoms as they blew past the corner of the hut.

Look, it was this or nothing, that's why I haven't gone mad. The only choice was another forty years in penal servitude with *Balalaika* just a mention in the dusty record books, *Mission abandoned,* won't you get that into your bloody head?

Seven.

Six.

Five.

"Four seconds," I told Marius.

We shifted our packs, settling the canvas straps.

Three.

I let my eyes rest on the snow where the light was brightening, and took joy from it, joy also from the cool kiss of the flakes as they landed on my upturned face and my eyelids as I closed them just one more time.

Two.

Opened them again to look across the camp under the tall floodlights.

One.

To look across at the shape of the huge diesel generator as the hand of the tin clock moved to zero and the sky was lit with a blinding flash. A moment later, there came the shuddering *whoof* and the whole camp was blacked out.

We began running for the wall of the thousand-foot massif.

23
Overhang

I DROVE THE PITON INTO THE SEAM and tested it with the rope but it pulled down at an angle and I drove it in harder, tested it, found it good and hauled up.

From three hundred feet the camp was lit with fireflies as emergency lamps came on. Flames still reddened the sky from the generator's diesel fuel, and black smoke rolled in waves between the huts.

Snow drifted past us from the east side of the massif, more heavily now, shrouding the moon, giving us a smoke screen on the face of the rock.

"Haul up," I called down to Marius, and felt the rope grow taut.

I'd got Andrei, the half-Mongolian smithy in the forge, to make me twelve pitons two days ago, adapting them from pit gear and grinding four of them into bird beaks in case we needed them. Of course we'd need them; we'd need a lot of other gear—hooks, dowels, free biners, pulleys, bolts, jumars—but all we'd got was what we could get, just the pitons, two broad-faced hammers and two weighted picks made from rusty steel—the ones we used all day were impossible to take from the pits; they were counted whenever we knocked off. The rope had been easier to get away with from the stores, hemp, 12mm, recently delivered, no fraying in it.

Andrei had made the pitons and the picks for me at the forge. He was massive, seven feet high, all muscle.

"From the city?" I'd asked him. His great oval face dripped with sweat.

"I am from the city, yes."

"You've got people there? Relatives?"

"My mother." He leaned on his five-foot hammer, watching me, his eyes crimson from the heat, an animal smell coming from his goathide apron.

"She okay?"

"She is okay. She is an old woman now. Why do you ask me?"

"I've been managing to get some mail through to the city."

"You must have friends."

"Right. I need you to do a bit of metalwork for me, Andrei."

"I've got enough work." He turned aside and spat, then wiped his face with the rag he kept in his apron.

"I could let your mother have some money."

"You haven't got any money."

"I'd have it sent to her through my friends in the city."

"How much?"

Sparks flew suddenly from a coal. "One thousand US dollars."

Andrei's eyes narrowed. "That is a lot of money."

"Yes."

"A lot of work."

"No. You've also got to say nothing about this."

He tilted his great head, sighting me along his nose. In a moment, "Very well. I say nothing. A thousand dollars. But must be paid in rubles. People will try and steal from her."

"In rubles, then. She can find somewhere to hide them."

Drips hung from the end of his hooked nose, like tiny rubles in the light of the forge. "Under the bed."

"No. I'll get my friends to show her better places than that. Leave it to me, Andrei. No one will steal from your mother."

That day he began work on the twelve pitons.

I could hear Marius now, hauling up from below, his breathing audible, too audible. Christ, we'd only just started.

"You want to rest?"

He thought before he answered, didn't want to say yes because of his pride, so he compromised: "Maybe for sixty seconds."

"Don't rush it." In the wind I heard his pick clinking against the granite. *"And don't drop anything."* Eventually the guards would search the terrain below the massif. They would search *everywhere.*

There was a lot of noise going on below us now: the klaxon horns still sounding the alarm, the dogs barking, engines starting up, the PA system relaying orders to the guards as the big gates swung open in the far distance and three snow tractors rolled through it with their headlights sweeping across the snow. Beyond the west side of the camp I could see shadows moving and the glint of eyes in the lamplight as the wolf pack watched the confusion for a while and then began loping away.

"Marius?"

"I'm ready."

I adjusted Max's lamp on my forehead, where I'd strapped it with a strip of canvas, and hauled up on the pick and searched for the next seam in the granite, rejecting three or four tricky placements before I was satisfied and drove a piton in and slung the rope, testing it, finding it good and hauling up.

"When you're ready!" I called to Marius, and felt the rope tighten.

Four hundred feet, as a rough estimate.

"Five minutes rest."

Marius didn't answer, was out of breath again, and I secured the line for him. A few feet below me, he was half-covered in snow from the east wind as I was, not looking up at me, hanging with his head down, his brow resting against the rock face, could have been dozing, praying, I couldn't tell and I wasn't worried: he was safe enough on the line.

The camp looked pretty now, a Christmas scene, with the flash-lights lighting the snow as the search continued among the huts. The klaxons were silent at last but the dogs were still baying, freed by their handlers to work the terrain, could have been given the scent already. After the explosion and the resulting blackout, the huts would have been ringed with guards called out for the emergency, and a general roll call could have been ordered at once as a precaution.

Dmitri Berinov, Hut 19. *Missing.*

Marius Antanov, alias Nikolai Parek, Hut 12. *Missing.*

The rope felt good under my hands, the rope and the pitons and the rock face and the near-darkness. Here we were safe. Here was the difference between freedom and the closing in of the war-trained pit bulls, their jaws ready to maul if their handlers couldn't call them off in time, the wolf pack circling outside the wire if we'd ever managed to climb it, the first search vehicles just in time to drag us back to the camp still alive, then the orders issued in the morning for the head-shaving and the shackling before we were held down across the vaulting horse in the gym for twelve lashes as a preliminary to being thrown into the solitary confinement cellars still bleeding and with a ration of black bread and stale water for two months, three, until the commandant was satisfied that the message was understood by the rest of the prisoners: This was Gulanka, and there was no escape.

You *still* think I was mad to go for the final chance? Then that's your bloody business.

I looked down at Marius. "Ready to haul up?"

He got his head lifted and looked at me. "What? Yes," got one hand tightened on the rope and handed me the piton he'd pulled out.

In another fifteen minutes we'd climbed another two hundred feet at a rough estimate, the placement easy enough with good deep seams and no dirt or dead moss in them, no loose blocks, the wind remaining at constant force and the snow flurries more of a help as a screen from below than a hindrance here, our lungs getting used to the thin air and Marius holding up as best he could.

Then we met the overhang.

Marius was looking up from below me, wondering why I'd stopped.

The curve of rock jutted six, seven feet from the vertical, hiding the faint light from the sky, and ran east and west without a visible break.

"Oh my *God*," I heard Marius say.

I took a minute to rest, to think. "We get these, sometimes," I told him.

He was quiet now.

Six, seven feet of granite brooding above my head, cutting us off. I reached up and ran my hand over it, having to lean backward over the drop.

The surface was bare, seamless.

I heard Marius again. "So we go sideways?"

"No."

"We've got to."

"We can't."

"For God's sake, why not?"

"Moving sideways across the face is always dangerous. In any case we don't know how far we'd have to go, how far the overhang goes. It could be fifty yards to the east and we might take the west, and find it reaches for five hundred."

The wind buffeted the rock face now, tearing at his voice. "But we can't go *over* it."

I went on feeling for seams, fissures, even cracks. "According to professional practice, yes, we can. Even if we tried going sideways it would slow us up, and time's critical. We've got to reach the top of the massif and get away overland before the search vehicles are in the area tomorrow—with the dogs."

"It's snowing too hard for that." He was close to me now, Marius, wanting comfort. His breath steamed in the rays of my little lamp.

"This wind could die in the night and by eleven in the morning there could be sunshine."

Decision, make a decision, my fingertips sliding across the freezing rock, coming away numbed. But there weren't any choices.

"I'm going to go sideways," Marius said, his throat tight.

"You're not going anywhere," I told him. The adrenaline was on full force now and I could think better.

"I can't do anything else," his voice came.

"Marius, hook your fall-arrest line to your harness. Now."

"Where?" I'd had him rehearse it fifty times, and he'd forgotten: You've heard of stress.

"To the front." I didn't want him pitched forward against the rock if he came unstuck.

"I'm going down again," he said, "some of the way. Remember the ledge we crossed, where we rested?"

"Marius, I want you to get this. I'm taking you to Moscow. I'm not dropping you off this cliff for them to find your body in the morning and learn *exactly* where I am. All we've got to do is get to the top of this massif, one foot at a time. *Get there*, you understand? Keep that in your mind."

"I knew you'd lost your reason, Berinov. I told you."

I fished out another piton and drove it in for a footrest and pulled myself up against the curve of the rock, unhooking my pick and reaching higher with it, scraping with its point, searching for anything I could find.

It took minutes before a narrow seam caught at the pick, but it was there, and I hauled up. "Move with me, Marius. Keep close." I got the hammer and drove a piton in, hard, weight-testing it. But the lead line was still taut. "Marius!"

"I can't!" His tone was lost now, desperate. It was a case of extreme funk, and I understood that. To look up at an overhang at night has put fear into hardened pros unless they're perfectly prepared. We weren't.

But I'd got to take Antanov with me. He was a man with a life to live, and he was Natalya's passport to freedom.

He was also the key to *Balalaika*.

"Marius, think about Moscow. Think about your sister. Think about destroying that bastard Sakkas. All that's going to be possible as soon as we reach the top of the massif. So think about *getting* there. Think about *being* there."

Okay, Max had nodded, his eyes bright on me in the shadows of the huts. *Okay*. But Marius didn't answer. He was praying now, I knew that.

"Marius! Tighten your lead line and—"

Then he passed out and I felt a jerk on the line and knew that he was swinging over the seven hundred foot drop with the weight of a hanged man.

24
Sakkas

THE WIND WAS WHIPPING AT GALE force across the massif
and we lay huddled together against the risk of hypothermia
and frostbite.

I'd put a compress bandage around his head but he still hadn't
moved or spoken, and I was hoping to God amnesia hadn't set in.
At intervals I kept asking him his name and he stirred at last.

"Name?"

"Yes. Do you remember your name?"

"Of course. Marius."

I went slack with relief. It was all locked in this man's head,
Balalaika.

"We're moving on," I said.

"Through this?"

"We've got to."

The snow was blinding, but the last of the moon's light was dying
in the west and we steered by it toward the railroad station that I
knew was six miles away. Before morning we climbed into a freight
car as the train slowed for the gradient.

Marius had asked me just once as we'd lurched through the snow,
"How did we get to the top of the massif?"

"I found a chimney in the rock face."

"How did you get *me* past the overhang?"

I thought of the intensity of the cold in that dank chimney,
slivers of ice lining its sides, digging into my back as I bridged my
way up, tension in the muscles of the calves, tension in the shoulders,

218 · *Adam Hall*

taking deep breaths before each move, tension because of the drift of air, and the crack of moon haze above that might be from a mouth too narrow for a man, too narrow even for a helpless ferret in the field. Then suddenly I was there, in the wind again, swinging out onto a shelf and seeing that the angle eased above me now; from here to the top would be a breeze, a scramble, if I could get Marius this far. I drove a piton in, then two more for an anchor, then lowered myself into the mouth of the chimney for the descent, my back sore now against the rock, to where Marius was hanging, still limp, like a fly in a web.

The chimney was harder the second time, with no rope. I needed it, you see, for the pulley system. To bring Marius up. It's not in the guidebooks, hauling a dead weight up a chimney with a hemp rope and three approximations to carabiners hammered out of old steel in a labor-camp forge. I would not recommend it, no, as a technique. The wind slapping now against my face, the arm and shoulder muscles singing, then burning, glad of those days swinging the ax at the seam of nickel in the mine, the extra hours in the gym. Wondering how the precious contents of Marius's skull would survive the upward passage against the unforgiving rock. I might strain at the hemp rope till my hands bled onto my boots and the blood froze there, blending with the flakes of snow, hearing the thud of his back against the granite wall over the shriek of the wind, then letting the piton take the weight while I took three sharp breaths, four, and heaved again, but if Marius couldn't remember *everything* about Sakkas's business empire, then *Balalaika* would die, though he might live.

I could have told him all that but I didn't.

"I don't remember, but there wasn't any choice."

We were three days moving south toward the city, hunched and rocking under a tarpaulin, the only shelter we had from the wind chill, getting through the last of the rations we'd brought from the camp.

We had no money but a guard at the station in Moscow showed mercy and threw down two kopecks and told me to get my friend to a hospital: The bandage was black by now with dried blood.

I left Marius propped on a bench while I went to telephone Legge.

"Did they recall the DIF to London?"

He recognized my voice.

"Yes."

"I want him back here."

In a moment, rather formally: "I'll try it and get him for you."

"I also want Croder here."

Another brief silence. The ferret in the field doesn't move a Chief of Signals around like a pawn on a chessboard.

"I'll have to go through the DIF for that, of course."

"Listen," I told him, "these are your direct instructions: Tell Croder I want them both out here by the first available plane. Tell him I'm bringing home *Balalaika*, but he's got to be here to take it over—it's too big for anyone else to handle."

"I'll do what I can but—"

"*Get them.* And listen, I'm sending a woman to you. Antanova, the dancer. Get her to London under protective escort as soon as she shows up, but not through the airport—she'll be hunted. Tell our people to keep her safe until further instructions. Is that clear?"

"Yes."

"Meanwhile, I want the DIF here, and the COE, *both of them.* I'll be watching for their plane."

I shut down the signal.

There were just three of us in here sitting in baroque armchairs like members of a London club. Now in an atmosphere of dust and shadows and brass blackened with age—this was the old British embassy, now derelict, the rendezvous Legge had chosen for us.

Croder and Ferris had flown in an hour ago, courtesy of a clear runway. It would soon be dawn.

"Let's cut straight to the chase," I said. "Here's the deal. I'm bringing the mission home and it's all yours. You've got *Balalaika* in your lap. I can give you the names of seventeen leading members of the Duma who either help control the Moscow mafiya or who are deeply in its pay. Nine of them, incidentally, are at this moment planning a militarized *coup d'état* through the former GRU designed to bring down Boris Yeltsin. I can give you the whole of Sakkas's organization and modus operandi from St. Petersburg through Moscow to Vladivostok and even from there through Beijing, Tokyo, and New York."

I got up and walked around a bit, disturbing the dust as I toyed with the tassle of one of the big velvet curtains.

In a moment Croder's voice came from the shadows.

"And the deal?"

I turned and looked at him.

"I want Sakkas hit."

I saw Ferris look up but he said nothing.

"We can't do that," Croder said flatly.

"That's a bloody shame," I told him, "because that's the deal."

"There's no provision in the constitution of the Bureau to take human life. You know that."

"Then you don't get *Balalaika*."

Croder's claw hand hit the arm of his chair as he got up to face me. "Why do you want him hit?"

"What else would *you* do with him?"

"Get him to London and slam him into jail for a start."

"You'd never keep him there."

"In solitary confinement during the investigation."

I swung away, swung back. "With a strong guard?"

"As you can imagine."

"There isn't any jailer who wouldn't accept a million pounds sterling from such an eminent prisoner and clear out to Monte Carlo. An inside escape job would cost him ten or twenty million. Last year his income was two billion US dollars. Or he'd kill his way out as he did before if he had to. There is no *way* you can keep that man in captivity, and once he's free he's going to start all over again back in Moscow, and I am *damned* if I'm going to let all the work or the effort I've put in come to nothing. And think how nice it will be to go to the prime minister and say you've pulled out the plum after all."

This time I turned my back on him, looking up at a faded portrait of George VI, cracked with age.

Then Croder astonished me. "If you want a hit made on Sakkas, you'll have to do it yourself."

I swung back to look at him. "There's no provision in my constitution for taking human life, either. I've done it only twice, and each time it was to avenge a woman. But I'd set it up."

"Difficult." Ferris's quiet voice came from the armchair for the first time. "And terribly dangerous."

"This trade isn't tiddlywinks."

"You'd have to isolate him."

"I think I can do that."

Croder spoke. "We haven't got a hit man in Moscow. Or anywhere."

"Three of Legge's men are trained snipers. One simple shot from a rooftop is all we need."

"I couldn't condone it."

"I understand that, just let it happen. And do the soul-searching afterward. Or do you want me to dump *Balalaika* in the Moskva River?"

It was still the pitch dark of a winter morning when I left the derelict embassy. There was only one phone call left to make. I'd called Natalya the night before at the theater to tell her Marius was free.

"He can't be," she'd said in a rush of breath.

"He escaped three days ago."

"From *Gulanka?*"

"Listen," I said. "This frees you, too. Make a note of this address and get there as soon as you can. Do *not* drive your car away from the theater.

Get a taxi—if it breaks down or runs out of gas, stay inside and ask the driver to get you another. Do *not* show yourself on the street—Sakkas's bodyguards will be hunting for you. The people whose address I've just given you will protect you and get you to London. You'll go by train to St. Petersburg and fly from there. In London you'll be looked after until it's safe for you to come out and resume your career. Look for me in the audience one night. I want to see you dance again."

Now it was time to phone Sakkas. I got a minion on the line and said, "Tell Sakkas that Marius Antanov is back in Moscow."

A few moments later an icy voice said, "I don't believe so."

"He escaped from Gulanka three days ago and he's ready to blow you."

His voice was cool and alert. "Who is this speaking?"

"You don't know me. I'm just a businessman and I have a deal for you."

"How much will it cost?"

"A hundred million dollars."

"And do I get the girl back?" he said.

"Of course."

I gave him the rendezvous.

The Mercedes limousine was punctual, coming to a halt on the opposite side of the street from the abandoned fire station. Other cars followed, spilling their occupants under the neon glow of the lamps. I counted eighteen guards, each with an AK-47 slung from his shoulder. The doors of the Mercedes remained closed.

I crossed the street, aware of all that firepower concentrated on me. The tinted glass of the rear window slid down six inches as I approached. His blue eyes, like chips of ice, bored into me.

"Where's little Marius?" he said.

I pointed at the firehouse. "He's inside with three lawyers and a banker. They're waiting to draw up the contracts to transfer the funds to a bank in Switzerland."

"What's in it for you?"

"I get a cut."

He looked past me at the building through the flurries of snow. A light from the first-floor window shone dimly through the gloom. For a moment a figure was silhouetted there. He raised a hand in salute. Marius. Even in a bulletproof vest it was a risk. He was a brave man.

"Bring him down," said Sakkas and stepped out of the car. The snow landed on the black sable of his coat.

I shrugged.

"I'll bring him to the door."

The nerves tingled at the back of my neck as I turned and walked over to the building, because here was the moment of truth: If Sakkas distrusted me he'd have only to make a brief signal and have his guards blow me into shreds and walk back to his car, but it wouldn't be in his interests or he wouldn't have come.

It was a single shot from a 1.2 mm Parabellum Deerslayer, I would have said, a man-killer at any range.

I walked into the firehouse and slammed the door on the confusion outside. A fleck of debris hit the rusting fire-bell and left a faint note floating on the air.

Coda

BY JEAN-PIERRE TREVOR

I AM HIGH ABOVE THE DESERT AND the thermals created by the 115-degree heat pitch the 737 around. The prepare-for-landing tone sounds, so I sit down and start slow breathing to calm myself. Flying makes me nervous.

From my window at 17,000 feet I can see where I'll be staying—an Arabian horse ranch down there in the baking desert. This is summer and the Arizona desert is one of the hottest places on earth. In a few minutes we will be landing at Phoenix Skyharbor International. About 200 miles south of here, buried in the sand dunes of Buttercup Valley, are the remains of the plane that was used for the film *The Flight of the Phoenix.* My father wrote the book in the sixties and was brought out from France as technical director on the production.

The turbulence increases as the plane slows. I jot some thoughts down, notice how clammy my hands are. I am also nervous because of what I am about to face. I pray it won't happen.

I am going to visit a dying man known to millions of people as Adam Hall, the creator of Quiller. He is also my father, Elleston Trevor.

Arriving at the ranch under burnt skies, I greet Chaille, my father's wife, who has been battling by his side during his illness for the past two years.

I go into the living room, the walls framed with book jackets, mostly of the Quiller series, and then into a darkened room. The only sounds are from a machine that keeps a special air mattress inflated, the humming of the air conditioning and a bell tinkling in Katrina the husky's collar. Resting on a mound of pillows is my father.

Softly I say, "Hello."

His eyes open slowly. "Hello, JP."

I stroke his forehead.

Outside the summer storm clouds are gathering. I look at this spectacular display of power and think: Please heal my father. I pray for a miracle and a small voice inside me says: Let him go if that is his wish . . .

Yet he wants to live so much. And *Quiller Balalaika* is pages short and this weighs heavily on him. I offer to set up a laptop so he can write. He says yes. I sit on the bed next to him and we try for a few minutes, but he is too weak. Part of me resents Quiller because he reminds me of the shield my father has had to keep in place all his life. Maybe if Quiller was vulnerable he wouldn't exist. And right now my father is the most vulnerable I've ever seen him, so I'm very confused.

The next day when I go into his room he looks like someone who has had a huge burden lifted from his shoulders.

I take his hand. "Hello, Papa."

"I'd like to work on the book if I may, JP."

"Of course. Just give me a minute, I'll get the laptop."

Chaille tells me that for three hours early this morning they talked of his distress at being stuck between life and death. It has given my father the spirit to write more.

We begin. There are long moments of silence as he creates Quiller and I look at his etched face, backlit from the desert light. Sometimes whole minutes drift by when I feel I am holding a flame that has been burning for years and the slightest breath will extinguish it forever. Then a word or a sentence, then more silence. The nurses know he is writing and stay in the living room.

"That's it."

My father speaks the words in a slow voice. He turns as I turn and we look at each other, a few inches between us, he on his throne of pillows, me with a shaking laptop on my knees.

I hold his hand and burst into tears, for the significance of the words—"That's it"—is too great. There's only one person I know who could show such unimaginable restraint and wrap up a whole life with those two words. I will never forget this moment.

I press some keys to shut down the computer and stare at the screen, which has never looked so black. I mumble something, go into the living room and tell Chaille he has finished his book.

Later I go into his office. The floor is covered in research material, city maps from Russia, letters from the Pentagon, plot notes are stuck to the walls. I look around. His worn black karate belt on a hook. Incense sticks. A police and fire scanner. Paintings by Chaille. *KGB Death and Rebirth* on the floor. Two Boken martial-arts training swords on the wall. On his desk are quartz crystals and fool's gold from the Arizona mountains, a manual on interrogation, a small bowl of protein wafers, an acupuncture needle, Tibetan chimes and a spinning disc with prismatic colors. My father likes things that sparkle.

I sit at his desk for the first time. In front of me, on the shelves spanning the entire room, is his life's work.

On the desk is his typewriter which he will never use again. Dust is already gathering on the keys. This is too much and I sit here in a veil of tears. There is something so horribly final about this typewriter that will never form words again. And when I look at the awesome body of work in front of me—over a hundred novels, dozens of foreign editions, the awards, ten motion pictures—I see a labor of more than fifty years of creating worlds for other people to share. I realize I am looking at my father and I feel buried in grief.

I return to his room. All I want to do is take his weary head in my hands and hold it for a long time, but I don't. I lean forward, put my face next to his.

"I've always loved you," I tell him.

"I've always loved you, too."

It floods out of me.

"Go ahead, let it rip," my father says while I hold him in my arms.

Chaille and I sit on his bed, my father between us. We talk about his leaving. In the Rembrandt light of the desert evening reflecting off the outside wall, I sit next to my father and time doesn't mean much anymore.

He slept better last night and wears his red kimono. His eyes are open and look at somewhere far beyond the walls. He might hear the wind chimes outside.

Slowly, over the following hour, my father turns his head slightly around and upward, focusing on something not in this world. Chaille and I don't say much. Are words important now?

Just the three of us in this room. Waiting for a signal.

He stays looking up into his Universe, like Wednesday's child, shallow breathing, almost not visible, but still there.

Chaille and I are on either side of my father. There are almost no sounds—Katrina's bell collar, our breathing. I pray.

My father lies under a lake of pink blanket looking like a noble Tibetan monk. Charlie, the plush bear I bought him, on his knee.

"It's safe, you're safe," I say to him.

I briefly look at Chaille because I don't think I saw his last breath. She looks back, not certain.

Another breath.

I hold mine.

My father swallows twice, gently with no sound.

Chaille says something to me but I don't hear it.

Now it comes. The storm breaks loose in my body and I bury my face in his pillows.

Finally I understand the meaning of the last words of his last novel, *Quiller Balalaika* . . .

At 4.10 P.M. on July 21, 1995, my father spread his great wings and took his final flight.

On July 31, Chaille and I took my father's ashes in a beautiful casket to the top of a 7,000-foot mountain in northeast Arizona where we sipped Fernet Branca—Quiller's favourite drink.

JEAN-PIERRE TREVOR
Los Angeles, September 1995

Afterword

BY CHAILLE TREVOR

QUILLER BALALAIKA BEGAN IN MEXICO AT a cancer clinic for brave people whose doctors, like ours, gave them little hope. Between therapies, in chronic distress, Elleston worked on research and plot. It was summer, 1994.

Elleston's hand-size tape recorder was always within reach. Shaving, during breakfast and lunch, ideas entered the back of his mind. He noted them on the recorder, Quiller's deft moves. Refusing to submit to the misery of circumstances, Elleston worked, practiced his Spanish, and joked with the nurses as if pain and weakness were not even an issue. Masses of research material covered the single table in our room: cancer study and research for *Balalaika*. He collected, read, marked, and filed pages and pages of notes.

Before the writing of a novel, Elleston was fascinated by investigative material. He would order books, street maps, perhaps a sample traffic ticket or a train table. He contacted residents on the other side of the globe, chatting, asking questions, getting facts and a feel for whatever shadowy corner of the world Quiller inhabited. Elleston felt that he wrote best about places he'd never been. Location became alive filtered through his imagination. At home in his study, behind his spacious blue-green desk with its photos of me, small stones, a glass cube, and other sentimental tokens, he was in another world, transported to the smells, faces, and streets of Katmandu, Laos, or Moscow.

With pace and plot, Elleston wrote of ordinary people facing extraordinary situations. Characters were challenged to the depth of their being. A sense of order, discipline, and dedication became brightly apparent in some dark world. Ethics held fast in corrupt circumstances. These heroes knew what was important to them, and they accepted a problem—even the most dire—for the opportunity to see its other side: a solution.

At first there were few signs. Then one by one, symptoms began to compromise and handicap life as we had known it. I grew to watch every gesture, every look of pain or weariness, every change in his body, the way he walked. I looked to his eyes; I looked in his eyes all the time to see where he was. Sometimes I'd see his face twist in pain. In the next moment, knowing I was watching, he'd pucker out his lips and with hands held up in a clawlike position, look left and right like a defiant gorilla, wanting me to laugh, breaking my heart.

Elleston arrived at the clinic in massive pain, with me at his side like a scared she-wolf frantically attending her crippled mate. I looked at the gentle Mexican doctors, fire in my eyes, TAKE AWAY THE PAIN!

They did. After two months, color came back into Elleston's face. He could walk without pain. It was time to fly to Los Angeles for further medical reasons, then home.

Elleston was so relieved to be back in the United States doing American things: lunch at Marie Callender's, an afternoon in a theater watching *Forrest Gump*. We breakfasted in a sunny country coffee shop.

One morning there in a booth by the window, Elleston began to tell a World War II story about men in the RAF, some funny thing they did. Unusual for him, he began to laugh at his own humor. Then laughter shook into crying, quite out of control to his amazement, like a storm passing through his body, shaking loose all the tension accumulated there.

Home. Problems still clung tenaciously, but we were determined to rebuild our lifestyle and make a new future.

Elleston wrote a love letter to me about making changes so that he could deserve through the efforts of his inner intelligence many more years in our small, beautiful world. The bottom lines read: *"Thou shalt elect a thing and it shall be bestowed upon thee, and light shall shine upon thy ways . . . This do I then elect. . . ."*

Elleston immediately went to work at his processor, determined to produce four or five pages of *Balalaika* a day. *Thou shalt elect a thing and it shall be bestowed upon thee. . . .* Quiller tells himself in his determination to find Marius and take him back to Moscow.

We continued with the programs begun in Mexico. Elleston meditated, visualized, read, listened to healing tapes, and climbed into an ozonated body bag every day. We acquired various juicers, an ozone ultraviolet water-purifying system, countless herbs and health products. Our kitchen looked like a pharmacy. 7-14-X, Coley vaccine, holographic repatterning, acupuncture, reflexology, hypnosis. . . . Elleston left few stones unturned.

"I feel a big breakthrough coming on." Many times he said that, only to suffer another drop in blood pressure, another trip to the emergency room. Nausea, edema, utter weakness continued to plague his days and try his spirit.

"I don't know what to do," Elleston said in a rare moment of despair, his face in his hands.

At times you can come very close to despair, and that's the most dangerous thing of all, except panic. You can take your time over despair, but panic is quick acting, deadly. I've never given in to panic, but yes, I've come close to despair. (Balalaika)

Day after day, Elleston fixed a nice breakfast, enjoyed it, lost it, rested and, hardly having the energy to talk, went to do "four pages today."

There have been times in my life, in my career—which is my life— when I've known that I've placed myself outside reality, committed myself to achieving the unachievable. It's very dangerous, but on these occasions there is no choice. (Balalaika)

He grew weaker. Even a wine bottle was difficult to lift. Elleston didn't drink wine these days, but he liked to pour mine, just as he liked to sit at the dinner table though he could eat next to nothing. Getting in and out of the car took enormous effort. I'd slowly raise one swollen leg into the Lincoln, then the other. On arrival, he'd sit for ten minutes or so, summoning the energy to lift himself out of the seat.

All year long Elleston had looked forward to the Bouchercon Convention in Seattle, and a five-city author tour was planned to promote *Quiller Salamander.*

The Bouchercon was a week away.

I was determined to take this trip that he'd been looking forward to since the last Bouchercon. The gods dare not deny his plans or force a dead-tired body to limp down airport corridors. "Thou shalt elect a thing!"

The night before our flight he fell into bed, weak and aching, not expecting to be able to leave in the morning. After rubbing his back, arms, and legs with liniment, I packed our bags.

The next morning Elleston got out of bed and walked without pain! The edema was almost gone; his energy back! The angels swooped down, picked up Elleston, and we flew off for Seattle.

On the second leg of a four-hour flight he looked good, was bright and writing with no back pain, weakness, or nausea. A miracle.

The marathon of airports and flights was topped off that night by a dinner for authors hosted by his publisher, Otto Penzler, at the charming La Buca Restaurant in downtown Seattle.

What would his New York contacts and friends think seeing him so thin? Elleston didn't want them to know of his disease for fear publishers wouldn't give him another contract. Taking a chair rather than standing to speak before a group, he explained that he had fallen from one of my horses and was recuperating.

No looking back now. After two weeks at home, we took off again for the five-city author tour stretched between California and Texas.

In bookstores Elleston was treated like the master he was. Awestruck fans waited in long lines, their arms full of the precious books they'd collected for years. Signing stacks of novels, Elleston shook hands and chatted for hours on end.

On the sidelines people asked me, "What is it like to live with the man who created Quiller?"

Elleston was an elegant Englishman who liked white and never owned a pair of jeans until he moved into a totally different lifestyle: my much-lived-in house, dogs, horses, dirt roads, a pickup truck. He was a gracious gentleman of an Old World demeanor for whom manners were a way of life. Never would he pick up his fork before I took a bite or sit before seating me or not rise when a woman entered the room. At the same time, another side of him was as playful as a schoolboy. If he was going to the grocery store, I wanted to go along just for the fun of it. What kept him young, I think, was his flexibility, his ability to change and make a new life, to keep moving on to the man and person he wanted to be. Elleston looked twenty years younger than he was. A black belt in Shotokan karate, he was fit and strong, absolutely charismatic.

Draped around each other like newlyweds we were sometimes asked, "How long have you been married?"

"Since yesterday," he'd say.

Intimacy was very important to Elleston. He believed that a man really becomes a man through his love and life with a woman.

At home, feeling better, Elleston renewed his passionate commitment to survival. He had the energy now to see more people, healers, doctors, and explore more alternative programs. Every morning he was up at 6:30, then off in his Mark VII to see a round of therapists. His dog, Katrina, and I ritualistically fetched the car and saw him away. In the afternoon, Elleston was back in his study creating *Balalaika*.

As if this were not enough to show his commitment to living, Elleston became passionate about hobbies: coins (he attended a coin show), stamps, antiques, investments (he bought a TED spread), sunflowers, trees (he joined an arbor society). A Spanish guitar was acquired; a workbench built. I bought seeds, pots of flowers, and made little pens to protect the baby trees. Coin, antique, business, and health magazines cluttered the house.

"Isn't life exciting?" he'd say, delighted with the thought of his projects, the pleasure of strumming his guitar and having pretty things to look at. Proudly he'd show me his bright coins as they arrived in the mail. He had selected them so carefully.

January of 1995, intense intestinal pains gripped Elleston for two days.

At 5:00 A.M., on a dark, rainy morning I drove him to the emergency room.

Quiet, resigned, Elleston lay waiting in the tiny cubicle. Pain took him away from himself and his surroundings, the doctors, nurses, and questions. Hours later he was moved to a hospital room. No improvement. I went home to feed animals and have a mid-afternoon breakfast.

On my return I found Elleston upright in bed engaged in lively conversation with Marcia, the nurse. He, his witty and eloquent self, was back! With pain gone, he turned his attention to leaving. Hospital staff wanted to put him in a wheelchair. Not Elleston. He was going to *walk* out of there. At the entrance, we left Marcia with an invitation for dinner.

Talking to Elleston about working less, taking time to eat smaller, frequent meals, about making his body a priority, made him angry. He spoke about the tight wire. A relentless sense of obligation to his publishers and readers kept Elleston on a tight wire. He was driven to get *Balalaika* finished and delivered.

"You're working too hard. Save your energy."

"What for?"

"The rest of your life."

Swing lustily, feel the muscles play, sustain the morale.

"I'm going to do four or five pages today." On and on Elleston wrote, like running a marathon with no strength.

But, I believe, when Elleston was writing, walking down the

streets of Moscow in drifting snow, *glimpsing the shadows, hearing the distant footsteps,* facing danger with Quiller's grit and grace, he escaped cancer's grip. Through Quiller, he was telling himself about the *thought of life's continuance against great odds.*

Nothing had been like this before.

We must strive, must we not, my good friend, to play the game and at whatever cost? What else can we do when we're thrown the bloody ball? (Balalaika)

Every morning he was off to a therapy or two. Good people, "a flock of angels", as he called them, did their utmost to help. He'd return home full of optimism and excitement having just met with a new man or woman. Our hopes rose on the waves these people created. "I have never seen such a beautiful spring," he said.

With waning strength, Elleston tried to live each day fully. To acquire things was to invest in life: more TV stations (we installed a satellite dish), more sunflowers, coins. . . . When he picked up the phone to talk to the investment brokers, his voice was immediately strong and sure. I'm sure they suspected nothing.

For a few days Elleston thought he was improving. "Let's go for sushi Tuesday," he said brightly. We never made it. He became still weaker, sliding his feet to walk, falling into chairs as he sat.

There was a thousand-foot cliff with a six- or seven-foot-high overhang. Elleston didn't know how to get Quiller to the top. He admitted that.

Another part of Elleston did know. *There wasn't any choice.* One must rage, rage against the dying of the light. *Think about* getting *there. Think about* being *there. (Balalaika)*

At the sound of a buzzer Elleston would force his bone-tired body off the bed and into his study. He'd type a page then set the timer again and lie down.

Finally a therapist for whom he had high regard insisted that he not enter his study for four days. I couldn't press the point, but she could. After ample protest, Elleston broke down with tears of relief, or grief.

On that day, Quiller was left on the cliff with Marius on the line *swinging over the seven-hundred-foot drop with the weight of a hanged man.*

These were the last words he typed.

He was spending all day and night in bed now. I asked him if he'd like to see JP, his son.

"I'm not dying!"

We had decided to check into Scottsdale Memorial. What makes such times heartbreaking is not the misery, but grace holding fast. Hardly the energy to stand but he must shave, wash his hair, wear good clothes. "No, not that shirt, the clean blue one, please." He was determined to arrive at the emergency room well groomed and dressed. I helped him all morning.

Finally settled in a room, Elleston was ready to see Jean-Pierre who had flown in from Detroit to see his dad.

Elleston didn't think he was strong enough to undergo an operation. Mayo doctors did. They gave us hope. We took it. The "one-and-a-half–hour" operation lasted four and a half.

JP and I were hovering over his bed when a tall vase of red roses arrived. Rather mystified, I looked at the card. *"Para los bravos!"* He had arranged for the flowers to be sent to the three of us, "For the brave ones!"

When he felt like himself, Elleston's style and humor were ever present. A nurse walked into his room and burst into laughter. There he was sitting up against the pillow, dark hair neatly combed, wearing his Ray-Ban sunglasses. He looked like a cool secret agent. Engrossed in the telling of a story he had everyone—me, too— "falling about" in tears of laughter.

About a week after surgery, Elleston's heart began racing. As always he knew what he wanted: no drugs, no ICU; he was not going to be moved from his room. The nurses and doctors were beside themselves and on the phone to JP and me. Clearly Elleston wanted to be left alone. JP and I agreed. Elleston told them that he knew how to slow his heart down with meditation, which he did. In the morning he called to reassure me, "All systems are go."

When energy allowed, Elleston was busy reading, studying about cancer, on the phone to his investment bankers, or trying his best to find out where his English publisher was vacationing in Europe. Before leaving, the man had spoken to Elleston and told him to take his time in finishing *Balalaika*. Elleston wanted to send him flowers.

More than two weeks passed in the hospital room, graced by Elleston's civility, but plagued by suffering: creases etched by pain in his forehead, a swollen arm, utter fatigue. "Thirty more pages. I almost made it," he said weakly.

There was nothing more doctors could do. "They wanna kick me outa here," Elleston announced.

On the way home Elleston talked of being on his feet in four days and looked forward to seeing *Macbeth* on the VCR. Also, he asked me to have flowers sent "to the angels at 3C, please."

Elleston became weaker, no appetite, nausea. He was chased by pain, bedsores, body pain, bone pain, excruciating pain caused by the GI tube. Depressed, discouraged, "It's miserable," he said, "Where's the .45?"

All along and still nurses greeted him with bright smiles and great respect. They were moved by his spirit. Incapacitated, but he apologized for being unable to rise when they walked into the room. "Can we get you a glass of sherry?" he asked.

After an agonizing day that had been an incessant physical-emotional nightmare to me, we were talking about coins or something. Suddenly it was in him to smile and say as he used to, "Isn't life fantastic!" I was stunned. Every good and miserable moment is lived, faced with Quiller-like mettle. The grip of disability, the humility to which a dependent patient is subject, the boredom of lying in bed day and night couldn't crush his zest for life.

"I'm going to fight like hell" was the first thing Elleston said one morning. He felt certain that his body would rally beneath the power of his unrelenting will. Adversity was to be met with super-human effort. He would not go quietly into the night, but rage and plan and build a way out.

His was a heroism of mind to face anything at all, particularly his own anxieties. The situation doesn't matter as much as the state of mind brought to it, the collection of mind to rebuild and fly out of a personal desert. I saw tears of love, furrows of pain, and eyes full of sorrow, but I never saw fear cross his face.

The hills were on fire. Outside, the mountains glowed orange with massive brushfires, but inside, in that quiet bedroom filled with flowers and lit by candlelight, it was an important time to be with someone.

Jean-Pierre returned and Elleston perked up, happy to see his son and resume their boyish banter.

A friend lent us her laptop computer. JP, sitting close to his dad, typed words of *Balalaika* as Elleston spoke slowly, his mind ever sharp and sentences flowing like poetry.

One reads Elleston's words not only for plot—his novels seethe with plot—but for the sheer beauty of strong, lean, poetic writing. His words are drawn from feeling like the bold, few brash strokes of a confident painter who doesn't need to define edges.

For two days and nights Elleston sat up in bed, trying to ease the coughing caused by congestion in his lungs. All night long he coughed.

"Call Dr. Kimbel," he said very early after a difficult night. "I have pleurisy. I can't breathe. I need to go to the hospital."

There are times you know you have to say something with no idea how, so you start spitting out words with the hope that they'll find their way to a meaning you feel overwhelmed to express. I couldn't just talk about death. I'd already done that. I had to drive to the bottom of his heart, and mine, an acceptance of death. Not maybe.

He could not go back to the hospital. His struggle had to stop. It was okay to die—not a failure at all, but an act of courage to consciously let go and slide into another world, to go toward the light, not rage against a dying of it. It was okay simply to *be*— alive, relaxed with JP and me in the sort of "love bath" we'd created.

On and on I spoke of these things, crying into Kleenex while he looked at me with thoughtful dry eyes.

"It's not easy," he said.

Elleston didn't want to fail anyone or himself. Self-control, self-discipline, resolve, refusal to surrender had always been the only answer. I was asking him to surrender, not to try to do anything.

"Your body knows what to do. It will be easy."

His first reaction was, "Well, I won't linger." As usual he wanted to be in control, to decide when to move where. But there were greater forces at work; he could trust them, some wisdom. Dying would be easy. I knew it would be.

"Yes, linger. There's still much to say and share."

For almost three hours we lay there talking side by side like two battle-weary warriors, one with a mortal wound in his side. I was emotionally exhausted and he looked like a haunted child.

Miraculously the coughing ceased. He no longer tried to breathe deeply into his lungs, but relaxed. Breaths became shallow, steady, appropriate to the condition of his body. His face softened. A look of quiet contentment came over him and a lingering half-smile, "like a wise old Indian," as JP later observed.

Everything changed. Elleston was calm and strong. His mental wheels began turning. Quiller taking control. He had changed his course but not a sense of purpose.

We would not go to the hospital. "Please cancel Charlotte." (Her therapy was scheduled in about an hour—8:00 A.M.). Instead: "When JP wakes, have him bring in the laptop. I'm going to finish *Balalaika*."

Mid-morning father and son got to work. Looking through the window, deep in thought, Elleston carefully pronounced each word in his clean, honed style for JP to peck onto the computer. Hours passed.

A fleck of debris hit the rusting fire-bell and left a faint note floating on the air.

"That's it."

Balalaika was finished. A master's career was over.

That afternoon Elleston slept peacefully. No coughing at all.

Who's to say what worlds are visited as death approaches. Elleston knew he was beginning a new life. Making plans, still *living*, he spoke of wanting to study Shakespearean acting and to become involved in the art of mind-body healing, like Deepak Chopra. He talked about people he admired, like Elisabeth Kubler-Ross and Forrest Fenn, and reminisced about our wedding at the Fenn Gallery. Then he asked me to fetch a piece of paper and began to dictate an invitation to a "Barn Party! . . . . with champagne and hot dogs and la musica Español!" He knew people would gather to remember him. He wanted us to celebrate.

Next, he quoted Shakespeare, lines that express the repose of death he now allowed himself to feel. "The innocent sleep . . . that knits up the ravell'd sleave of care."

Two days later, on the twenty-first of July, Elleston awoke in the night to tell me vividly about a woman and a cottage as if he'd been there. "Do you think I'm crazy?"

"No, of course not."

In the morning he seemed uncertain which world he was in. "Have I died yet?" he asked.

JP and I stayed with him throughout the day, talking sometimes. He greeted an acquaintance. Late afternoon we were on either side of him. The shallow, calm breathing hardly existed. Then he twisted his head to look upward, eyes open, conscious. His body shuddered. A breath moved in his throat, then gently slipped away. He died with my hand on his heart feeling its last beats.

"Is he gone?" JP asked.

"Yes."

JP and I took Elleston's ashes to the top of Ziegler Mountain, which overlooks my mother's ranch in the White Mountains of Arizona. Elleston loved a view. Standing on boulders by an ancient twisted tree, one can see over miles of wilderness and hear only the wind. JP and I lifted our glasses of Fernet Branca toward the distance and toasted the flight of Elleston's spirit.